The Hand of Justice

Book 3 of the Tony Signorotto series

Phil Copsey

in case of emergency press

We are proud to acknowledge the Traditional Owners of country throughout Australia and to recognise their continuing connection to land, waters, and culture.

We pay our respects to their Elders past, present, and emerging.

We support recognition, reconciliation, and reparation.

The Hand of Justice

Book 3 of the Tony Signorotto series

Phil Copsey

in case of emergency press
https://www.icoe.com.au
Travancore, Victoria
Australia

Published by in case of emergency press 2022

ISBN 978-0-6453751-6-9

Dedicated to the most elite police officer of all:

The General Duties Member

Phil Copsey

Table of Contents

Chapter One

Marco Toscano leant against a metal railing on the footpath outside Flinders Street railway station in the heart of Melbourne and gazed idly at the myriad of pedestrians heading downtown in the early morning rush.

They reminded him of ant-like creatures swarming through the streets all heading for their little office nests where they would feel secure and happy before making the trek back the same way to where they had come from in another eight hours. He shuddered at the thought that it could ever be him in that situation keeping down a day job. Never. Life was too short and there were too many things to do. Too many scams to run with.

At the end of the day, Marco Toscano was a two-bit hustler with big ambitions who liked nothing more than a bourbon and coke in one hand while he watched over illegal card games that he organised for the Vietnamese communities from the western suburbs.

Marco was an average card shark who had come to realise that there was good steady money in the organising of the games rather than playing with chance and losing. Occasionally, he would gamble in the dens where there were not only card games but also cock fighting. He supplied the venues, cards and under the counter booze. Whatever else they did he didn't concern himself with. The illegal part for him came with the fact that he was taking a percentage of the 'bank' funds. He wasn't running these for charity. The fact that he could get busted for the sale of the alcohol was also a factor, albeit a small one. One big trouble with running these shows was that sometimes it was very hard to tell if some of the punters were over eighteen — another illegal problem.

Gambling of any sort in the Vietnamese communities was like heroin addiction.

At twenty-eight years of age, he had been around card games, both legal and illegal most of his life. His father had been a gambler and an alcoholic, but it never stopped him taking young Marco to some of the biggest illegal card games that happened on a regular basis over the western side of the Westgate bridge.

By the age of ten, he had watched his father make and lose fortunes. He wasn't prepared though for the shock, after a particularly bad loss at a packed back yard 'card and cock' night when his father pulled their battered old Ford to a sudden stop on top of the Westgate bridge. Marco thought that maybe his dad had drunk too much again and was just going to throw up, although he had never seen him cry before like he did that night. One minute his father was outside the car and before Marco realised what was happening, his dad had clambered up and over the rail and just disappeared before the little boys' eyes. Marco had sat there terrified for what seemed like an eternity before a police car pulled up behind him and two policewomen gently took him out of the car and placed him in theirs. They then drove him away from the last place he had ever seen his father. For some psychologically unknown reason he had borne a hatred of police ever since.

Standing on the corner, he knew he couldn't go back to his old haunts in the west to run card games anymore. The money was very good, but he was coming under the eye of the Footscray CIU and local police way too much. He had been hiring Air B and B's, but the cops were getting very smart and kept a close eye on all rentals because of wild parties being held. Illegal card games being held in Air B and B's really made them sit up and take notice. They knew he was the main organiser of the games, wherever they were held, and had charged him twice with gambling and alcohol offences. He wasn't going to push for third time lucky. He wanted to keep in touch with a lot of his regular players so that he could still get his regular four figure retainers from the games. What he had to do was change locations to somewhere over north of the city. He just needed someone to back him with a location. The trouble was that he didn't know anyone this side of the bridge.

Thinking over his options, he had been idly staring at an Asian beggar sitting cross legged and with bowed head on the opposite side of the road outside Federation Square. Suddenly a giant of a man approached the beggar, squatted beside him, and held his hand out. Marco thought this benevolent male was going to give the beggar some money. What happened next made him look intently at them both. The beggar quickly handed the male an envelope. The man stood and walked away and headed towards another beggar outside St. Paul's Cathedral. Marco saw the same procedure take place.

A very curious Marco Toscano decided to follow the big man. After watching him take five envelopes from five beggars stretching from Federation Square all the way up Swanston Street, the man turned into Victoria Street with the envelopes and climbed into the driver's seat of a late model black Mercedes Benz, pulled out into the traffic, and headed towards Collingwood. Not before Marco had taken down his registration though.

Something told Marco to try to find out who this person was. Either the beggars were being scammed or they were working for him. Marco didn't really care. What interested him was that the man was doing something illegal on the city side of the Westgate Bridge. Room for thought if he could get someone to find out who the car was registered to. A vague plan was germinating in his brain as he thought about who could help him with this. Who owed him a favour? Who indeed?

Chapter Two

Senior Sergeant Tony Signorotto sat behind his desk, which he referred to as his 'mahogany foxhole,' on the ground floor of the Carlton Police Station. He was slowly scrolling his way through the long screed of emails which seemed to go on forever on the monitor of his computer. He hated reading through the list, but he knew it was his own fault. He kept telling himself that he had to stop using the phrase, 'keep me in the loop.'

Since becoming a Senior Sergeant and being put in charge of the largest metropolitan police station in the inner suburbs of Melbourne, he had insisted with his Superintendent and close friend, Phil Stone at Divisional Headquarters in the city, that he wanted to be a hands-on Officer in Charge and not one that just delegated down through his Sergeants. Not that he didn't have very competent Sergeants at his station, because he did and drummed that requirement into any person with three stripes that wanted a piece of the action at Carlton. He trusted them all. It was just the fact that he himself had been a three striper at his beloved station for several years, before Phil Stone convinced him to go for the vacant Senior Sergeant's position that had come up due to the ill health retirement of the incumbent Officer in Charge. He knew he couldn't completely let go of the day-to-day hands-on style of policing of this United Nations melting pot.

Most Senior Sergeants positioned their offices away from the general running of their stations because they had too much to do to be distracted by the constant ebb and flow of citizens that came in to report, cry, complain or in general just bitch about their lives, which they knew themselves that there was absolutely nothing the boys and girls in blue could do to help them with. They just wanted a shoulder to lean on or an ear to listen. None of them ever thought for a millisecond that the member they were haranguing with their concerns had their own problems, be it at work or home. No, that blue uniform was the last bastion between sanity and chaos.

Tony Signorotto had swapped his office with the Sergeants office to give them some peace and quiet so they could complete their own paperwork and look after the group of wide-eyed Probationary Constables that each of them had been given to supervise and protect for their first year 'in the job,' so they didn't quit through stress or even worse, not turn up for their shift one day because they had overdosed or hanged themselves in some dark and lonely place. The modern-day police officer didn't realise till he or she had walked the streets of a city night and day that sometimes the blue uniform wasn't impervious to both projectiles aimed not only at their bodies but also at their minds. It was not a pretty world out there.

Tony was a police officer's police officer. He loved station life but at times he had to take a step back and get his own correspondence completed. No one else was responsible for signing off on the boss's work. Quickly looking through the station's personnel roster, he noticed that one of his best Sergeants, Kate McLaren, was on duty upstairs.

Kate had been at Carlton for about a year now and had not only proved herself worthy of the rank she held but she had also been presented with the Police Valour Award for her part in the capture of a lowlife gangster who had been the so-called mastermind behind a daring raid on a police convoy that netted him three thousand nine-millimetre pistols that were headed to the police armoury. He didn't have them for long and was sentenced to thirty years imprisonment. His time lasted only shortly before he was found dead at the door to his cell with a shiv in him. She had stood between the gangster, 'Big Al' Lombardi, and freedom and dared him to shoot her. Prior knowledge that the pistol he held at her chest would not fire helped her bravado, but it was still a guessing game at the time. To her though it had been a calculated risk worth taking.

As he pressed the internal number for her desk phone and waited for his Sergeant to pick up, Signorotto scanned his emails. One caught his attention. It was from Phil Stone and detailed the arrival in a few days' time to Carlton of a new Sergeant. Puzzling over the fact that he knew nothing about any new arrivals, Kate picked up.

"Yes, boss," she answered as she looked at the flashing OIC's number on her phone.

"Coffee? See you in the mess room. Got time?"

"Absolutely. On the way."

Before heading to the mess room, Tony printed off the email regarding the new arrival so he could show it to Kate. What raised alarm bells with him was that this transfer was nothing to do with the normal channels where he would be asked for an input on the applicant. This member wasn't an applicant, and in fact, Tony read that he was being transferred from the big country station of Bendigo as a Detective Sergeant to Carlton as a uniform Sergeant. This warranted a phone call to Phil Stone.

Walking into the mess room he realised in a heartbeat why he valued Kate McLaren as one of his Sergeants. As she was reaching for two coffee mugs on the shelf, a young Constable stood and quietly tried to remove himself from her presence. A very sheepish look spread across his face as he almost made it through the door past Tony.

"Constable Larkin," Kate said in a commanding voice with her back to him.

"Yes, Sarge," he replied a tad too quickly.

"That report about the minor damage to our Divisional Van will be on my desk by three o'clock this afternoon. The report will include the reason why it got damaged while you were out of the vehicle and away from a radio while you watched football training at Princes Park."

"Yes Sarge. It will be."

"If it isn't Constable, then you won't be knocking off at three. You will knock off when you have finished it and I have read it. That is if you want any sympathy from me at all as to why you were watching bloody Carlton train. Bunch of losers. Swing your allegiance over to Melbourne, my beloved Demons, and I might look at the paperwork through rose coloured glasses. Mind you, I want to see credit card proof of your new Melbourne membership with the report. Off you go."

"Sarge, that's bribery. Isn't it, Senior Sergeant?" the young trainee member said with an appealing look at his boss's face.

"Without a doubt," the lifelong Carlton supporting Senior Sergeant replied so as his Sergeant could hear. "I think I would just tell the truth and say that you were patrolling the car park and a football kicked by some Carlton superstar came thundering over the fence, hit the side of the van and you couldn't do anything about it. Sounds good to me. But do get it done by three because otherwise I might have to put you on a three-month foot patrol around the Carlton flats dealing with all the druggies there. I know what my choice would be, so don't waste a minute of your precious time and don't bother to stop for lunch. Decision made, eh?"

The young member made a bee line for the nearest computer as fast as he could.

A smiling Tony Signorotto looked across at his Sergeant. "They have respect for you, Kate, but not for that football team of yours."

Kate McLaren smiled and slid a cup of black coffee across to Tony as she sat at the table. Tony slid the copied email across to her before speaking.

"Kate, have you heard of a Detective Sergeant by the name of Ricky Bobrov? Apparently up at Bendigo CIU or was until he got his marching orders back into uniform and a stint down here at Carlton."

"Only one way that happens, boss," she said, reading the printout. "Big time disciplinary problem. Takes something untoward for a member to be put back in uniform. First thing he loses besides his anonymity is his CIU allowance. That would hurt his hip pocket big time and, no, I've never come across the name before."

Tony held his coffee mug to his lips and slowly blew on the hot liquid. "The email came in from Phil Stone without a follow-up phone call. Think I'd better give the good Superintendent a ring."

"No need. The good Superintendent is here," a familiar voice said from the doorway. Both the seated members turned to see a concerned looking Phil Stone walking towards their table. "Time for a coffee also. I suggest we adjourn to a quiet room that doesn't have ears and have a serious chat about the contents of that email I sent."

Chapter Three

Tony Signorotto led the way into an empty office at the rear of the police station where he knew there would be no eavesdropping by other members. The office was mainly a storeroom, so members gave it a wide berth lest they were told to tidy it up. Both he and Kate McLaren sat themselves on the edge of two disused desks and gave their Superintendent inquisitive stares as he stood in the doorway and looked out into the passageway before closing the door.

"Don't give me that look, Senior Sergeant. All is about to be revealed," a quietly spoken Phil Stone said.

"That's what I'm afraid of. Obvious question, Phil. Why is he arriving as a uniformed Sergeant and not coming back to the city as a Detective Sergeant? Has he stuffed up that badly that he is losing his suit, his CIU allowance and his cushy job up the country? Disciplinary move?" Signorotto asked.

"In a nutshell, yes. As you can guess by the surname Bobrov, he's of Russian background but born here. Been in the Force for eleven years and has done stints in the city and South Melbourne. Promoted to Sergeant two years ago at Footscray. Had already completed Detective Training School as a Leading Senior Constable so only stayed around Footscray long enough to grab a Detective Sergeant's position when it came up at Bendigo. His name had already been mentioned in dispatches at Footscray regarding illegal gambling dens. Not busting them but floating around them."

"Nothing too strange for being around those suburbs. What bombshell are you going to drop on us, boss?" Kate said eagerly.

Phil Stone gave his Sergeant a cold stare before continuing.

"Thanks, Kate. Let me finish. I'll know you'll have questions. It wasn't my choice to have him sent here when I found out the complete story. If I had my way, he'd have been kicked so far out of the job he would have landed in the unemployment queue at Centrelink." Phil Stone said with a voice that had gone up an octave or two.

Both Tony and Kate sat still. Tony especially, had not seen his Superintendent this annoyed for some time. This Bobrov character was already getting under his skin and he hadn't even arrived at the station. Stone continued in a much lower voice.

"Sorry, but if there's one thing I can't stomach, it's a bent copper. Anyway, two years ago, in Footscray, the Casino Squad did a raid on a big illegal card game where a Russian that was running it was charging five thousand a head to get on the table and taking a big percentage from the bank for doing so. He got busted and when he was questioned about how he got hold of the premises to run such a large game, the boys found out that he came from St. Kilda and didn't have any real local contacts in Footscray. Turned out he did, but not on the street. In the bloody job! Seems it was Bobrov who gave him the contact for the empty premises to hold the game."

"How did Bobrov, a Leading Senior Constable, find him a big empty house to hold his event?" an incredulous Tony Signorotto said to Stone.

"Not a house, Tony. A bloody factory in Yarraville and home to a firm called Stoddard trucking that did regular runs across the Westgate bridge and interstate to South Australia and Western Australia. When the Casino boys dug a bit deeper, the owner of Stoddard's was giving Bobrov exclusive use of the upstairs area in exchange for first up notification re any inspection or weighbridge sites that the local Highway Patrols and Vic Roads were carrying out. The Russian wouldn't say what Bobrov did for him but it's obvious he gave a monetary kick back for use of the factory."

"A few fines for overweight rigs or crook logbook entries wouldn't be too much for a long-haul trucking firm to get worried about. Par for the course I would have thought," Kate said.

"That's what you'd think, Kate," Stone said with a crooked smile on his face. "Until a couple of the other local trucking firms got together and approached the Yarraville Highway Patrol boss. It didn't take Einstein to figure out that whenever there was a blitz on the road by us or Vic Roads that Stoddard's didn't run their rigs on those days. Subsequently the Highway Patrol kept a close eye on Stoddard's and jumped all over two of their rigs that rolled out early one morning about five hours before there was a scheduled weighbridge and inspection site being opened. They pulled them over at Lara and dissected both rigs. Low and behold, they found that they both had sealed compartments within their fuel tanks. Got to give it to the Highway boys, they are like a dog with a bone when they tackle something that upsets them. The Casino Squad decided to join forces with the Drug Squad when they realised a copper was involved in the background. Rather than take him in they stopped short by busting the trucking company."

"Surely Bobrov and the Russian deserved their whack?" Kate said unimpressed.

"Very hard to join up all the dots for prosecution on the drugs side. We believe the Russian is involved with other stuff down here and are monitoring him closely. Ethical Standards decided to 'kick Bobrov upstairs' and passed him on his Sergeants papers to get him out of metro Melbourne. They created a vacancy at the CIU in Bendigo. The boss up there is ex Ethical Standards. They have been waiting for him to trip himself up and see if he linked up with the Russian again," Stone said.

"Understand all that, Phil, but what happened at Bendigo?" Tony said.

"Gambling big time at the local tracks. Nags, dogs, trotters. You name it. He's now in debt for big sums to some of the local bookies. There was a meeting between the Chief, Ethical Standards and Crime Command and just before they elected to cut him loose, they decided to bug his mobile to see how he would handle the debt pressure. Sure as God made little green apples, they found he was ringing his Russian mate to see if between them they could get a gaming house going. The Russian's name by the way is Pavel Antonov, Russian mafia and a very nasty piece of work who the Department and the Feds believe is involved in a large scale begging scam in Melbourne involving illegals from Asia."

"The bookies up at Bendigo wanted their money, surely?" Kate chipped in.

"Ethical Standards knew they couldn't ignore the complaints completely, so they put him on notice and made him arrange a payment schedule from his wages to keep the locals satisfied. It gave them a reason to put him back into uniform and get him back down here where we believe he will get in contact with Antonov again. They don't just want Bobrov for something minor. They believe, because of him losing his CIU allowance and having to pay back the Bendigo bookies, he will try something big. They reckon they can get two birds for the price of one and here at Carlton there is a lot on display with all the different cultures. A new playground for him. We know what the Vietnamese community are like with gambling. It's in their blood. Bobrov thinks he has just got off with a severe reprimand and being put back into uniform and everything will be right in time," Stone said with raised eyebrows.

"Besides being an obvious crook and gambler, what other surprises can we expect? It's one thing keeping an eye on him, but if he tries any standover tactics or comes the heavy around here, I don't give a stuff about Ethical Standards. I'll stop him dead in his tracks if he tries anything on with local traders or restaurants," a snarling Tony Signorotto said to Phil Stone.

"The reason we are giving him a bit of rope is that wherever he has been stationed, he has actually done his job without too much drama. The job is just an eight hour fill in for him, some say. Hasn't involved any others in his gambling and has never been accused of approaching other members for money. Big bloke but has never come the heavy with anyone inside or outside the station. Just treat him as a sympathetic welfare case. If anyone asks about how he got to Carlton the way he did, just tell them that he asked to come back to uniform. He won't want to go into details about his gambling background. No doubt some stories will follow him down here. Just jump on them quick if you hear members talking about him."

"So, besides all this, who is going to monitor him after hours? We can't be with him twenty-four seven, and in all honesty, Phil, I won't be encouraging any of my troops and that includes the Sergeants to be socialising with him. I have to say right here and now, I don't like my station being used in some sort of spy network. When is he arriving? Where's he going to live?"

"I'm not happy either, Senior Sergeant," a clearly frustrated Phil Stone replied. "Welfare have set him up in a rent reduced flat in Flemington. The cover story from them is that we are a caring Department. You know, warm and fuzzy. They will look as though they are bending over backwards to rehabilitate him."

"In one way I don't care about him, but if he must work here, I am duty bound as his Senior Sergeant to treat him fairly. The only people that will be bent over and shafted will be him and ultimately me as his boss," Tony Signorotto said with a raised voice.

"Points noted Tony, but my hands are tied. Tenth floor has spoken so that's the end of the discussion. Comes down to this really. He can either pull his head in or continue with his bad habits," Phil Stone said as he glared at an uncomfortable looking Kate McLaren and a seething Tony Signorotto.

Silence engulfed the small and now overheated room before a calmed down Senior Sergeant spoke.

"Okay. We win some and we lose some. Obviously, I've lost this round. Looking at you though, Phil, you don't look entirely happy either?"

"As your Superintendent, Senior Sergeant, I am here to advise you of a situation. As a lifelong friend and supporter of this station you know I'm not happy about it either. I'd sack him in a heartbeat if I could."

Kate McLaren could see the tension dissipate with this comment. She was glad these two old warriors would never have a falling out over a crooked cop.

"Okay. Sorry Phil. It's just that I love this place and the people in it. To have a snake thrown in here means we will have to be on our toes every shift. Getting back to after hours, do you have any monitoring processes in place?" Tony said with a contrite voice.

"Mate, I'd be a very unhappy Superintendent if you just accepted this without a fight. This place has a fantastic reputation for looking after it's area. I'm as proud of that as anyone and I never cease telling it to those above me in town. And God forbid if you think for one minute that I won't have him covered, you'd better think again," Stone said smiling at them both.

"Don't keep us in suspense," a now relieved Tony Signorotto said.

"I've got Mick York and Johnny Petran from Melbourne Divisional Response tagging him after hours for the first couple of weeks. Big ask, but I insisted with the bosses that they have unlimited overtime for it. Hopefully due to his lack of money, he will make his move soon. They will be all over his Russian arse. By the way, he arrives in two days' time."

Before Tony could say anything, Kate spoke.

"Nothing ideal about all this boss, but there's one thing the three of us have in common that will sort this Bobrov out."

"What's that, Sergeant?"

"A deep, deep hatred of bent coppers!"

Chapter Four

Ricky Bobrov stared at the peeling and cracked bedroom ceiling of the old flat that the Police Welfare Department had provided him with in Flemington. Laying on the rickety bed, he couldn't make up his mind if he owed the Police Department a debt of gratitude or hated the situation he now found himself in. In truth, it was probably both.

Even though he still had a job as a uniform Sergeant he realised that the money coming out of his now diminished wage because of his return into uniform would make for a very frugal lifestyle in Melbourne. The obvious basic fact was that he just couldn't bring himself to give up gambling at the tracks just because he had been transferred.

He knew he could literally just take a punt on backing a few runners at Flemington, Caulfield or even on the dogs at Sandown Park, but if he didn't get some winners past the post, he'd really be in trouble. The Department would still garnish his wages to the banks back in Bendigo to service his debts to the locals up there and he would be surviving on next to nothing. Welfare wouldn't let him even have this accommodation for too long. For the time being he may have to give up the nags and any other animal on four legs he could bet on and just knuckle down at his new station. The first part of this thought process was soon eliminated. Track betting was now a full-time obsession with him after hanging around country race clubs for the past few years. He realised though, that Melbourne was a very multi-cultural city and there would be ways of raising cash without the Department knowing. He needed to feed his habit without drawing suspicion, so he would continue to perform his police duties to the best of his ability, however it was only a means to an end and he knew that his career, although he needed to keep it, wasn't the be all and end all of his existence. Track gambling had taken over.

Getting off the bed, he decided to do the right thing and phone into Carlton to see when he would start duty. He was owed a couple of days off and he would be telling them he wanted to take them immediately. Not that he'd give the roster Sergeant a particular reason, it was just that there was a mid-week race meeting coming up at Caulfield and a Saturday meeting at Flemington. Priorities first. He smiled to himself thinking that it was ironic that Welfare had really taken him from one gambling situation and placed him about one kilometre from the most famous racetrack in Australia. The home of the Melbourne Cup, Flemington.

Glancing at his phone, he saw an unfamiliar number which had left a voicemail message. Deciding he could deal with that later, he tapped in the number of the Carlton Police Station. The call was picked up in quick fashion.

"Carlton Police. Constable Bishop speaking. How can I help?" the young sounding female said.

That was answered quicker than anything at Bendigo.

"Yes, this is Detective Sergeant Bobrov," he automatically replied, forgetting that he put the title of detective in front of his rank. "Can I speak to the Senior Sergeant, thank you?"

"Sorry, Detective Sergeant, but Senior Sergeant Signorotto is in a meeting. Can I put you through to the Sergeant's office?"

"If you wouldn't mind," he replied.

The connection went through and as it did, Bobrov spoke first just as a female answered.

"Detective Sergeant Ricky Bobrov. Who am I speaking to?"

"Ah, I think that is Sergeant Bobrov, isn't it? You are speaking with Sergeant Kate McLaren."

Silence ensued before Bobrov spoke.

"Ah yes, my mistake. I was wanting to find out when Senior Sergeant Signorotto had me starting and what portfolios he has assigned me. I'm owed a few days off, so I'd like to take them now before I start."

"Already have the Sergeants roster done, Sergeant Bobrov and unfortunately you'll have to wait for those rest days. This is a very busy place, and a lot of our Sergeants are tied up with arrests and subsequent court hearings. I've got you down for 0700 hours start tomorrow morning in the Watch House and inquiry counter for the next week. You'll be able to meet up with the Senior Sergeant in the morning. He is always here at seven o'clock to make sure everything is running smoothly and to get a de-brief from the night shift."

Bosses don't get in till at least eight, he thought.

He spoke with a calm voice.

"I thought with my experience in the crime area, he would give me that portfolio. Am I correct in thinking that?"

"Negative to that. We have several Sergeants who are ex CIU and one of them has that portfolio. He has you down for training purposes now but with your track record, excuse the pun, you'll have to sort that out with him." There was another silence before Kate continued.

"Sergeant Bobrov. The Command structure here at Carlton which includes the Sergeants, know your story. None of the other ranks have been told. We are more than prepared to assist you and see you succeed at Carlton, so I thought starting you at the 'pointy end' of the station would be best. This way you can get to meet some of the public you will be looking after for the next few weeks before you get rotated onto night shift. You'll need to start all over again, don't you think, before you would be eligible to get the detective title back?"

"Obviously that rank will have to wait a while. Let's see how it all plays out," a flattened Bobrov said slowly with a hint of anger in his voice.

"Okay. We will see you bright and early at 0645 hours then. The morning shift Sergeant is expected to be here for the night shift de-brief. That is a 'given' with our boss. Oh, and by the way, the title of Detective is not a rank. It is a title given to a CIU member. It is not a promotion to a rank."

"Thanks for reminding me, Sergeant," Bobrov said, barely containing his anger now. "See you tomorrow. Can't wait to meet you."

Bobrov slowly took his mobile phone away from his ear.

Going to have to put that bitch in her place.

Stepping outside the door of his flat, he started to walk down the street to get something to eat at the same time as he hit the voicemail button on his phone. Coming to a halt on the footpath after listening to the message, he slowly spoke to himself.

"Marco Toscano. Where do I know that name from?"

Chapter Five

Ricky Bobrov made sure he was on time for his first day at Carlton. In fact, he got there at six-thirty in the morning to beat his new Senior Sergeant in. It was to no avail. Tony Signorotto had arrived even earlier.

Bobrov was making himself a cup of coffee after being given directions to the mess room when his new boss walked in.

"Sergeant Bobrov I take it?" Tony Signorotto said from the mess room doorway without making any effort to approach him.

"Correct, Senior Sergeant. Ricky Bobrov reporting for duty. I was advised to be here bright and early," he said, taking a few steps towards the big uniformed Senior Sergeant that loomed large in front of him. He put out his right arm in a gesture to shake hands.

Signorotto stepped forward and placed his right hand in an outstretched gesture, palm downwards so when Bobrov shook his hand, Signorotto's was on top and his below.

The dominant handshake theory, Bobrov thought. *Let the games begin.*

Signorotto noticed that even though his hand was on top of Bobrov's, the grip was returned with the same strong measure that he had given the new Sergeant. He let go and walked over to the kitchen bench to get his own coffee. He only spoke after he had finished making his morning brew.

"Come with me, Sergeant. We will go to the shift handover and then upstairs to my office so we can have a little heart to heart chat."

"Sounds fair," Bobrov replied.

Spinning around to meet his junior member eye to eye, Signorotto replied.

"Oh, have no fear. I'll be fair with you Mr Bobrov. I'll also be very honest with you."

During the night shift handover to the day shift, Bobrov noticed that Signorotto read all the reports from the night shift thoroughly and asked several questions of his crew in relation to them covering their patrol areas as often as they could between jobs. He also picked up that in the few quiet times throughout the night, the crew dedicated themselves to random car searches and licence checks. They had made a couple of suspects turn their cars inside out for them with minor drug possession charges being laid. When he was handed the sheets by Signorotto, he could see that the crew had given themselves very little downtime. They had only come into the station twice. Once for a quick meal and the second to back up the station crew when some drunken fool had staggered into the watch house thinking it was a local hotel demanding a bed and a meal for the night. He got fifty percent of what he asked for — the bed behind bars.

From speaking to the tired crew and then to the eager day shift duo, he could tell this was a well-run and pretty happy place to work. He had never worked at a station where the Senior Sergeant was a permanent fixture at the morning shift change. Not that it made an iota of difference to Bobrov because he didn't plan on staying more than the minimum eight hours it took him to get out of the blue monkey suit. He had just finished reading the nightshift reports when Signorotto spoke quickly to him.

"Upstairs in five minutes. My office."

Ricky Bobrov walked into Tony Signorotto's office four and a half minutes later. He stood calmly as his Senior Sergeant sat behind the big desk reading the personnel file that had arrived at Carlton the day before from Bendigo. A full minute passed before Signorotto placed the file down and looked at his new and hopefully temporary Sergeant.

"Bobrov. Russian, I take it?"

"The heritage behind the name, but not me, boss. Never been there and have no real interest in the history of my forebears," a smiling Ricky Bobrov said, looking directly at Signorotto. "Do I call you boss or Senior Sergeant?" he said, trying to throw the conversation in a different direction.

"Either one. I don't do first names with my Sergeants unless I initiate it, which is hardly ever."

"Spoke to one yesterday by the name of McLaren. Wouldn't mind getting on a first name basis with her. Bit of a hard arse I'd say," Bobrov said with a leering grin.

"You'd say, would you?" Signorotto said raising his voice an octave and giving Bobrov a stare that would cut through steel. "Don't think my Sergeant McLaren, VA by the way, would have time for your sort. Let's get that straight right now, Sergeant. You'll find that if you do the wrong thing by anyone at this station, the rest of my Sergeants will most likely take the situation into their own hands well before I hear about it. To be honest, that is the way I would expect it to be. I told you I'd be straight up and honest with you, Sergeant Bobrov. This is Carlton and although we might have a few problems down Lygon Street at Trades Hall from time to time, they share the same motto that this station swears by."

"Which is?" Bobrov replied in an uninterested tone.

"Touch one, touch all. Get the message, Sergeant?" Signorotto said with a harsh tone before continuing.

"I was against you coming here from the get-go. My station is staffed by hard working police and civilians. I have absolutely no time for a member who has been put back into uniform because he can't control his bad habits, in your case, track gambling. You've not only disrespected the hard-working members of Bendigo CIU, but you've also let down the Bendigo community. The only thing that is keeping you employed by Victoria Police is the fact you have shown by your record that, believe it or not, criminality aside, you are capable of doing your job. Why the Department has helped you out with a financial pay-back package is beyond me. They probably just don't want any bad PR coming their way. What have you got to say to that?"

Bobrov had been prepared to cop some flack over the situation but he was realising more and more that he really couldn't give a damn. He was getting no joy from his job and he realised he liked his off-duty pursuit more and more every time he went to a track. Like all punters though, he knew that his luck would come. Just a matter of time before he hit a big winner. Never did he stop to think that it was more than a hobby. It was becoming an addiction like drugs and alcohol, and there were plenty of coppers who had ended up kneeling and gnashing their teeth before those Gods.

Having been through all this before with Ethical Standards, he wasn't going to go through it with this true-blue believer who already knew the story about Bendigo. He was just going to run out the same line from now on. He was over it all. He knew he needed his job for the time being but once he was back on his feet, he would pull the plug on the Department. He would do his job, but it was not going to be his priority.

"I've been through all this with Ethical Standards. It's between them and me. Enough said. I'll cop my fair whack and perform my duties. I believe that's all you can ask," Bobrov said letting out a big sigh.

Tony Signorotto raised himself up from his seat, walked around to the front of his mahogany foxhole and slammed the office door, causing his civilian assistant Veronica, who had a desk close by in the next office to let out a loud exclamation of fright. Walking up behind Bobrov, he spoke very quietly into his ear.

"Usually, I have an open-door policy in my office. I do not intend to belittle you in front of all the troops because only myself and my Sergeants know your full story. The one thing I will say is this Sergeant Bobrov. You have an extremely chequered past and you don't seem to care too much. In the long run, I will treat you the same as I treat every person under my command, but if you so much as put one foot out of line here or involve anyone of my team in any of your nefarious schemes I will be all over you like a cheap suit. Do you fully understand the implications of what I am saying Sergeant?"

Bobrov just nodded his head.

"Answer me Sergeant. Don't just move your head like a bobble doll."

"Loud and clear, Senior Sergeant."

"You can call me boss like I said before."

"I'll stick to Senior Sergeant thanks," Bobrov said turning to Signorotto with a cold stare.

Signorotto returned to the other side of his desk and stood facing Bobrov and placed both his hands on the leather inlay before looking him directly in the eye. Bobrov didn't blink but just returned a blank thousand-yard stare over Signorotto's right shoulder. It was then that the Officer in Charge of Carlton knew he had a real problem member on his hands.

Bloody hell, Phil Stone. This bloke is a real case. I just know it.

"Enough for now, Sergeant. Get down to the Watch House and inquiry counter and try to show some interest in your job. As far as the troops go, they have been told you are here on a temporary transfer down from Bendigo because you have a sick relative in Melbourne. Why Ethical Standards are looking after you is beyond me."

"Yes, Senior Sergeant," Bobrov said, slowly exiting the office.

A real fucking old school type, this one. Seven and a half hours to go and I'm out of here.

Tony Signorotto was still standing and privately fuming seconds later when Kate McLaren walked slowly past his door looking at Bobrov's back.

"Kate, a minute please," he called out to his Sergeant.

Kate McLaren walked into the office smiling and pretended to check the hinges on the old door.

"No damage here. Veronica's nerves are a bit jumpy though and her blood pressure has gone through the roof. Not like you to lose your cool, boss. How did it go with the Russian Revolutionary?"

"Not funny Kate. This bloke has issues. I'm not saying dangerous ones but it's obvious that he couldn't give a stuff about the job. I only want him working down there with senior members. Even if it means not giving him a portfolio at all, I don't care. Those rest days that he's owed, give them to him now. The less time he is here the better. If he's going to stuff up like the Department thinks then let it be outside of here. I reckon that the track gambling bug that he has picked up and owes big money on will be too much for him down here. The Divisional Response guys will have to be on their toes I think, Kate."

"As long as he keeps straight in here. The Sergeants won't put up with crap," Kate replied.

Chapter Six

The back flip from Kate McLaren to Ricky Bobrov regarding his request for his owed rest days that he had brought from Bendigo came late in the day while he was behind the inquiry counter trying to ignore as many public inquiries as he could whilst trying to palm them off to the two young Constables under his command.

"The boss said you are to take off those four days you're owed straight way, Sergeant," a polite but succinct Kate McLaren said to him when she came downstairs. She could tell by the look of the young members that they both wished he would disappear in a puff of smoke immediately. She had seen it all before with members who were trying to work as a team but were failing because of one idiot who would not pull his or her weight.

"Why the change of heart?" Bobrov replied.

Kate looked him in the eye. "Ours is not to reason why."

"Fair enough. I'm not complaining, but you did say it was too busy for me to take them."

"As I told you. I do the Sergeants' roster, but the Senior Sergeant signs off on it," Kate said as she turned and left the inquiry counter area. She didn't see the older female who had just entered the station and was standing waiting her turn at the counter.

Nice long weekend coming up, he thought.

Ricky Bobrov didn't dwell on why he had been given the days off. He was just happy because it meant he could now get to the race meeting that was coming up at Flemington next Saturday.

His enthusiasm for Police work wasn't matching that of the two counter inquiry members, whom he believed pandered unnecessarily to the whims and fancies of all and sundry that wandered into the station. Looking up at the clock on the far wall, he saw that there was about half an hour before his shift finished. Even though he could see that the two young members were busy with inquiries and the phone was ringing off its hook, he ignored a request for assistance by one of the frustrated Constables and was about to head off to the mess room for a coffee, while also disregarding the older woman who was waiting.

"I'm off for a coffee you two. See you in a few days if you are lucky enough to work with me again," Bobrov said with a dismissive voice, without a backward glance, as he headed away before being brought to a sudden halt when the waiting female's voice boomed across the entrance area.

"Excuse me, Sergeant. I'd like some service here and seeing you are the only one who is obviously free, I'd like it from you."

"You'll be right luv. They'll get to you," came the flippant reply.

"No, Sergeant. You'll get to me right now, thank you," the now seething female replied. "My taxes pay your wages and I'd like to see those same taxes at work, if you don't mind. These young members are busy, and you obviously aren't."

Turning to face the female civilian, Bobrov spoke in such a derogatory tone, it made the two other civilians, and the Constables stop their conversation and stare at him.

"I'll decide when I get to you. Whatever you're here to complain about can't be too serious otherwise you would have phoned in. We don't want to see our old age pensioners have to shuffle down to their local station for nothing," Bobrov said glaring at her.

The female replied with an answer that left him searching for words.

"I can't hear you because of the ringing of the unanswered phone at your abandoned counter, Sergeant." The look on the face of the female civilian turned from one of disbelief to that of rage as she stepped forward and fronted Bobrov.

"Listen to me you rude prick. I didn't come in here to complain about anything. I actually came in to have a cup of coffee with my very good friend and former colleague, Senior Sergeant Signorotto who I can see standing directly behind you. I was going to ask you if you could just let him know I was here, but it looks as though he has been standing there listening to our conversation, doesn't it Senior Sergeant?"

"That will be enough, Sergeant Bobrov," Signorotto barked. "You are making it more difficult for yourself every time you open your mouth around here. Finish up, get out and come back next Tuesday morning with a whole new attitude. However, before you go, I'd like to introduce you to a former member of this station, Leading Senior Constable Jill Norton, VA. Yes, Sergeant, this station has one former female Valour Award recipient and one current one in Sergeant McLaren. Look at the wall in front of you," a furious Signorotto said as he also stepped forward and eyeballed the now wilting Sergeant.

Bobrov hadn't taken any notice of the two framed photos near the clock, because the only thing he had been looking at on the wall during his shift was the clock as it ticked down the hours remaining in his shift. When he did examine them, he saw the two framed pictures of Kate McLaren and Jill Norton in their uniforms proudly displaying their Valour Award medals.

Signorotto continued. "Their pictures are there because they were and are outstanding members of this station and have prided themselves in looking after the citizens of this suburb. Something which I don't think you can relate to!"

Ricky Bobrov could do nothing but move his guilty looks from Jill Norton to the framed pictures and back again. Eventually he spoke.

"Ah, yeah, right. Hi Jill," he stammered.

Jill Norton walked straight past Bobrov without replying to the half-hearted attempt at a greeting as Tony Signorotto indicated for her to continue to the mess room before turning to speak.

"Sergeant, you have twenty minutes left of your shift today. Forget the coffee and help those members. I don't want to see you again until 0700 hours Tuesday morning."

Trying to climb out of the hole he had dug for himself, Bobrov attempted a feeble reply.

"Thanks for the days off, Senior Sergeant."

"The station's pleasure," Signorotto replied with a voice that sounded like gravel being crushed as he followed Jill Norton down the hallway.

Stepping into the room behind her, he was met with an avalanche of words from the feisty veteran member.

"You sit on the transfer boards for members to this station. How the hell did that useless excuse for a Sergeant let alone a Victorian Police Officer ever get past you? I hope you're not back on the booze, because if you are, I'll rip you apart, son," the red-faced visitor let fly with. You've been off it for years now with help from a lot of people."

"Jesus Christ, Jill. Of course, I'm not back on the piss and it bloody well hurts that you think I am," he said as he waved his arms towards her in an attempt to calm down his old work mate who was spilling more coffee than putting it into the two cups that she had got out of the cupboard. A relieved Jill Norton took a breath and continued.

"Well, you had better come up with a good explanation about that stupid, embarrassing fool out there. It's one thing having a go at me, but he did it in front of two other civilians. Two young Constables were flat out while he was doing sweet, pardon the French, fuck-all to help. I'd been standing there watching him, the lazy bastard. If that had been my inquiry counter, I would have reamed him good and proper," Jill said as she sat down abruptly at the table.

"Not my doing, Jill." Landed on me by Phil Stone just now and I can tell you I'm not happy about it. Can't go into a lot of detail, but what I can say is that he is a temporary discipline transfer from Bendigo CIU."

"I can well understand it if that is the way he speaks to people. It might be an idea to keep him out of the public eye," Norton said with a calmer voice than she used in her previous outburst as she handed a mug of coffee to Signorotto.

"I'd love to keep him away from the public altogether, but I can't unfortunately. He's come to us with rest days owed and I've already had a run in with him this morning about his attitude. I've given him his days off to get him out of here and give me some time to think of what I will do with him next week. Stuffed if I know though."

"What's the discipline hitch?" Jill said with a curious look on her face.

"One of the usuals when it comes to coppers. Gambling. Or to be more precise, on-track gambling. Owes money to the bookies at Bendigo. To make matters worse, the Department in its infinite wisdom has let Welfare set him up with a flat in Flemington, a stone's throw from the front gate of the racetrack. How they think I can run a station with this prick here is beyond me."

"You know my attitude, Tony. Look after you and yours first then help those that need help. If he gets caught in his own crossfire then bad luck. Your job is the welfare of the other members under your command. Simple as that. If this bloke has been put back into uniform so the bloody toe cutters can land a big fish then that's their problem, not yours."

"There's more to the story which I can't go into, Jill and I know you'll understand after working with me for so long. Ethical Standards are the puppet masters pulling the strings from way above my head. He's the puppet and I'm providing the stage."

"Sounds to me like he should be on a stage and heading out of town pronto, mate."

Tony Signorotto nodded his worried head at Jill Norton before taking a large mouthful of coffee.

Chapter Seven

Ricky Bobrov stepped off the train after it pulled into the Flemington Racecourse station. He was dressed in a pair of new black jeans and casual shirt. The most important item of his apparel though was a comfortable pair of shoes that would take him around the famous betting ring many times this race day.

He had finally decided to ring the number that had been left on his phone and was surprised when the person who answered had brought up their past association almost immediately. Bobrov had run through the so-called meeting many times in his mind before he had arrived at the track. He thought back.

Marco Toscano. You're not some crook I arrested a few years ago at Footscray, are you? Or was it the time the Gaming Squad was coming in through the front door with a battering ram? It was in Droop Street. I'd had a bad night on the punt. We jumped a couple of fences together and legged it to your car. Told you to ring if I could pay back the favour. Now I remember!

Bobrov didn't forget faces and Toscano's image had come floating back. It couldn't be much of a favour owed for a quick exit. The incident was history, and he knew that Toscano couldn't get any traction out of it. He told him to meet him at the Makybe Diva statue on the lawns in front of the grandstand near the winning post, and as he slowly walked towards the famous racehorse icon, he recognised the small but muscly figure that had helped him out a few years before. He got on the front foot immediately.

"Long time, Marco. How's life been treating you?"

"Not too bad, Ricky. Always looking for the next big break like most."

"Aren't we all. I'm not at Footscray anymore. You still around the old traps?"

"Nah, mate. Getting a bit warm for me around there. Your mob's been coming down hard in the last year or so. You're lucky you left, or you might have had to make a few more quick exits. You still in the Force?"

Bobrov gave Toscano a long hard look before he replied.

"Marco my friend. You helped me out once and I'm grateful, but as you know, it is ancient history so don't expect miracles from me just because I may owe you a very small favour from the past. Let's get that straight right here and now. The answer to your question is, yes, I am still in the Force and I'm now a Sergeant at Carlton so let's cut to the chase. What do you want?"

As Toscano began speaking, neither of them saw the punter about thirty metres away raise his phone in their direction to start snapping some photos of them together.

"Fair enough. Let me know now though if I'm speaking to a person who still likes to make some extra tax-free money with some inventive ideas which maybe on the other side of your blue line. Just money ideas, not drugs or anything."

"You wearing a wire?" Bobrov shot back as he took a step closer to Toscano.

"No fucking way," Toscano said before turning around. "Mate just thought you might be interested in something. If you were, I just need some information on a number plate. Not to worry, I'll be on my way. All good. Have a good life, Ricky."

After Toscano had taken a few steps away, Bobrov called out.

"Okay, okay. Come on back. I don't mind spending some time listening. Bear in mind, I have only been at Carlton a few days so I'm not really up to speed on the area if you are looking for a safe house for a card game."

Toscano slowly turned back and spoke.

"That could be another possibility for sure, but what I was after was a name from a car I saw in the city the other day. It made me realise that over this side of the bridge there are a lot of business opportunities for a couple of smart lads."

Ricky Bobrov's interest was piqued with the last comment.

"What type of business opportunities, Marco? You never know, I might be interested in a new venture also."

Marco Toscano then quietly told Bobrov about the beggars in the city and him following from a distance watching the person obviously doing some sort of business with several of them all the way north up Swanston Street.

"Interesting," Bobrov said after the story had been told. "If all the beggars you saw are Asians, then I'd bet someone is controlling them and has their passports. Could be quite a big operation that you've seen and most likely a very profitable one. Trouble is, it could be something that you might not want to go near. Maybe too big and profitable. Tell you what I'll do, I'll check out Vic Roads for the details of the car and I'll be back in touch. In the meantime, I'm going to have a nice day here at Flemington with the ponies."

As Toscano walked away, he turned and spoke.

"Might be worth it financially for me to have a look around Carlton for a house for a card game or two. Would you be in on that or am I speaking to a blue believer?"

"Mate, blue believers are just football followers from Carlton. I couldn't give a toss about football so, no, I'm not a blue believer regarding football or my job. I play a straight bat when I'm at work, but I can tell you, the way I've been treated recently I haven't been a believer in the uniform for some time now. A few extra bucks are okay by me. Gives me more time with the ponies. Let's keep in touch. If Carlton is like all other police stations, they'll keep a holiday register."

"What's that?" a quizzical Marco Toscano asked.

"Some of these dumb citizens tell their local police when they are away on holiday in the belief that the troops will actually check on their houses and patrol their streets at least once or twice a day. They have no idea of what workloads stations have. Be lucky if the cars can go past once a week if that."

"So, what you're saying is that you can let me know when a place is empty for a week or so for a possible card game?"

"Catching on quick. There's another race meeting here next week. Even if I'm rostered, I'll call in sick and see you back here, Marco," Bobrov said as he put out his hand to shake with Toscano without realising at the same time several more photos were taken of the meeting and the shaking of hands.

Marco Toscano walked off towards the railway station with a smile on his face.

Chapter Eight

Superintendent Phil Stone was sitting down to Sunday dinner with his wife when he looked across at the dining room sideboard and saw the flashing screen on his work mobile phone. He deliberately left it on silent at home for the sake of his wife and family who had endured years of having their time together ruined by 'The Job.' He had a feeling that this call would not be good news. Picking up the flashing mobile, he spoke.

"Superintendent Stone speaking."

"Sir, Mick York from the Divisional Response Unit here. Sorry to annoy you. There was no answer at your office, so I presume you are having a well-earned rest day?"

"No problems, Mick. I thought you may be ringing after I gave you that surveillance job. Good news or bad?"

"Well, I think you are going to have to do a bit more work on our colleague, boss. Bobrov spent virtually the whole of Saturday at the Flemington races and from what Johnny Petran and I could see, he spent all the time going from the betting ring back to the finishing post watching his money go down the. He didn't even stay for the last race. I'd say he went through a sizeable amount of money yesterday."

"Was he by himself all day, Mick?"

"No. That's the interesting thing and really why I'm ringing you. At the start of the day before the first race, he met up with a muscly looking little guy about the same age. They were down on the grass in front of the grandstand and talked closely for about twenty minutes. No back slaps or that so I'd say it was a planned meet. In the end they shook hands and went their separate ways. Bobrov to the betting ring and this other dude went back out of the course and caught a train back to the city. Obviously not a punter on the nags. We got plenty of photos of them together."

"Great Mick. You're my eyes on the ground. Did it look dodgy at all?"

"If I was a betting man, excuse the pun, I'd say it was some sort of business type thing. Looked like a lot of talking being done by both parties."

"Can you get those photos circulated amongst some of the troops and CIU areas. Let's see if this head is known. Only the ones of him though. I don't want Bobrov getting a heads up on the photos, so don't show them round Carlton."

"Way in front of the game there, boss. Johnny and I thought we'd go back through his old haunts at Bendigo and Footscray without letting anyone in on the fact that there was a copper involved. We hit pay dirt with a member of Footscray CIU. He pigeonholed the little bloke straight away. His name is Marco Toscano. Hasn't been active recently but is known around the traps as a mid-level arranger for some big rolling card games throughout the western suburbs."

"Rolling card games? What's that mean?"

"They play some high-stake card game in one house and have another on standby in case they get a whisper of our boys kicking in the door of the first place. They roll out of one and continue the game in the other. When they are on a roll, they must keep gambling. They are like addicts except it's money and not drugs. Winning is their drug. They don't mind pulling up stakes and shifting if they keep winning, or in some cases losing. People like Toscano like to have their games covered, and I can guarantee you that our mate Bobrov would have been involved in some of this shit when he was back at Footscray. Without giving anything away boss, I had a beer last night with a couple of ex western suburbs boys who, with a bit of nudging in the right direction, didn't have a good word to say about Bobrov. If ever they were glad someone got promoted, it was him. Meant he had to move on. No one trusted him."

"Thanks Mick. Job well done. I'll have to think this one through carefully. Bobrov's back at work tomorrow but I might just get you to check what he does next weekend if I can. Overtime for this isn't a problem, tell Johnny. In the meantime, I will try and get something going on the inside."

"No problems, boss. If this bloke is as bent as I think, he'll need to be watched twenty-four seven I'd reckon. We'll work him around the clock with or without the overtime. Don't want his sort in the Force."

"Welcome aboard the Phil Stone train of thought, Mick!"

Chapter Nine

Sergeant Ricky Bobrov walked into the Carlton Police station fifteen minutes before the start of his Tuesday morning shift.

After checking the Sergeants roster, he noticed he had been put down for a correspondence shift for the day. He knew he had some overdue paperwork from Bendigo CIU and a day in the office would help him get the registration details of the black Mercedes that Marco Toscano had seen regarding the beggars in Swanston Street.

Bobrov wasn't stupid when it came to ways of getting around the increasing security of Police computers. He knew that if he logged onto a work computer to find out the owner of the Mercedes, his name would be red flagged by Vic Roads. All Police who were on suspension or had been moved in their job like him were constantly being monitored by the Department. The Registration Branch would immediately throw back the inquiry to the Ethical Standards Department and they in turn would send it down the line to his Senior Sergeant. Given the fact that he hadn't even been out on patrol at Carlton, it would send a loud ping off Tony Signorotto's radar.

Fucking Police Force that fears itself. Bobrov thought.

An hour into a very light check of his outstanding paperwork he put his plan into action. He saw that the night shift crew had put in a list of registration numbers whose drivers had been given breath tests the night before at a random breath testing station. These numbers had to be checked through Vic Roads for any outstanding warrants or fines and if so, passed onto the local police station. To do all that checking during the night with the number of alcohol and drug tests that was demanded of the present-day General Duties members would have meant that they would be tied up for hours during their shift. Obviously, any suspect cars or drivers that were given tests were dealt with there and then. The Government though didn't want the average punter held up for too long. Votes at the next election were crucial. All members knew it was a political statistics game that was constantly being played by whoever was in power. He grabbed the list off the clipboard and walked over to Kate McLaren.

"Kate, I haven't got a lot on my plate so I might as well do the Vic Roads checks. They'll take an hour or so."

"How many are there on the list?" Kate inquired.

"Hang on and I'll count them."

Bobrov counted twenty-six registration numbers and then called out as he walked away with the list.

"Twenty-seven all up. Won't take long."

"Okay. Just make sure you enter them all on the official preliminary breath test request list then they won't be asking why it's you that's submitting the form. They'll know it's all about breath tests," Kate said looking over at Bobrov.

"Not to be trusted, eh?" Bobrov replied with a sneering look at Kate.

"You're the one under a cloud mate, not me."

Bobrov sat down at a computer just as a young Constable was putting a cup of coffee down next to it with the intention of continuing his own paperwork.

"Sarge, I was already working on…"

"Well, I'm here now sunshine, so take your coffee and find somewhere else."

"But I'm halfway through typing up a statement."

Bobrov looked at the computer screen and with a quick couple of movements of the computer mouse, the young Constables' work disappeared.

"Hope you saved that, son. Now go away and start again or come back in an hour when I've finished."

The Constable picked up his coffee, glared at Bobrov and stormed out of the room.

Kate McLaren jumped up from her desk and strode over to Bobrov.

"You do that again Sergeant and I'll personally drag you up before the boss. That member must have that statement ready by the time he finishes today. That was no way to show leadership."

Bobrov shrugged his shoulders and started to enter the registration numbers as Kate walked over to the fuming young Constable and spoke to him.

"Don't worry. The boss is keeping a close eye on that new Sergeant. If he isn't finished in an hour, you can give your written statement to me, and I'll get the boss's secretary to type it up."

"Thanks, Sarge. I do want to get away on time this afternoon. I've got football training."

Bobrov wasn't interested in the conversation between McLaren and the Constable. He was only interested in adding a final registration number to the inquiry list. The twenty-seventh and last number was the one that Toscano had given him.

About fifty minutes later, Bobrov had just entered the Toscano inquiry as a number from the previous night's breath testing statistics when Tony Signorotto put his head around the corner of the correspondence room and called out to Kate without even looking at Bobrov.

"Kate. Off to headquarters. Meeting with Phil Stone. Something about manpower."

"Okay boss. Switch your phone through to me if you want to."

"Already done. Ricky, what are you doing today? Hope you are fixing up your Bendigo stuff. I want all your crap from up there back there."

Bobrov was working up a dislike for Signorotto but smiled at him when he replied.

"Just doing last night's stats for the breath testing. About to send them off."

"Make sure they are on the right form. I don't want return phone calls, thanks."

Bobrov looked at Signorotto at the same time as hitting the send key on the last number.

Signorotto turned and left as Bobrov saw the reply come back to him. He immediately spoke out loud to himself, but not loud enough for Kate McLaren to overhear.

"Well, well. Pavel Antonov. My old mate from Yarraville. What scam are you running these days? What have you been up to that would make Marco Toscano follow you right up Swanston Street? Something interesting, I'll bet."

And something that I want to know about my Russian friend.

Bobrov wrote down the details and was pleased to see that the address was in Moonee Ponds. Just up the road from where his digs were.

Chapter Ten

Tony Signorotto didn't like going into headquarters in the city. Too hard to get to through the traffic and too many officers walking around, who, in his own words, 'couldn't find a crook if they saw one floating in their soup.'

One of the few that he had the utmost respect for was his old friend Superintendent Phil Stone. They trusted each other implicitly and Phil was only too keen to attend anything that happened at the Carlton Police station or for that matter, anything in Carlton, especially at Dom Santino's famous Italian restaurant in Lygon Street, the scene of all celebrations both happy and sad for past and present members of the Carlton Police family.

After navigating the necessary but infuriating electronic security nightmare in the city headquarters and finally arriving at Phil Stone's office, he not only saw the seated Stone behind his desk but also a younger member whom Signorotto himself had taken under his wing and trained at Carlton.

Senior Detective Max Tyler stood up and smiled as Signorotto entered the room and put out his hand to shake hands with his former mentor.

"Been a while, boss. Great to see you," Tyler said warmly.

"You too Max. How's life as a big city detective treating you?"

"Always on the go. Just like at Carlton. Head down, bum up."

When Tyler had arrived at the old Carlton Police station, Phil Stone had given Tony Signorotto a mentoring role over the raw recruit. It was not only to knock a few edges off Tyler but more importantly to get Signorotto back on the straight and narrow and off the booze. The then Sergeant had hit the bottle due to the result of a car chase gone wrong which resulted in a local hoon being incinerated. Signorotto and Tyler had been through a lot since then, sorting through the sewers and scum of the old bluestone suburb. Mafia wars and criminal takeovers had been fought and won. It had been a brutal, eye-opening introduction to life on the streets for the young Tyler and he had Signorotto to thank for his position in the Force. Tyler would be forever grateful for the chances he had been given.

After a few memories and 'war stories' had been shared not only by Signorotto and Tyler but also by Phil Stone, whose name had also been etched in Carlton Police folklore history, Signorotto looked slowly at his old friend Stone before he spoke.

"Okay, Phil. What's going on here?" You didn't ask me to come into the ivory tower to reminisce about days past or to offer me tea and biscuits. Something is pinging on my radar and is starting to smell more off than Yum Cha in Dom's Italian bistro. What have you dragged me in for, Superintendent?"

A surprised look passed between Tyler and Stone before the latter burst out laughing.

"You must need glasses in your old age, Senior Sergeant," Stone said pointing at the epaulette on his own right shoulder before redirecting his hand and pointing at his name badge on his navy-blue shirt.

The 'penny' suddenly dropped with Signorotto. Phil Stone was no longer wearing the crown and one pip of a Superintendent but the crown and three pips of a Commander. With a quick glance at his name tag, he couldn't see the word 'Acting' next to the word Commander, so he knew immediately that Phil had been promoted to the higher rank. He couldn't help himself with his next remark. Something that could only be said between old friends and people who had gone into battle together.

"Get those out of a Corn Flakes packet, mate?" he said indicating the shiny new epaulettes Stone's shirt was displaying. "Couldn't they find anyone else to promote, you old bastard?"

Stone stood, leant on his desk and stared back at Signorotto before replying.

"I resent those comments, Senior Sergeant. Well, at least the one about being old," he said and started to grin.

Tony stepped up to Phil and grabbed him in a bear like hug.

"Mate. That is fantastic news. You deserve it so much. When did this happen?"

"I've known for about a week, but honestly, I've had more important things on my mind."

"Where are they packing you off to Commander? I suppose that what's more important to me though is who is my new Superintendent?"

"Well, they've created a new position of Metropolitan Uniform Commander, so that's good for all of us. I'll stay as your overall boss, but I don't know who the Superintendent is below me."

Turning to Tyler, Signorotto spoke to the young Senior Detective.

"Did you just spot the new rank as you were passing the office?"

"Ah, no, not really, I…"

"No, of course you didn't. Your office is way downstairs. You got called up here for a reason. What's going on here, Superintendent, sorry, Commander? What other little surprises are you going to pull on me and Senior Detective Tyler here?" a suspicious sounding Signorotto said slowly just before Tyler spoke again.

"Ah, Sarge, it's just that" …Max Tyler said before being cut off with a wave of a big arm from Tony Signorotto.

"Let the good Commander speak now, Senior."

Stone looked at Signorotto and a red-faced Tyler before speaking.

"Sorry Senior Sergeant. It's Acting Sergeant Tyler now, who will be stationed at Carlton from the start of the next roster," the Commander said to a now dumbstruck Tony Signorotto. "Let me explain and I'm sure you will be more than happy with your latest acquisition."

"I wanted you both here so we can all be on the same page about this, Tony. Max has been up here for half an hour because I didn't want to have to go through the whole Ricky Bobrov spiel with you again."

"Yeah, understand that, Phil, but what's with sending Max over to us? We have a full complement of Sergeants. Not that I mind Max going up for the role. What's your plan?"

"Well, the three of us and Kate are going to keep a very close eye on Bobrov. I wanted to bring Kate over here this morning, but I saw on your roster that she and he are the only two Sergeants on at Carlton this morning. Tony, you'll have to brief her when you return. I'm sending Max over as an upgrade so that Bobrov can get close to this young, inexperienced Acting Sergeant who will naturally be pumping him for advice on everything from parking tickets to looking after members. I know that many of your troops at Carlton know Max already, so it won't come as a surprise to see him coming over for a couple of months of upgrading. Max is basically going to be a uniformed under-cover member reporting to you and to me. Now let's go upstairs to Degani's and get a coffee and I'll fill you in on what our friend Ricky Bobrov was up to last Saturday at the Flemington races."

An hour later as Tony and Max shook hands on the ground floor prior to going their separate ways, Tony spoke.

"What with the Divisional Response guys and us looking at him, I'll be very surprised if we don't discover Ricky slipping up at some stage. It may be that either he is back with his old mates or someone has discovered he is back in town and maybe wants to team up with him or just wants a police favour now and then. Phil had told me over the phone the other day that some of those Bendigo bookies are still savage on him, not just for still being in 'The Job' but because the Department has given him a get out of gaol card with that repayment scheme. Anyway, I'll have a word to Kate and start you on the roster."

"I was thinking," Max said to his soon to be boss. "Why don't you arrange for a bit of a party at Dom's for Commander Stone's promotion and because I am the junior Acting Sergeant, I'll have to work the shift with Bobrov so all the other Sergeants can crack an invite? Not that I want to miss the party, but it would be a good opportunity to have eight hours with him in a one-on-one work situation."

"Good thinking, Max. We can party together later if we trip him up. I'll see how our old friend Dom Santino is set up for Saturday week. That's into the next roster so Kate can swing the changes. Let Ricky play the benevolent Sergeant showing poor you the ropes about being a supervisor."

"Talk soon, boss. I've got a heap of paperwork sitting on my desk, so I'd better get back to it."

Tony Signorotto went down the lift to the underground police car park but thought to himself as he did.

Don't like these meeting at racetracks. Nothing good comes out of them.

Chapter Eleven

Ricky Bobrov left it until late the next night to go for a walk to Moonee Ponds. In fact, he left it till almost midnight.

He had no intention of going to the address that he had written down from the Vic Roads database because he knew the type of person he was dealing with. If Pavel Antonov was the same as a couple of years ago in Footscray, it would have been a pointless visit. He knew he would not be at home if there was the hint of a card game going in the back of any café in Puckle Street, Moonee Ponds.

The shopping strip was well known for its coffee shops which, alongside coffee, served up a large range of cakes and pastries by day and cards and drinks by night. The local Police went by the theory that it was better to keep the illegal games corralled rather than for them to spread further along Mt. Alexander Road. This way they could keep their own resources to a local area. The Moonee Ponds CIU could keep an eye on the crooks in their own backyard.

It was sort of a mutual agreement amongst the card game participants that to 'poke the bear' would be detrimental to their nights of pleasure. They were aware that if they ran a 'banker' at one of the games who everyone knew was the main organiser taking home a percentage from the house as well as charging a table entry fee it became an illegal operation, however, to attract big punters, the bank had to be loaded, otherwise with the money some of the players wanted to put on the table it was wasting everyone's time. They were all big boys and if they kept the winnings and losses to themselves then the local Constabulary wasn't going to interfere.

The other thing that kept the rozzers away was the uncertainty of who the punters would be. Many a Greek heritage politician or celebrity had participated in the big games on their way home from a hard day at the office at Parliament House or an appearance on the television. Gambling was a way of life for these people. Quite a few Parliamentary pensions or wages had been whittled down during the wee small hours over a smoky card table in the back room of one of the cafes.

Memorising gamblers habits had become second nature to Ricky Bobrov as he had ducked and weaved his way through many a big game back in Footscray, so he didn't bother peering through any of the front windows of the Puckle Street shops. He went straight to the back alleys that ran behind them and the surrounding car parks. It was only a matter of time before he found what he was looking for—the black Mercedes-Benz with the registration number he had been given by Marco Toscano. It was parked just to the rear of *Espresso Taverna.* Along with the late model sedan were two seven series BMWs and a Maserati Quattroporte. This was obviously no small change card game.

Bobrov settled himself against the side of the Mercedes and lit a cigarette as he thought of the best way to attract Antonov's attention. Minutes later he dropped the butt onto the gravel and ground it under his shoe at the same time as grabbing the driver's door handle and attempting to open it. That was all that was needed to set off the ear-piercing alarm that sat under the bonnet of the black sedan.

Within seconds, the back door of *Espresso Taverna* burst open, and the large frame of Pavel Antonov appeared under the motion sensor light that had come on automatically, lighting up the back yard. The big Russian stepped forward brandishing a small aluminium baseball bat which was semi-raised in his right hand. Behind him several other men were spilling out the back door.

Taking several steps towards Bobrov, Pavel Antonov suddenly saw the police identification wallet that was being held directly in front of his face. Bobrov's voice cut through the air with the sound of authority.

"Police. Settle down everyone. I only need to speak to Pavel here. There are no issues with your game so go back inside and keep playing for those matches. Pavel is an old friend of mine whom I haven't seen for a while. I thought this might be an ideal time and place to catch up."

Everyone stopped in their tracks and slowly, one by one, backed up and re-entered the café, leaving Bobrov and Antonov facing each other in silence.

"Ah, Mr. Bobrov. I don't forget a face. To what do I owe the pleasure? It had better be good because, policeman or not, there are no witnesses out here. No witnesses to the beating I may very well give you for attempting to steal my car. Your word against mine."

Ricky Bobrov slowly put his police identification back into his jeans pocket.

"Sorry about my unusual style of invitation, Pavel, but there is something we need to discuss — and discuss in English. Not Asian gibberish like your people speak to you in Swanston Street. How about you and I sit in your chariot and have a chat?"

Antonov took his car keys from his pocket and pressed the door release. Upon opening the front door, he tossed the baseball bat onto the back seat and faced Bobrov.

"If you are the same Bobrov, we can talk. If not, I will take care of you, police or not!"

Chapter Twelve

"It's funny how people come across each other, isn't it, Pavel?" a smiling Ricky Bobrov said as they sat next to each other in the front seat of Antonov's late model Mercedes Benz AMG GT.

"You haven't just come across me, Bobrov. You have come looking for me," Antonov said in a heavily accented reply.

"True, Pavel. I'll tell you the how and the why now. I was given this car's registration number by a third party from my past. He wanted to know who owned this rocket ship after seeing you drive it away from Victoria Street in the city a while back. Without boring you with too many details my friend, he tagged you all the way up Swanston Street as you visited your little Asian beggar friends sitting along the way from Federation Square to Victoria Street."

Pavel Antonov's eyes narrowed as Bobrov finished his story. It was after ten seconds of silence that Antonov spoke. In doing so, he leant across very closely to Bobrov and squeezed his arm.

"I would suggest that you and your 'third party' forget everything about what you have just spoken of. Policeman or not, it would be very bad for your health if any of my Russian associates knew of what you have just said. Who is this 'third party' person that is interested?" a clearly concerned Antonov asked in a hushed tone.

Ricky Bobrov's self-preservation instincts kicked in immediately when he glanced at Antonov who by this stage was pressing even more firmly on his arm.

I've hit a nerve here and I think I'd better back off. Way out of my league, Bobrov thought before Antonov continued, his face within inches, smothering the policeman's face with the fetid smell of garlic and caviar.

"I will not waste time with you over this, Ricky. If I don't mess with the bosses of the Russian mafia in Melbourne, then I suggest you and this other person should not either."

Ricky Bobrov knew he had stepped into a minefield by mentioning the beggar operation. He wanted nothing to do with the Russian mafia.

"Pavel, you have my word that it won't be spoken about again and I shall tell the person. If it concerns you, then it concerns me."

"Ricky. You owe me nothing and I owe you nothing. Just forget everything and remember, as an outsider, not to get involved in anything that makes my bosses a lot of money."

"Pavel, what he told me is very sketchy and was only of mild interest to him. What he saw could never land anyone in court. It certainly hasn't been reported in any official capacity. You know as well as I do that Vic Pol hasn't got the resources to get involved in anything like that. It's just hearsay from one of my fizzes to a copper," Bobrov boasted. "I really don't care what you and your kind get up to."

"Then this conversation is over, and I will return to my social card game," Antonov said as he reached for the handle to open the driver's side door before being stopped suddenly with Ricky Bobrov's next words.

"Are you interested in a business deal? A House of Cards deal as we used to say a while back."

The old saying referring to a clandestine card game brought silence to the car's interior for a short time before Antonov turned and looked at Bobrov.

"A straight question, Ricky Bobrov. What side are you on? Our side or the police side, eh?"

The reply came back immediately.

"Two sides actually. Our side and my side."

"What happened to the police side?" Antonov said staring straight into the black eyes of the policeman.

"At work only, Pavel. Keeps me employed, although I dare say one more bad move on my part and I will be lining up at Centrelink for a handout. Outside of my job I work for me and my friends and when I say work, I mean for good money."

"I will only ask you this once, Ricky Bobrov. Are you recording this little chat?"

"No way, Pavel. I just want to see if you may be interested in some upmarket card nights that you, me and my other associate could make a decent score from?"

"Ricky, Ricky. I have a card game going on here," Antonov said indicating the back of the restaurant. "What's the difference with yours?"

"Let's say I can arrange some far more salubrious premises in Carlton than the back room of a smelly restaurant here or some shitbox house back on the other side of the Westgate bridge. A place where you could greet your friends in a far better manner. Now that I work this side of the bridge, I can organise much better premises. Carlton is a very wealthy suburb where the residents don't always spend all their time at their grand houses. They holiday for weeks on end both interstate and overseas leaving the safety of their homes to the Victoria Police. I just happen to keep an eye on these premises, and I can pick the eyes out of the appropriate ones where a game can go on without notice. We invite people who are respectful and wealthy. By the looks of you and your mode of travel you like the finer things in life and if the three of us can run this little scam successfully even for a few months or so, I know we can make big money. Different days from the ones out west. A bit more up-market than dealing with trucking companies and factories."

"Interesting days indeed. Too many people though and too much risk. I leave the drugs to the gangs. Who is this associate of yours?" Antonov said quickly to put Bobrov off guard.

Bobrov knew that to keep Antonov interested he would have to give up Marco's name.

"A western suburbs boy by the name of Marco Toscano. Was a mid-level organiser around Footscray. Helped me out of a situation once."

"I do not know the name. How many involved in this idea?"

"Right now, just the three of us. If we work this right, it will be beneficial to all of us."

"How do you think it will operate?" Antonov said with an interested tone.

"You get the clients to the first game after I have gone over all the groundwork for an empty house of high quality where the owners are away for a reasonable time. It will be a house within a boutique area of Carlton or North Carlton with no prying neighbours over a weekend. Some of these snobs have bought or built houses around the area where it is very quiet. That is the type of house I want. We only need do it three or four times over say six months, and if by the look of yourself and your car, you would be up to floating the bank for the first one, we could get it off the ground nicely."

Antonov wasn't fazed by being asked to be the banker, which pleased Ricky. He was on the repayment plan for the bookies at Bendigo and had no spare money. Losing at Flemington a couple of days before also put the squeeze on his finances. He waited for Antonov's reply.

"How much do you think for the bank?"

"If you put up twenty K and got some real high rollers in, it would work. We need some names who like to take risks but at the same time are hopeless card players."

"What is this Toscano getting a cut for?" Antonov spat back with.

"When I find the right house, he will be sussing out the neighbourhood over a few days to make sure it is right for us. He can then arrange the players pick-ups and drop-offs afterwards. We don't need strange cars around the area, and we want your guests to think it is a bit like a gangster's night out."

"It could work, but we don't supply drugs. My associates are top businessmen and a politician or two. They cannot play cards to save themselves and are willing to lose money if they go home feeling like they've been treated like royalty. A change of scene from the back of a shop to a decent residence. Keep talking," Antonov said.

"I will be there also. I'll make sure there are no patrols anywhere near our game. A lot easier now that I am a Sergeant. We can figure out the percentage cut from the house for us but naturally you will take a larger share if you bank the first game. We'll put in a non-refundable entry fee of say five thousand each. We will see what happens after that one if we want to keep it going."

"I want to meet this Marco Toscano first, Ricky. I don't trust anyone with an Italian name. No definite promises yet. We three meet."

"Done. If you like, we can meet at the Flemington races next weekend. Better to meet in public than in private. Okay with you?"

"Ring me later in the week," Antonov said as he pulled a gold Mont Blanc biro from his suit and wrote his number on an empty cigarette packet before handing it to Bobrov. Without another word he indicated for Bobrov to get out of the car before he locked it and sauntered back into the rear of the café.

Chapter Thirteen

Max Tyler's arrival at Carlton as a uniformed Acting Sergeant was a surprise to many of the younger members stationed there.

Most of the more senior ones knew that Max was a rising star in the eyes of the Department, so no one was surprised to see the young detective being given a stint of uniformed upgrading to enhance his CV.

It took only thirty minutes of storing his correspondence and uniform items before Ricky Bobrov approached him in the locker room.

"Ricky Bobrov mate. You are?"

"Max Tyler, Ricky. Great to meet you. Been at Carlton long?" Max said without any hint of knowledge of the rogue Sergeant's background.

"No. Only a week or two. Came down from Bendigo. Took a position up there after being in the CIU in Footscray," Bobrov said without stating the fact that he hadn't been transferred to Carlton in the normal manner. "Bit quiet up there for me. Wanted to get back into the action down here. You're an upgrade. Where from?"

"Oh, I was stationed here a few years ago but got a detectives position in town. Bit of a surprise to be given this upgrading, but I thought I'd better grab it for my career opportunities. Must admit though I'm going to use this to my advantage without busting myself."

Man after my own heart. Bobrov thought.

"So, you'd know Signorotto and that bitch McLaren?" Bobrov said with a sarcastic tone to his voice.

Max Tyler went straight into undercover mode with his reply.

"Yeah. Signorotto was my Sergeant here. I've worked operations with both. Signorotto's a real hard nose old style. Stickler for rules. Between you and me, McLaren is good but a real grandstander too. I was involved with her getting a Valour Award a while back and I reckon she only got it because she's female. I could have done what she did, but I was left with cleaning up the scene where the crook killed one of ours back down the highway. You remember that Highway bloke who got run over?"

"I remember the cop getting killed and the story in Police Life about her getting a VA. You don't reckon she should have?" Bobrov said quietly as he turned around to make sure there was no one else in the change room eavesdropping.

"All I'm saying is that it was a team effort, but, typical of the Department these days it ended up being a female headline," Tyler said whilst reminding himself that he had to tell Kate the story he was spinning so that she could become a bit more hard-nosed around him.

"Any others besides those two that I should know about, if you get my drift? I like to run my own race without bosses hanging over my shoulder," Bobrov continued in a quiet tone.

Trying to nurture the fellow detective comradery, Tyler continued.

"Yeah, so do I. I like the upgrading bit. Can always do with the extra dollars. Put a bit into the ponies recently without much reward. There was a lot of freedom being in the CIU and out in a suit all the time. You'd know what I mean? Never had to touch my wallet," Max said with a quick wink in Bobrov's direction.

Ricky Bobrov stepped over to Max's open locker to continue talking in a lowered tone.

"We could work well together, Max. You sound as though you know what you want out of this department?"

"The job's a good one but my motto is that everything in life has to be to your own advantage as far as I'm concerned. They know me here, but from work only. They don't own me after hours, mate."

"We'll get on well. I'll see if we can work a few shifts together. See you around," Bobrov said as he slipped quickly out of the change room after giving Max a solid pat on the shoulder.

Max took his time unpacking. Before heading upstairs to the Sergeants office where Kate McLaren was sitting, he made a quick mobile phone call to her to give her an update on the conversation that had just transpired in the change room. She forced herself not to laugh during the call as she glanced at an unknowing Ricky Bobrov sitting at his desk nearby. When Max entered the office, Kate began her routine.

"Welcome aboard, Acting Sergeant Tyler. Have your roster all ready for you for next week. Hope you haven't got a social life? I know you and that blondie Constable Schaeffer are an item but don't expect any favours about rostering from me."

"Just as well she's on four weeks leave then, eh, Kate?"

"Mr. Tyler. As an Acting Sergeant and new to the upgrading, I think it would be appropriate to address me as Sergeant. Cut out the equal bit because we aren't equal. I have the rank and you're just playing at it for a while," Kate said rising from her desk, coffee cup in hand and heading towards the mess room.

Max stared at Kate's departing back.

She's obviously got the bitch role down pat. Max thought smiling to himself.

"She's a hard-faced bitch," Bobrov commented from his desk.

"Like I'm really going to take a lot of notice of her, right?" Max shot back as he raised a middle finger at the departing Sergeant.

"You really don't like her, do you?" Bobrov said.

"She's good at her job but I just think she goes over the top with the Sergeant thing. She was in an office at headquarters before she got here. Never seen an angry man until her medal incident. Gone to her head I reckon."

"Seems to be in tight with Signorotto though," Bobrov said looking at Max inquiringly.

"Yeah, she would be. This gender equality crap. She's female and she knows the Company policies like the back of her hand. That's what it's all about these days, isn't it?" Max queried Bobrov.

"You and I think alike, Max. If we play our cards right and stay off her shit list, we might be able to have a good time here together. There's an old saying Max. Here for a good time, not a long time."

"You got it in one, Ricky," Max said as he put out his hand to shake with his new best friend.

Chapter Fourteen

"Sorry Acting Sergeant, but that's what happens," a steely voiced Kate McLaren said directly to Max Tyler after he questioned not being able to attend Commander Stone's celebration party.

"Luck of the draw I suppose," Tyler replied sarcastically.

The raised voice of the new Acting Sergeant caused other members of the office to look up at the now virtually toe to toe Sergeants. Trouble was brewing.

"Nothing to do with luck at all," A visibly agitated Kate McLaren spat back. "You are the only Acting Sergeant here, so you are basically at the bottom of the pecking order. You along with Sergeant Bobrov, a late comer to Carlton, will be working the car and the station on Saturday night. What part of that don't you understand Acting Sergeant?" she said with the emphasis on the word acting.

Max Tyler kept the verbal exchange going.

"But I've known Commander Stone longer than you. Why don't you do the Saturday night shift?" he said in a voice which effectively penetrated through to the Senior Sergeant's office all the way down the stairs. Tyler and McLaren stood like a scene from a western movie in typical Mexican stand-off mode. Tony Signorotto entered on cue.

"I don't know what's going on here, but I won't have arguments between my Sergeants. I can bloody well hear you both down in my office. What's the issue?" he said glaring from Kate to Max.

"I'm just trying to explain to this upgraded member, that because of his position here along with Sergeant Bobrov, they won't be able to attend the function for our new Commander on Saturday night," she said, also looking from the upset face of Tyler to the completely blank face of the seated Bobrov who suddenly spoke.

"Fine by me, Sergeant. I don't know him so I'm happy with working the car and station."

Tony Signorotto fired up as he pointed directly from McLaren to Tyler.

"Both of you in my office now."

Kate McLaren made a point of brushing past Max quickly so she could be the first down the stairs. She collapsed into a chair as Signorotto closed the door behind them all and sat on the edge of his desk.

"You two should join actors' equity. Ten out of ten for the performance. Very convincing."

Both Sergeants smiled broadly at each other before Max spoke.

"He definitely thinks I hate you, Kate. He barely speaks to the others but is all over me after I told him I like to look after myself and do things my way."

"Yeah, I've noticed that. Seems to be trying to form a two-man club. He keeps his cards very close to his chest, if you'll excuse the pun. He thinks you are a kindred spirit."

"I did drop it in conversation that I've done a bit of money on the ponies so that probably endeared me to him even more."

"I'll back you on the junior Sergeant stance Kate with next Saturday night. Let's see what happens. Also, Max, I want you to record him if you think you must. I want this whole mess back with Ethical Standards. I know Phil's in a bind, but my priority is looking after the straight members of this station, not taking the place of the bloody toe cutters. They can figure out their own ways of finding shit out about him. You two go back up and I'll supply the back up," Tony said before opening the door. Minutes later he re-appeared in the Sergeants office.

"Okay, listen up everyone," Tony said to the four or five Sergeants that were at their desks.

"What Sergeant McLaren says goes. Junior or most recently arrived Sergeants will look after the station this Saturday night. End of story. If I'm not here at the station, then consider Kate to be the next in charge. I won't have any more efforts at undermining her authority. She does the rosters so that should make you keep sweet with her. We don't have a second Senior Sergeant here at Carlton due to shortages across the state, so as far as I'm concerned, Sergeant McLaren is to be looked on as my second-in-charge."

With a sweeping icy stare around the room, he left the Sergeants office, but not before he noticed a slightly stunned look on the faces of some of the younger Sergeants. He felt bad about his little spiel and he hoped that the Ricky Bobrov saga could be a thing of the past very soon.

Kate McLaren stood, making an exaggerated swipe at her mobile phone, and stepped hurriedly out of the door. Ricky Bobrov got up, crossed over to Max Tyler's desk and spoke.

"Well, I think we both know who the boss's favourite Sergeant is, eh Max?"

"Mate, let her have her little victory. You and I will be running the place come Saturday night," Max said with a grin towards Bobrov as he chewed on the end of his biro.

"Yeah. We might have to do a patrol of our area and make sure our citizens are all home safe and sound in their mansions," Bobrov said returning the grin with a devious one of his own

Chapter Fifteen

As Max Tyler and Ricky Bobrov slowly trawled their way around the more affluent streets of Carlton, it became obvious: Bobrov was looking for something specific. It made Max all the more grateful for the support of Kate McLaren in devising the Saturday night roster. She had left an experienced crew on duty at the station while others were at the party. He was hoping he didn't need any sudden backup if Bobrov did something stupid.

Bobrov had made sure that the troops on afternoon shift were fully briefed on their duties. When darkness came, he had grabbed the keys to one of the patrol cars and announced to the inquiry counter senior member that he and Max would be out on files duties for a few hours. The member had found this a bit strange as those duties were specifically tasked to one of the Senior Constables at Carlton. Added to the fact that Bobrov had not taken any of the files with him except for the Holiday Book made Max suspicious also. The Holiday Book was the one listing properties around the Division where people had notified the police that they would be away from their premises for an extended time while on holidays or business.

"You really interested in these places or are you just ticking the boxes to keep in the good books with the bosses? The Holiday Book isn't one of your portfolios. It's assigned to one of the other Sergeants," Max said.

"Just want to get to know the area Max. Also shows Signorotto that we've been out and about."

"We're not really checking them though, are we? It's not as though we are getting out and rattling doorknobs on any of them. Not actually walking around and checking security," Max said slowly.

"Signorotto and McLaren won't know that," Bobrov said as he slowed then stopped outside a large Edwardian styled house located between a small shop and what looked like an old boarded up bakery in Faraday Street. "Now that you mention it though, it might be worth having a walk around this one. The owners are overseas for a month or so according to the book. In the bloody Bahamas would you believe. This place looks like a burglar's dream."

Max Tyler didn't quite know why, but he had a feeling in his gut that this house was of particular interest to Bobrov. Others from the Holiday book he had only driven past.

He immediately got out of the car to have a look. The detective in him told him to look at everything Bobrov was looking at without making it obvious.

On one side of the impressive residence was an old corner shop, now barricaded up. In years gone by according to the faded lettering on the brick work, it may have been an old bakery. A bluestone alleyway ran down one side. Next to that was the house Bobrov was interested in. On the other side of the house was a small factory displaying the name '*Bridal House of Carlton. Designers of Bespoke Wedding Gowns.*'

Max pretended to be interested as he casually observed what Bobrov was inspecting. Bobrov looked quickly over the side fence of the house then for some reason looked intently at the printing on the front window of the wedding premises. After that he walked up and down the alleyway paying particular attention to the windowless brick wall of the old bakery. Neither of these inspections had any relation to the house itself.

Max was full of unanswered questions, but he made his way back along to the front window of the wedding dress shop. What was of any interest? The blinds were drawn and the only thing to read other than the name of the premises was the gold embossed lettering and numerals on the front door giving the Monday to Friday trading hours. He quickly took out his phone and photographed the information without letting his partner see him. As he put his phone back in his pocket, Bobrov appeared from the alley and spoke.

"Okay, Max. I think we've seen enough. Looks like a nice quiet safe place."

Odd thing to say, Max thought.

Getting into the patrol car, Bobrov took the Holiday Book and casually placed it on the back seat.

"Let's hit some eateries in Lygon Street and see what we can get with the old blue suit discount," Bobrov said.

"Better off looking for freebies in Brunswick Street tonight I reckon, mate. Stone's party is going on in Lygon Street at Dom's bistro. Don't want to get caught out doing the five-finger discount."

"You're like me, Max. Tell them nothing and take them nowhere. Fuck 'em all, I say. Just thinking also. Only put a couple of those house checks on the Running Sheet. Don't worry about the last two. Don't want to look as though we are working too hard, or they'll expect it all the time," Bobrov said with a laugh.

As they drove into Brunswick, Max did as he was asked but made sure he memorised the Faraday Street address. He needed to run all this information past Tony Signorotto on Monday.

Chapter Sixteen

Ricky Bobrov was feeling nervous.

The introduction that he had arranged between Marco Toscano and Pavel Antonov at the Flemington Sunday race meeting had started off quite amicably, but by the third race he could feel the tension between the two growing.

Antonov was willing to discuss a possible future card night deal but was not going to be questioned continually by Toscano in relation to the begging scam. Antonov took Bobrov to one side.

"Ricky, we came here to talk business. I did not come here to have this little Italian throw questions at me about something that doesn't concern him. I know you found me through the car registration which he gave you, but he needs to shut his mouth. It won't be healthy for him if he doesn't. You need to tell him to stay out of Russian mafia business or I will, and he won't like the way I tell him. I am beginning to dislike him. Understand?"

Ricky Bobrov was about to speak when Marco Toscano suddenly walked over shouting in a loud voice.

"What's the problem? Why the private conversations? I thought this was a three-way deal?"

"I'll tell you right here and now Marco. The thing I run in the city is not mine. I run it for the Russian *Bratva*. To you that translates into the words *Russian mafia*. Keep your nose out of it before it gets cut off, understand? Do not ask me any more questions. You are out of your depth. If you want to talk to me about Ricky's idea for the card game, we will do so," Antonov said with a tone of finality in his voice.

"Might be so, Pavel, but that begging scam looks profitable."

Antonov pushed Ricky out of the way, grabbing Marco's arm in a bear like grip before looking around to see if anybody was watching them. The two bored looking, scruffily dressed punters nearby were ignored by Antonov. Johnny Petran managed to snap off a couple of photos of the enraged Antonov without being noticed.

"What part of 'mind your own business' don't you understand, little man?" Antonov said as he continued to squeeze Toscano's arm.

Bobrov stepped between the two quickly, yelling at Toscano before the situation got worse.

"For fuck's sake Marco, shut up. I did not come here to try to muscle in on something that the Russian mafia own. I want to talk about a possible site for what could be a very profitable card night for us and all you can go on about is that begging shit. You've been told to forget it, now forget it. I think I've found us a house so let's work on it."

Toscano stepped back as Antonov let go of his arm.

"Fine, fine Ricky. I just thought maybe we could help each other with a couple of schemes," Toscano said.

"Toscano, there is no 'we' in the street stuff. It's non-negotiable, that is unless you want a visit from some very nasty Russian friends of mine," Antonov said with conviction in his voice. "Card game only or I walk!"

Silence overtook them as the fourth race neared the finish line. Ricky Bobrov tried to ease the tension by talking about the race.

"Shit. There's more of my bucks gone on that race. The one I backed will still be running when the next race starts. Now let's get down to what we are here fo—some mutual business. I'll get us some drinks and then outline a plan that should work. You both okay with that?"

Bobrov waited for the other two to nod their heads before going to the bar.

Why do Italians always have to have the last word? he thought.

On return, he handed Marco a Crown Lager and Pavel a large vodka on ice. To keep the afternoon on an even keel, Ricky stuck with a can of coke. The last thing he wanted was this deal to go off the rails before it had started. This could be his one chance to make enough cash to set himself up for other things.

"Okay, I've found a perfect place in Faraday Street in North Carlton where the owners are away until late next week. No nosey neighbours and a quiet area on a Saturday night. If we do this, I am running point, understand? Marco, I want you to arrange the booze, cards and transport. No drugs. Pavel, with a week's notice can you get let's say six good punters? Marco and you can work out the Uber side of things because we don't want unfamiliar luxury limos parked around the place drawing attention to the house. No private cars at all. The question remains Pavel if you could run the 'bank'. Is twenty K too much for you to float?"

Pavel Antonov replied slowly.

"As I told you when we met, Ricky, no problem with a twenty K bank. I take fifty percent of the profit because it is my money. You two do what you like with the other fifty. I need assurances that my customers are given top treatment. Top line Ubers and alcohol. Can you promise me that, Ricky? They will want the night to go from about ten till about five in the morning. Have you checked the premises thoroughly? It must be classy inside."

"Pavel, it will be a classy night. The house is empty now and I have the code for the security system. On Tuesday night I will make a personal inspection of the inside and the outside. Don't worry, I have my reputation on the line here also. Right next to it is an alleyway which we can use. Your customers will want for nothing. The only thing we need is for you to win big, Pavel. Don't care how, but it has to be big and no complaints from your punters when they lose," Bobrov said.

"I'll play them off against each other, so they'll all look good, but by the morning they'll be desperate to get their money back. One of them won't of course. I've got a few heads in mind but I won't know till later in the week. They'll pay a five K table fee. They won't mind when I put the stakes up late in the morning. That's when I take control of things. When I am the bank, I make sure I win," Antonov stated coldly.

"How are we divvying up the other fifty?" Toscano said nervously as he listened to the talk of possible big money. Ricky Bobrov jumped straight in. He wasn't going to let Marco ruin things. Pavel was the money man in this operation.

"We'll carve up the entry fee three ways, so that is ten K each sheer profit. The rest will be halves depending on the night and how it runs. I'm the one taking the real risk here, Marco. You two might cop a big fine if things go pear-shaped but I'll lose my job and get charged. You just concentrate on the booze and cars. Pavel, when you find out who the punters are let Marco know what their liquor preferences are, and it'll be sorted. Dress up for the night, Marco. No western suburbs jeans and T shirt crap, either."

"I'll know by Wednesday who the punters are, and you can expect at least one State Government minister. No name, but you'll recognise him. I'm thinking a member of the Melbourne Club also," Antonov said.

Marco Toscano couldn't help himself when he spoke.

'We are all taking a chance here, Ricky, so I reckon it should be a third share each."

Pavel Antonov cut straight back in.

"I don't need this game, Toscano. I get by on other business interests and because of that I can put up twenty thousand. If you can find that sort of cash, then you need to put up or shut up. Understand, you little prick?" he said closing the space between himself and Toscano quickly.

Bobrov pointed his finger at Toscano at the same time as trying to remain calm with the man from Footscray. He raised his voice slightly as he spoke.

"Look Marco, you're either in or out. The minimum you'll take home is ten grand. If I have to put this off because you want to keep bitching, then good. I can find a replacement for you in a flash."

"Okay, okay. Twenty-five percent it is," Toscano said looking at Antonov. "Let's hope your associates are ready to gamble."

Antonov pushed his face closer to Toscano's.

"I don't work for nothing, okay?"

"I have both of your phone numbers, but I suggest you get a couple of cheap throw-a-ways with false names and new numbers. Send me a couple of texts with half the number in each to be safe. It's now Sunday and I'll be in touch Tuesday. I already have a burner phone the Department doesn't have a clue about. Text me all the details of what you're doing, day or night. We need to get a move on with this because the people who live at the house will be back halfway into next week. Pavel, five punters only, and I need to know who they are. If there are police files on them, I don't want them in this. Cleanskin bunnies only who don't mind losing a wad of cash on the night," Bobrov said looking at his two accomplices.

"I can let them win occasionally, but I will pick out one to hit hard early in the morning. He'll be tired from the table," Antonov replied smugly.

A high rolling card game night with no hassles is what I want, Ricky Bobrov thought.

"Let's get our own parts organised and I'll call you Wednesday," Bobrov said.

Antonov shook hands with Bobrov but walked off, ignoring Toscano.

"Fucking Russian moron," Toscano said quietly, walking off in the other direction.

Chapter Seventeen

Ricky Bobrov got to the station bright and early on Tuesday morning. There was work to do—and it wasn't Police work!

Bobrov was glad that Kate McLaren was on a day off because he didn't want her hovering over him checking his workload during her shift. He would make sure his out-tray was higher than his in-tray before he had finished for the day. McLaren might hold the same rank as himself, but anyone could see that she and Signorotto were as 'thick as thieves.'

He spent the first few hours checking station paperwork including the running sheets from the various patrol units, members roster duties and the entries into the property book plus other mundane but necessary checks and balances that kept the station ticking over.

One entry in the property book caught his eye. It had been made the day before and was for an amount of five hundred dollars that had been found in Argyle Square, wrapped in a rubber band, and brought into the station by some honest citizen. Bobrov couldn't believe it. If he'd found that amount of money, or any money for that matter, it would have gone straight to the bookies at the nearest racetrack. Some people were so honest they were stupid.

At one stage he even made an appearance at the front counter when a call came from a young Constable downstairs, that there were quite a few people wanting to make various inquiries and he was by himself. If there was a chance that lending a helping hand would be seen in any way by Tony Signorotto as a positive move, then he would take it.

Around lunch time he put on a plain jacket over his uniform shirt, told another of the Sergeants that he was going down to Sam's Deli of Delights for lunch and headed out the door.

Besides the fact that he needed a break, his reason for the walk was to make two phone calls. The first to Marco Toscano and the second to Pavel Antonov. It was time for a logistics check with his two new partners.

Walking out of the delicatessen, he sat on a bench across the road in the park, unwrapped the triple decker ham, salami, and cheese artery blocker that Sam's was famous for and took a bite as he flicked through his speed dial and rang the new number for Marco Toscano.

"Mate, how's your end going?"

"Yeah, good. Spoke to Antonov. I've ordered the high-end booze and some limo Ubers for seven punters," Toscano replied.

"Why Ubers for seven? It was meant to be five," Bobrov retorted.

"Talk to your friend Antonov. Obviously, he didn't take any notice of you," Toscano said with a sarcastic tone in his voice. "Are we getting together before then?"

"I've got Friday night off and Saturday because I put my hand up to work last Saturday night. Get to Naughton's hotel in Royal Parade at seven. Talk then, okay?"

"All right. By the way, that fucking Russian can stump up the money for the booze and..."

Bobrov had cut Toscano off mid-sentence. He was more concerned with Antonov's disregard of his request that there be no more than five punters invited. He jumped straight onto the phone to the big Russian.

"Ricky mate. How are you? All well?" a happy sounding Antonov said first.

"Listen Pavel. I said no more than five punters. Marco said you have seven. Not on. Cut two loose, understand?" Bobrov said with a serious voice that did not translate into the uncertainty that he felt.

"One is a friend of a big punter I am bringing. It's okay, I'll vouch for him. Take it easy, Ricky. Cool it."

Crunch time! Ricky Bobrov knew that if he didn't take control now, Antonov would try to control Saturday night.

"Listen to me, Pavel. It either stays at five or the night's off. With us three it's eight. I make the rules on this. I found the house. If it goes off okay and we find somewhere else for another game, I'll re-visit the numbers. Tell your punter that I'll consider his mate next time. No more discussion."

A long silence ensued before the gravelly voice of Pavel Antonov returned.

"Okay, Ricky. This time only. You find a bigger house for the next one. If I upset my punters, there may not be a next time. They are also used to having things their own way. For now, I have the names of the players for this Saturday. You listening?"

Bobrov replied. "Yes, I am running this one, Pavel. Let's keep it nice and tight. Go ahead with their details."

Antonov read off five names. They included one politician, two captains of industry, one eminent doctor and a well-known sports star.

"What information did you give them so far?" Bobrov said quickly, moving off the subject of the number of punters playing.

"I gave them the 'one-off, gold-plated card night, five thousand bucks non-refundable' etc. etc. Also, that we will arrange transport and the booze, which reminds me that we have to talk about Marco."

Bobrov had an inkling of what was about to transpire.

"Did you and Marco have words over who was paying for the booze?"

"Ricky, you know I'm putting up the money to float this night and I can handle the initial outlay for other things, but I won't be told to add to the twenty thousand bank because, as that little shit put it, 'you're a rich bastard. You pay first up.' I've had enough of him, Ricky. Keep him away from me."

"I'll speak to him Pavel. Leave it with me. I'll give Marco the money," Bobrov said, thinking at the same time that he didn't have the money to do that.

"Ricky, I don't really need this gig and I am thinking this Toscano is a real western suburbs amateur. He expects money for no risk, and if he crosses me again, I will deal with him myself. He knows I am *Bratva*."

Bobrov was listening to Antonov but couldn't take his mind off the distraction that Marco Toscano was causing. If there was to be a second game, he would have to be replaced.

"I said I will deal with him Pavel, okay?" A clearly frustrated Bobrov replied in a loud voice.

"You and I stick together on this Ricky, otherwise Toscano will be sleeping with the fishes," Bobrov said before disconnecting the call.

Bobrov finished his Sammy Special and returned to the station. Now he had to find five or six hundred dollars to cover the booze. He knew where to find it. He tried to ignore the career ending thought if he got caught.

Chapter Eighteen

Bobrov had to make his move that same afternoon. If he didn't do it now, he'd never do it.

Knowing that Tony Signorotto was heading out after lunch to a Citizens Advisory meeting up at the North Carlton library in Rathdowne Street, he bided his time. When he knew his Senior Sergeant had left the station, he snuck into his boss's office and removed the key to the Property Office safe, which was located in the storeroom.

Making sure that no one saw him entering the storeroom, he quickly pulled a pair of blue latex gloves from his pocket and slipped them on. He placed the key in the safe, opened it and searched through the items that had been handed in by the public. After thirty seconds he found what he was looking for—a clear plastic evidence bag containing the five hundred dollars that had been found in Argyle Square. Stuffing the money in his pocket, he closed and locked the safe, removed his gloves and quickly made his way back to Signorotto's office, returned the key and then slid back into the Sergeant's office. The one person he hadn't seen though was Veronica, the boss's secretary. She had quietly been going through some old files in a closet storeroom just near the Property Office. She had seen everything that he did. As soon as she could, the whole story would be re-told to her Senior Sergeant.

Sitting back at his desk he had a quick laugh to himself when he thought about that honest citizen who would have signed a claim form for the money hoping that if it could not be tracked to the proceeds of a crime or wasn't claimed in three months that they would be five hundred dollars richer. *Not this time you poor fool!*

What a surprise they had coming when the money couldn't be found when either Kate McLaren or Tony Signorotto found it missing in the weeks to come before it had to be shipped off to the main Property Office in the city.

Everyone on the station roster except those on Recreational or Sick leave would have to be questioned about the missing money. This would be one time when he didn't mind being a 'little fish in a big pond.' There were fifty-seven members plus six Public Service Support Staff on the roster.

Trying to concentrate on the station paperwork in front of him, he couldn't shake the nagging feeling that what he was planning with the card game was starting to throw up hurdles which needed to be jumped before he could get to the finish line.

In the past at Bendigo, it was just himself and the horses. Yes, there were the bookies also, but they had plenty of money. He never involved other Police members or shady characters who had criminal pasts.

Alone at his desk he realised that things were changing. This was a whole new ball game. One which he had instigated the moment he had looked up Pavel Antonov. He kept trying to forget that Antonov was a self-proclaimed member of the Russian mafia. That should have been warning enough. One part of himself said to back off now but the devil sitting on his shoulder and whispering in his ear said that this was the way to make money quick. With this and maybe one or two more card games he could get out of the Force, get rid of the bookies' payments, and set himself up properly. It never occurred to him that the Department was not only giving him enough rope to reel in some bigger fish, but also a bit to spare to hang himself with.

He had just involved a workplace full of Police members by stealing the money from the safe. In his mind the risk was justified. He had no money himself to buy the alcohol for the game and he didn't want an all-out fight between Toscano and Antonov this close to the night. He pushed aside the fact that his present lifestyle was solely due to gambling. No, it wasn't an addiction, it was his lifestyle. Some people like watching football, some liked gambling. Simple.

That's enough, Ricky. Think forward, not back!

His mind immediately went back to thinking about the present night and his getting into the house he had picked for the game. It was burglary, but that was of no consequence. The idea of being caught for any of this, getting the sack and charged with serious criminal offences and most likely going to gaol was not entertained. It was his right to have a better life. Forget the fact that he had ruined his old life by his own actions.

No. I'm not addicted to gambling. This needs to be done for my own lifestyle. This will work. Simple, he thought.

Slowly but surely the delusional world of Sergeant Ricky Bobrov was starting to wobble on its axis.

Chapter Nineteen

Ricky Bobrov wasn't about to take any chances when he visited the 'House of Cards' in Faraday Street that night.

He finished his shift and left the station quietly after changing into his civvies without announcing to anybody that he was going. He liked it that way as most members had become used to him. Even the crews at the front counter had given up expecting an answer to their daily farewells. The man was a loner. The only member he really talked to was Acting Sergeant Tyler.

Buying a coffee and burger from McDonald's at the Royal Children's hospital in Flemington Road, he made his way on foot into Royal Park near the Zoo, sat on a bench and enjoyed the late afternoon sunshine and the peace while he ate his meal.

At four o'clock he stood and slowly walked back via the side streets to his dingy Flemington flat. Once inside he set his phone alarm, lay down on the bed and went to sleep.

When the shrill alarm sounded two hours later, he woke up with a feeling of anticipation in his stomach. Although he was nervous, he was already getting a buzz from thinking about the night ahead.

Changing into a black T shirt, black jeans and a dark hoodie, he left the apartment and set out on foot at a quick clip back into Carlton. He knew the walk would pass in a flash as he would spend the time thinking about the layout of the house and the privacy factor that he needed. Not that he had been in there when he and Max Tyler did their supposed check of it in the days before, but he suspected from the size of the house that it would have all he required.

It was a long walk from his flat in Flemington to his destination, but he was paranoid about his old car being seen on CCTV around Carlton, so he left it in the street outside. He was just a citizen going for a late-night stroll.

When he arrived at Faraday Street, he could see that his choice of houses was a good one. Passing the closed wedding shop and the old bakery, which were in darkness, he walked quickly up and down the street and saw this was an area where people kept to themselves. A few lights were on in some of the better houses, but he knew if they kept the arrival of the punters quiet, they could get everyone in through the side gate without giving any notice to the neighbours.

Bobrov studied the houses across Faraday Street and thought that because the Carlton streets were laid out with such a wide expanse that most of the residents wouldn't even know each other. He had previously examined the Holiday Book for the house they were going to use and had seen that there were no notes about keys being left with nosey neighbours. The one item that pleased him was that the mail for the address was being forwarded to a business address in Port Melbourne while the owners were away.

Making his way down the side lane, he quietly undid the wooden gate. The owners had not put a lock on it probably thinking that if they had they would just hold up the police that would be doing the security checks. It still amazed him about the naivety of the average punter. Then again, the police *were* about to inspect the premises—but not for security reasons!

He had already removed his mini mag lite from the barrel of his service pistol back at the station and now placed the little torch in his mouth so he could illuminate the centre of the old sash window at the rear of the house. With a small flat headed screwdriver, he manoeuvred the semicircular latch connecting the upper and lower panels to the open position.

Quietly climbing in through the open window, he shone the small torch towards the front of the house and could see the expensive drapes that were covering the front windows were drawn. What he then saw was just what he wanted to see. A formal dining room with a large antique table and eight comfortable chairs placed around it. Off to one side was a small lounge area and through an open doorway he could see a large kitchen.

Bobrov would be telling his clients on arrival that this house belonged to a friend of his and he had only been given permission to use it if no other rooms besides the dining room, kitchen and toilet were used. If his punters wanted to smoke, it had to be done outside. The supposed friend had only given him the house if his wife didn't know. To add to the ruse, the players would be told that Bobrov was paying four figures for the house.

He knew that he could have got a house with airbnb but he did not want any money trail that could lead back to himself. Also, this was a classy house and could encourage the attendees to come to another game on a future date. They would never know that they were in the house illegally. Peering through the front curtains he was further pleased that the high brick front fence made this place virtually invisible from the roadway. Once inside, their privacy would be ensured.

Retracing his steps out through the window and the laneway gate, he walked stealthily back through the shadows of the night to Flemington.

Chapter Twenty

Tony Signorotto, Kate McLaren, and Phil Stone were seated in the new Commander's meeting room at Police Headquarters with several files spread across the office table.

The reason that Stone had called the others into the city was to get their advice on applications he was preparing to obtain more funding for equipment for the Carlton Police station. Even though he was about to become the overall Commander of several metropolitan stations he wanted to make sure there were no glitches when the new Superintendent sat in his chair. If Stone got in now and authorised several purchases, the new Superintendent would just be handed an already authorised 'tick' list.

Looking up from the conference table, Tony Signorotto saw the two scruffy looking individuals lounging in the doorway.

"Well, look what the cat dragged in," he said with a grin on his face as the two rough looking members ambled their way over to the table.

Phil Stone also looked up as his two members from the plain clothes Melbourne Divisional Response Unit, Johnny Petran and Mick York approached.

"What brings you two classy looking characters into Crime Central?" Stone said with pride in his voice.

"Geez, boss. Go easy on two down and outers, will you?" Mick York said with a smile.

"Down and out? You two have been putting in claims for that much overtime, your wages would float the National debt. Both of you could buy me, Kate and Tony out, I'd reckon," Stone said.

Laughter filled the office until Johnny Petran put up his hands in mock surrender.

"Got to keep up the payments on my Ferrari, people," he said.

"In your dreams, Petran," Kate chipped in. "What do you two lowlifes really want?"

"Actually," Petran said. "Thought you'd all like to know that some of that overtime was wisely spent on us last night. Nothing concrete mind you but just something pretty out of whack we thought concerning our fellow serving Russian."

The laughter died instantly as the three uniformed members shot each other quick, concerned glances, knowing that Petran was talking about their fellow member at Carlton—Sergeant Ricky Bobrov!

"Don't need three guesses as to who you're referring to, boys. Give us the good news and the bad news. Knowing you two, it'll be only bad news," Stone said, thinking all the while of the position the Department had put him and subsequently his Carlton team in with Bobrov.

"Got it in one boss," Mick York replied. "Thought we'd hang off his flat in Flemington last night as we'd just finished up another job early. Got there with a couple of coffees about nine thirty and had to quickly chuck them when he appeared out his door dressed completely in black. Shoved his hands in his pockets and took off back up Flemington Road towards Carlton."

"What happened?" Tony Signorotto said quickly. Mick York continued.

"I jumped out and started to tail him while Johnny drove around the block to get in front of him. He walked all the way down to the end and turned into Royal Parade. I kept up the dogging, but we didn't know how far or where he was going, so Johnny parked the car in a side street and then took over. Bobrov kept in the shadows as much as possible. Most people when they walk at night are keener to keep in the lit areas. Not this guy. We've done our fair share of tailing crooks and this guy was doing his best to know who was around him."

"Where did he end up?" Stone cut in anxiously.

"Well, I had to hang back because this guy was good," Petran said. "Tagged him into Faraday Street but then I lost him. Got Mick to come in from the other end on foot from the next block, but he had just vanished."

"Sounds pretty suss to me," Kate said. "If you were going for a late-night stroll, why go all the way back up there. He could have just taken one of the paths around the Zoo for a walk and it would come back to Flemington Road."

"That's why we hung around," Mick York said. "He wasn't doing a circuit, so we figured he'd have to be in or just off Faraday Street. We split up and covered a couple of blocks and lo and behold about thirty minutes later I spot him, head down, coming back the way he'd gone in. Question is, why walk all the way from Flemington to just go into Faraday Street? There's nothing in Faraday Street. Then he just goes back the same way, in and out of the shadows back to his flat. When he went to unlock his door, he scanned the whole area around him to see if anyone was there. Tell you what, boss. This bastard is up to something."

"Thanks guys," Stone said with a worried look on his face. "Another brick in the wall of the Ricky Bobrov saga."

"No problems, boss. Keep you updated, of course," Petran said as the two plain undercover cops took their leave.

Kate McLaren was first to speak after there had been a prolonged silence from them all.

"Next move?"

Tony Signorotto looked from McLaren to Stone then as he was about to speak, his mobile phone rang. After what appeared to the others to be a serious sounding call, he turned to them and spoke.

"That was my secretary at the station. Apparently, she spied Bobrov taking an exhibit out of the safe just before. She quietly tracked down what he had taken, and it turns out to be a roll of cash that was recently handed in. The only way he got into that safe was to take the keys from my office. This bloke is either seriously bent or has an addiction to gambling. I think we need young Max to get a lot warmer and cosier with Bobrov. We can't just rely on Johnny and Mick to let us know what's going on."

"Are you suggesting that he become a bit bent as well?" Stone said raising an eyebrow. "I don't want him in any way tied up with Bobrov's activities. Ethical Standards will chew him up and spit him out as quickly as Bobrov, and I won't be able to do a thing about it."

"Well, he's going to have to get closer with him after hours is what I'm saying. If that means getting a bit closer to the dark side, so be it. He's a big boy and knows when to back off if he has to," Signorotto said.

A sigh came from Stone as he stood.

"I've got to go to a meeting upstairs with the Deputy Commissioner now. I'll leave you to it," Stone said as he headed out the door.

"Kate, is Bobrov rostered on this weekend?" Tony Signorotto said, turning to his Sergeant.

"No, he worked that other Saturday night when we had the function at Dom's for Phil," she said looking at her Senior Sergeant.

"Okay then, I think we need to shake the tree a little bit. When we get back to the office, I want you to tell him that his roster has been changed and that he must work a patrol with Max Saturday night. We have the Italian film festival kicking off at the Nova cinema, so just tell him that I said we need some extra crowd control around the area. Tell him it has come down the line from the bosses in here. I'll tell Max in private. Let's head back."

The two officers headed downstairs to the carpark and began the short drive back to Carlton.

Inside their station, Kate headed straight for the Sergeant's office where she found Ricky Bobrov.

"Good news and bad news, Mr. Bobrov," Kate said with a sarcastic tone. "And there ain't no good news."

Ricky Bobrov looked up at her blankly. "What?"

"Not my decision, but the bosses in town want all hands on deck in Carlton this Saturday night because of expected crowds for the opening of the Italian film festival at the Nova cinema. Some big time Italian film star is going to be there. Unfortunately for you, that means you are now working on a car with Max Tyler."

"No, no, Kate. I've got this Saturday and Sunday off. The roster says so," Bobrov said raising his voice as a sudden sheen of sweat formed on his forehead.

"Listen, Sergeant. The roster gets changed with a pencil and rubber when Senior Sergeant Signorotto wants it changed. Don't argue with me. Take it up with him if you dare, but I don't think you will, will you?" McLaren spat back in the eye-to-eye confrontation.

The tension in the Sergeant's office was palpable. Bobrov's breathing could be heard by the other members who were seated at their desks with all eyes on the two combatants.

Kate was trying her hardest to 'poke the bear' as she continued to talk.

"Don't bother trying to swap with any of these others here," she said waving her arm to the other members. "They will be given jobs, too."

Ricky Bobrov lowered his eyes, picked up his paperwork and walked out of the office just as Max Tyler entered with a smile on his face. "You and me Saturday night, Ricky. Shafted again, eh!"

Bobrov brushed past Tyler without speaking, forcing Max to step out of his way.

"What's up his arse?" Max said in the direction of Kate McLaren as he winked at her.

"Don't know, don't care. Now I'll go and adjust those rosters."

Max Tyler knew there wasn't much he could do about the situation except try and reinforce his supposed friendship with Bobrov. The best way to do that he thought was to get him on his own somewhere. He walked in the direction that Bobrov had left in and soon found him in one of the downstairs filing offices. The papers that the disgruntled Sergeant had taken with him were in a messy pile on the floor. Max surreptitiously hit the record button on the micro recorder he had in his right pocket.

"Mate don't let that crazy bitch get to you. You and I can do whatever we like Saturday night. Stuff her," Max said as he leant against the door jamb looking at the obviously pissed off Ricky Bobrov.

"We worked last Saturday night and now we are being told to work this one. I've got things on this Saturday night, so she can get stuffed," Bobrov said.

"We can do what you like while we are out and about. I can cover you if you need. Just won't answer the radio."

"No mate. Bit bigger than that. Night out with some old mates. Card game and a bit of fun."

"Hey, always up for a game if there's some extra bucks involved. Blown a bit on the nags over the last few months," Max said hoping for more than just a nod of the head in return.

Ricky Bobrov looked long and hard at the eager face of the junior Acting Sergeant, never thinking for a moment that Max was trying to glean information from him.

"Max. Tell you what. Can't help you out now, but what sort of game are you interested in? Big, small? Some of my acquaintances are, shall we say, a bit on the high roller side of things. They stump up four figures for most games."

Max knew he couldn't back out now, so he replied in a quiet voice.

"Ricky. I owe a bit around the traps but if I knew I could get in on a private game, I could scrape up a couple of grand for the table. Are we talking just poker?"

Bobrov was torn. Did he trust this young copper who obviously was a bit of a tearaway, or did he tell him nothing? The thought that was uppermost in his mind was that he knew he had to dump Marco before there was trouble with Pavel.

"I'm taking a risk here, Max, but if you're interested in a poker night with some guaranteed winnings, it can be arranged. Maybe not totally above board but from the vibes I get from you, I think you would be across the idea. Yes, or no?"

"Bloody oath, mate. When and where?"

"Hey, easy on there partner. Can't do anything for you this weekend but I reckon if you want to help me out with some arrangements for the next one it will be profitable for you. Interested?"

"For sure pal. I don't mind bending the rules a bit. You cracked it because you have to work Saturday night and you've got something going?"

Bobrov stepped up to Tyler and put his hand out. Max presumed he was about to shake hands but when reciprocated, he was met with a shake of the head.

"No, Max. No handshake, I want your phone for a second."

"What for?" Max said in a confused tone as he slowly got out his mobile.

"Unlock it and show me the microphone recording set up."

Max Tyler realised that Bobrov wanted to see if he was being recorded.

Thank God for my other recorder. Max thought.

Bobrov looked closely at the phone and then handed it back to Max.

"Okay, we'll look at something next week. In the meantime, strictly between you and me, I won't be in on Saturday night no matter what the Ice Queen thinks. You good with that?"

"Not a problem. I'll just grab one of the downstairs crew. Don't bother to phone in, I'll just say I took the call and that you are really crook."

"You and I might work well together, Max," Bobrov said as Tyler walked slowly back out of the room with a conspirator's look on his face.

Standing by himself in the filing room, Ricky Bobrov realised that this was the first time he had involved another member in one of his schemes.

Very quiet alarm bells were ringing somewhere in the back of his head.

It'll work out.

Chapter Twenty-One

Ricky Bobrov had taken Max Tyler at his word and didn't bother ringing into the Carlton Police station to tell them that he was reporting sick for his Saturday afternoon shift. What could they do? Nothing. Members were always taking days off for all sorts of reasons, the usual one being stress, which was perfectly understandable when you considered the amount of pressure the average station Police Officer worked under.

Unfortunately for him, Max Tyler had informed Tony Signorotto and Kate McLaren of Bobrov's story for Saturday night which had resulted in another sit off on Bobrov's flat from early on the Saturday morning.

The plain clothes member's patience had finally paid off about eight o'clock that night when a suit clad Ricky Bobrov had stepped outside and started making his way along the same route back to where he had last gone a few nights before. Back to Faraday Street. This time though, Johnny Petran and Mick York had enlisted two other members of the Divisional Response Unit to be in Faraday Street with eyes wide open to confirm their suspicions from the previous 'dogging' exercise.

When Tony Signorotto had informed Phil Stone of Bobrov calling in sick after his shift had been changed, he decided to set up a mini-Command post in the downstairs conference room of the Carlton Police Station for the night and had told Signorotto and McLaren to be present. Signorotto had told the Saturday night crew that it was just an emergency radio exercise that Command in town wanted them to be in on and that they were not to be disturbed.

The call soon came through that the two extra DRU members had sighted Bobrov in Faraday Street as he was turning down an alleyway next to an old Victorian house in a very quiet part of the street. Stone picked up a police portable radio that he had taken from the equipment issue area and turned it to the secure channel that he and the DRU had agreed on.

"Johnny. Can you make sure someone is in a position to get photos of whoever or whatever goes in and out of that laneway. I don't care if you're there all night, but I want faces, registration numbers, deliveries, anything. Understood?'

"Absolutely, boss. Mick and I are in an old Transit van and will tag team with the other two. We'll be well out of the way but will have line of sight and I've brought the big Leica with the telephoto. Everything will be recorded. I want Bent Boy as much as you, boss."

"Thanks Johnny. We are going to wait the night out here at the station so any car numbers you get, shoot them through to us and we'll do the checks here. Photos too, if you can. Might as well stay busy for the night."

"Looks like the night might be starting soon, boss. We have a vehicle in the laneway already and it's a Dan Murphy's delivery van. Bobrov must have gone over a fence or something because he's re-appeared from the back of the Victorian house off the laneway. There's two of them… wait, the other dude looks very familiar. Yep, I've tagged him. It's that Toscano character he was at the races with. Got to go boss. Have to set up for the celebrity photo shoot," an excited Johnny Petran signed off with.

"Keep us up to speed boys," Stone said, turning to the others as Kate McLaren began to speak.

"Two out of three ain't bad but what's the bet the third guy will be Antonov?"

"Good guess, Kate," Signorotto said.

The three settled in for the wait. They all had plenty of paperwork to keep them going.

"Saturday night now Phil, and by the time you walk out of here on Sunday you will be a Commander."

Phil Stone didn't react. He was too engrossed in the fact that they were now basically running a Special Operation with this Command post and the observation van. A situation which had been started by Ethical Standards.

"Stuff this for a joke, people. I'm ringing the on-call Inspector at bloody Ethical Standards right now. He can get his arse down here and sit through this too. They started it and they can see what it's doing to a good police station."

Signorotto and McLaren smiled at each other as Stone picked up the direct line to D.24 communications and spoke quite tersely to the operator before hanging up.

"Gives me great pleasure in saying that some young jock of a Detective Inspector is about to be dragged out of a police retirement dinner and sent down here. He can witness the amount of time and work we are putting into one of their own cases."

Chapter Twenty-Two

A knock at the door of the Command post was answered by Tony Signorotto.

"Come in."

Max Tyler, who now was a spare member for the night since his partner Bobrov had gone sick, entered in front of a mid-thirties aged male wearing a dinner suit and a filthy expression on his face.

"Boss, this is Detective Inspector Ted Conlon of the Ethical Standards Department."

"Thanks," Signorotto said putting his hand out to shake that of the Detective Inspector. The offer was ignored.

"Why have I been dragged down here, Senior Sergeant? I was at the retirement dinner for Assistant Commissioner Jenkins and certainly didn't expect to end up down here at Carlton."

Phil Stone stepped into the room from the small kitchen area.

"Detective Inspector Conlon, I am Commander Phil Stone, so I suggest you ditch the attitude, take off the bow tie and join us while we listen to what's going down with one of your tagged members by the name of Sergeant Ricky Bobrov. Do you know the member?"

A suitably chastened Conlon replied quietly. "Sorry, sir. Yes, I am across the contents of Bobrov's file. I believe that you are monitoring the situation?"

"That's correct, Inspector. However, you are now going to spend some time with us monitoring a situation in Carlton where I believe your 'file' as you put it, is up to something illegal. At the end of the day, I don't want anything to sully the reputation of this Police station."

Kate McLaren rolled over an office chair as Conlon took off his suitcoat and tie.

"Do you have any grounds for thinking he may be up to an illegal activity?"

Tony Signorotto spoke. "We have had the DRU dogging him on a couple of occasions, today being one of them. Bobrov was rostered on for an operation this evening. I had his roster changed at the last minute to rattle his cage a bit and he was not impressed. Subsequently he went sick."

"Members go sick for a lot of reasons. Who took the phone call?"

"No phone call. He relied on Max Tyler here, who knows the whole story, to pass the message on to us. Max is basically cultivating Bobrov to think he doesn't mind breaking the rules, so Bobrov left it up to him to tell us he was sick. Even told him he was going to a card game with some mates. The DRU guys spotted him coming out of his flat in a suit and followed him back to Faraday Street which is where they lost him a couple of nights ago."

"What's happening now?"

"The DRU have eyes on him and a low life crook by the name of Toscano. Right now, they're transferring an alcohol delivery from a delivery truck into a house in Faraday Street."

Max Tyler turned quickly to the other members.

"What number in Faraday Street?"

Tony Signorotto picked up the portable radio.

"Johnny, Mick, come in please," he said into the hand piece.

"Mick York here boss. We've still got eyes on them."

"Thanks Mick. A question. What number Faraday Street is it? Max Tyler wants to know."

"Stand by," York said as he swung a powerful set of Nikon binoculars from the alley to the front of the house.

"Number forty-two," he said focussing on the large brass numbers on the high brick front fence.

Before he could ask Tyler why he wanted to know, he saw him hold up one hand as he turned and dashed from the office. Signorotto looked from McLaren to Stone questioningly. Both members shrugged their shoulders. Thirty seconds passed before Tyler re-appeared holding onto the Holiday Book with one hand as he furiously flipped to the last couple of entries. When he spoke, he had a smile of satisfaction on his face.

"Thought so. Number forty-two is here in the Holiday Book. Owners are away till next week. When Bobrov and I were out the other night he was checking houses in the book, supposedly for security. He got out of the car at this one only. Went up and down the alleyway checking the place out. When he got back in, he just threw the book onto the back seat and called it quits. We'd checked about six houses, but this was the only one he got out at and the only one he was interested in. He didn't want me to put this one, or the one before, on the log because he said he didn't want to look as though he was doing too much work on them.

"Who owns the house, Max?" Phil Stone said.

Max Tyler ran his finger down the entry page.

"A Carlo Genessi."

"I'm pretty sure that's the guy who owns Genessi Real Estate. They have a lot of branches around the northern suburbs. Very pro police. Active in a lot of charity work."

"That is him, Phil. I've had a bit to do with him with charity stuff for the Royal Children's Hospital. I know he lives in Faraday Street with his wife and three or four kids. Good family," Signorotto said.

Phil Stone went very quiet as he began to slowly pace from one side of the office to the other for at least a minute before he turned and confronted the group.

"The choice is, do we let him and whoever he is with commit what is a burglary now, which is basically us letting him commit a crime or do we nab him now that there is more to the story. Max, is there a contact number for Genessi?"

"Yes, boss. It's right here," Tyler said showing Stone the number. "He's in Italy according to this."

Phil Stone took the book from Tyler and handed it to Conlon.

"Okay, Detective Inspector. This is where you come in. I want you to ring him even though you have to probably wake him and run this all past him. Explain the bind we are in if we grab Bobrov now as against letting this play out. Tell him we are all over the scene, but we need his permission to let Bobrov carry on. Tell him that if there are any damages to his house, although I doubt there will be, that your department will cover expenses. There is a good chance that we might land some big fish in our net."

Conlon went into another room slowly and rang the number. It was answered after quite a few rings. Minutes passed as he spoke at length into the phone while the others looked through the glass partition. Stone turned and spoke to Signorotto.

"Tony. I'm doing it this way because I don't want any blowback on Carlton. This is a situation that was started by Ethical Standards and shoved onto us. If Genessi gives the go-ahead, we will run the operation, but I want Ethical Standards to get it authorised. Anyway, they can be front row for this."

Minutes later, Conlon re-appeared and spoke to Stone.

"He's okay with letting it run. Very pro police. He just wants us to get back to him when it's finished."

"You sign off on damages?" Stone said quickly.

Conlon looked directly at Stone and realised he could not argue with a Commander.

"Yes, yes. If there's damages, my department will cover costs."

Stone could be seen by everybody in the room writing down the answer to his last question. Just as he finished the notes, the voice of Johnny Petran came over the radio.

"DRU to Command."

"Come in DRU," Signorotto replied.

"Ring me please," Petran said.

Kate McLaren immediately punched in the DRU number.

"What's up Johnny?" Kate said as she turned on the phone's speaker.

"Just to let you know that when I spotted Bobrov unloading the grog, something interesting dropped out of his coat pocket. I think someone should go and check the number of portable radios that are currently in and out of the station. I think you'll find there is one missing because that's what he just dropped."

"Fucking hell!" Signorotto yelled furiously as once again, Max Tyler shot out of the room heading this time to the Stores office. "We can continue on this channel, boys. It's definitely a secure one, no matter what channel he listens to, he can't hear us talk. I'd say he has it on the city channel so he can monitor any local Carlton vehicles. To be on the safe side though, Johnny, if there's anything that you think is a high priority, just phone it in here to the Command post." Signorotto finished by slamming the palm of his hand onto the desk in frustration.

"Righto, will do," Petran replied.

Phil Stone turned to Conlon and spoke.

"Okay, Detective Inspector. Right now, we have burglary and most likely theft of police equipment. I know your department have set this bloke on a long leash because you wanted to see where he may lead you and I know that you have permission from the owner of the house to continue, but I think you'd better contact your own Command to see if they are okay with aiding and abetting a police officer to commit at this stage what looks like two or more serious indictable offences. Ball's in your court."

"Let me make another call, Commander," Conlon said heading back into the glassed-off area once more. Before coming out, Max Tyler returned and confirmed there was a portable radio that was unaccounted for. Minutes later Conlon came out and spoke to the group.

"Just had the Deputy Commissioner on the phone. His answer was that we still want some bigger fish out of this if we can. We're to let him have free rein for now, with us as the observers."

As Conlon talked, Phil Stone took notes. He had very little trust in the police who policed the police.

"Okay, as long as we are all on the same page, we'll continue," Stone said just as his desk phone rang shrilly. Stone picked up the receiver and listened. After letting a couple of expletives fly around the office, he hung up and faced the others.

"Never rains, but pours," he said wearily. "Apparently two people have turned up in separate Ubers to the laneway at the side of 42 Faraday Street."

"We had a feeling something was going to happen, but what's so special about the visitors?" Conlon asked sarcastically.

"Well," Stone replied. "The first one is a member of the Australian cricket team and the second is the State Labor Minister, Steve Bird. Mick York said they were both ushered through the side gate of number forty-two."

Conlon reached immediately for his mobile phone and was in the act of punching in a number on the speed dial when Stone reached across and removed it from his hand.

"No Inspector. No calls. I am now contacting the Deputy Commissioner myself. This is about to become a problem that is way above our pay scales. No-one leaves this office, and no-one uses their phones. Even you, Inspector. Understand?" Stone said giving a surreptitious wink to Tony Signorotto.

As Stone went to make the important call to the Deputy Commissioner, Conlon breathed an audible sigh of relief, glad that it had now been taken out of his hands and 'kicked upstairs.'

Suddenly, the portable radio next to Tony Signorotto blared into life with an urgent note in the voice of Johnny Petran.

"DRU to Command."

Signorotto picked up the radio and replied. "Go ahead DRU. All ears here."

"We have some more people of interest arriving."

Signorotto indicated urgently to Kate McLaren to hold Phil Stone from making his phone call. Moving quickly to her Commander, Kate shook her head rapidly from side to side and made a slicing motion across her throat to stop him.

"What is it, Kate?" Stone said with a puzzled look.

"More guests arriving at Faraday Street, boss."

Hurrying back to Signorotto's side, Stone heard Johnny Petran's voice.

"I can't believe that Bobrov had arranged all this. He's not that connected. He's not in a position to know any of these players. If this is a high stakes card game someone else has arranged the punters. It's a who's who down there."

The group looked at each other before Stone spoke. "Who've we got, Johnny?"

"Besides the first two who were Mike Rawlings from the Australian Cricket team and State Labor Minister, Steve Bird, the next three who rocked up in Ubers are two television personalities, one being Peter Vaughan and the other that old newsreader, Ed Palmer. Last but not least is one you'll all know and that is Professor Dung Tran, the big-time heart surgeon from St. Vincent's hospital. I reckon there is serious money going down here. Sending through pictures as I speak. Double check them as quick as you can and get back to me as to what your plan is."

"On it now," Signorotto said as the pictures started to appear on the internal email system.

"Hang on, hang on," Petran suddenly said. Guess who has come out into the laneway and escorted them inside. It's bloody Pavel Antonov."

Phil Stone spun around to Conlon. "Well, now we know Bobrov is up to his old tricks again. Just wonder if he realises that he's playing with a loose cannon from the Russian *Bratva*. I think now's a good time to have a long conversation with the Deputy Commissioner."

It seemed like an eternity before he returned ashen faced but smiling.

"The DC must be a Liberal. Said to go ahead with the night. He wants everything recorded. Political leverage, I think. Doesn't want anyone else involved but us, Johnny and Mick. Says he will talk to the heads of Ethical Standards once the night is over. Realises that Bobrov has become a small fish now that a member of the Russian mafia is involved."

An hour went by in which both the DRU and the members back at Carlton either watched the house or listened for updates. At about ten-thirty, Johnny Petran called in.

"Boss, I think whoever was coming to this shindig has arrived. I've been talking to Mick, and we reckon we could get down the side alley and possibly even onto to the roof of the old bakery and possibly get some shots of anyone who is there."

"Go for it, but don't take any chances," Stone said. "Just shots of any head that pops up. Don't take any of something that may be going on. You two can witness that yourselves and tell us later. Whatever we may think of this, it's going to involve a Minister of Parliament. Be careful."

"Roger that," the keen voice of Johnny Petran came back.

The Carlton crew bided their time drinking copious amounts of coffee and staring at the portable radio as time dragged on. It was almost two o'clock in the morning when Stone turned to Conlon and Signorotto.

"I think it's time we called in. What do you think?"

As Signorotto picked up the radio handpiece he jumped slightly as it crackled into life.

"York to Command," came the hushed voice.

"Go ahead, Mick," Signorotto said as he was crowded by the others.

"Okay. First things first. We have taken heaps of pics both from up on the bakery roof and through a gap in the fence. They obviously aren't allowed to smoke in there because that Toscano keeps loading up the outside table with cigars, cigarettes and booze and I can tell you it's all top shelf. Every one of those we named is there. We managed a long lens photo look through a slightly open side curtain and Bobrov is hovering around the table while Antonov is the dealer and the bank. There's an awful lot of money in this. Nothing on the table except hundreds and fifties. I'm talking quietly because we are in the alley heading back to the van and Toscano and Antonov are having a big argument over something. Bobrov is out there trying to sort it. He's been trying to pacify that politician and I think he's just taken him back inside. Bit hard to tell but Antonov and Toscano are going hammer and tongs at each other. Heard the word 'beggar' come up a few times but can't really make it out. We're getting back where it's out of the way."

"Okay, Mick. Give us a ring when you are back in the van."

Chapter Twenty-Three

Ricky Bobrov was a relieved man with the unannounced and smooth arrival of Antonov's high profile punters at the Rathdowne Street address.

He quietly stood back in awe as sporting, political, television and medical identities had arrived in the alleyway via separate Ubers and were greeted by Pavel Antonov as though they had all been friends for years. It suddenly dawned on him that this was just another high stakes game for Antonov and that he, Ricky Bobrov, was just a bit-player amongst a cast of stars in the evening's entertainment. It didn't overly concern him if at the end of the night he could take home a sizeable wad of cash for himself.

As the night progressed, his sharp eye picked up several deft moves by Antonov in his card dealings to the group. He by no means thought that he had seen more than a couple of the ways the money was being won and lost across all the punters. Antonov had them all by the balls. First one fortune, then another would rise then fall along with their hopes. They didn't lose too much before they won back some of it. These were not good players but just celebrities who wanted good entertainment. It was a thrill for all of them to be one of the 'bad boys' for the night. They were all very wealthy people and even the Australian cricketer had confessed to Bobrov that he was just using his spare 'good time' money that had been given as an under the table deal in conjunction with a new bat sponsorship for the upcoming Test series. The spare cash part was a little over two hundred thousand dollars which, to this young up and coming sports star, was just the cream on the cake for the sporting company concerned, slapping their sticker on his bats. The fact that the sporting company didn't even make the bats didn't faze him one iota. Some poor bastard back in India was the one who had slaved to make his weapon of choice and then for very little money. This was pin money!

He and Marco Toscano had paid close attention to any needs that the punters had asked for. The only time that one of them was denied was when the well-known heart surgeon had asked for a little area to be cleared on a coffee table so he could 'cut' his coke, but he was told he was on his own. Bobrov wondered if he approached open heart surgery with the same enthusiasm as he did with a line of the powder off the patio table. When it came time for a smoke break, everyone who wanted to adjourned to the rear garden area where there was a humidor containing Cuban Montechristo cigars and several packets of expensive Sobranie Black Russian cigarettes. Alongside these were a bottle of Blue Humour black truffle infusion vodka and a crystal container of Ledaig smoked whisky from the Isle of Mull in Scotland. For those that didn't like things Scottish there was also a bottle of Michter's small batch Kentucky bourbon. No expense had been spared.

Antonov played them all to a point where they wanted more. The thrill of winning and then losing had come and gone several times and Antonov knew these men survived on competition to remain the best in their fields. They were ready to keep going. Egos were coming into play. Antonov took his partners aside to speak to them quietly.

"Next half hour is crunch time. The cricketer is getting desperate, and I've seen his wallet. Stuffed with hundred-dollar notes. He owes the bank ten which I've generously allowed on the promise that he stays in the game. I'll have his wallet emptied out very soon. The old news reader is in for about fifteen and I want him up for another ten. With a small kick-in from the other wallets, I think we'll be on track to take about forty grand all up. The bank hasn't been broken so far and I don't think it will be. They think they can play but they really don't have any idea. Main thing is that we're going to make a sum and they're having a good time trying to beat each other. That cricketer told me of the money he earns. I am going to play him hard."

Marco Toscano couldn't help himself when it came to annoying Antonov.

"This as good as running an Asian begging scam in town, mate?"

A red mist descended on Antonov. It had been a long couple of hours trying to not only play the punters off against each other but to stack up a profit for themselves. He was tired. Before Bobrov could move, Antonov charged at Toscano, grabbed him by the hair and proceeded to drag him, past some bushes and down towards the garden shed at the rear of the back yard.

Bobrov wanted to follow quickly but couldn't because the State politician, Steve Bird suddenly approached him and began to speak.

"I overheard a comment about a begging scam in the city. I don't want to know anything about it. I can't be around people who are involved in this sort of thing, do you hear me?"

"Don't worry Mr. Bird. Nothing leaves here, okay? Just a misunderstanding between my colleagues. Why don't you go back inside if you're finished your drink and we'll continue with the game. You're on a bit of a winning streak from what I've seen. Let's get back to it, eh?"

The politician's eyes kept flicking back around Bobrov to the area where Antonov had dragged Toscano. Ricky quickly stepped up and draped an arm over the politician's and spoke in the direction of the other punters. "Alright gents, let's get back to it, shall we?"

They all began to walk back into the house, but Bobrov could feel Bird try and turn around, still trying to see what was going on down the backyard.

His mind was still spinning as all the punters once again settled at the table. The trouble was, Antonov had not re-appeared.

"I'll just go and see where our main man is. Back in a second," Bobrov said, anxiously heading back out the door.

Turning the corner to the shed, he saw Toscano on his knees with blood running out of his scalp, but more worryingly, out of both ears. As he watched, Toscano pitched forward on to his face amongst several pieces of broken terracotta pottery and lay still. Looking up he saw Pavel Antonov standing with the broken base of the pot in his right hand.

"What the fuck have you done?" a stunned and frightened Ricky Bobrov said to Antonov as he knelt next to Toscano and felt for his pulse. There was none.

Antonov tossed the piece of broken pot to the ground at the side of Toscano and spoke slowly.

"If he's dead, he deserved it. Too many questions from the little man. I warned him to shut up about my other interests."

A sudden cold shudder ran its way up the spine of Ricky Bobrov as he turned to the big Russian.

"He's fucking dead all right. Fucking dead. What the fuck will we do now? That politician will know he's missing because he saw you two come down here. What are we going to do now, eh?"

Antonov looked directly at Bobrov with cold reptilian eyes.

"He wanted more from the take tonight otherwise he was going to ring the Asian crime gang Police. A word of advice Ricky. No one threatens the Bratva. No one."

"What now?" A dazed Bobrov said.

"We go back inside and finish the night. I will make a phone call and this piece of shit will be dog food before the sun comes up."

Pavel Antonov took Ricky Bobrov by the shoulder and led him back up the path to the house.

Bobrov knew that Marco Toscano was beyond help. The only person who needed help now was Ricky Bobrov.

Chapter Twenty-Four

Ricky Bobrov's mind was elsewhere from when he walked back into the house. All he wanted to do was to finish the night so he could clean up and get out. There was only one way to do this he realised as he took Antonov away from the table for a quick talk.

"Pavel, I know nothing, okay?" The scared police officer said. "I saw nothing and heard nothing. The problem now is that I have to put this house back properly after the game is over. Put it back by myself now after what's happened. That's the problem. This game has to finish by four. Gives us time to get the punters out and for you to get your people in. Let these people know it's game over by four no matter what. You fix it," he said angrily.

Antonov looked at Bobrov and after a tense stand-off, nodded his head. Even he could see that although there was minimal cleaning to the inside, he had to get his Bratva associates to do the removal side of things. He went back to the game.

As the time approached, Bobrov could see that the cricketer was going to take the biggest hit in the back pocket. The others were down a few thousand, but he had noticed that the Right Honourable Mr. Bird looked like his name—he wanted to fly. Bobrov guessed that something was wrong, so at a short five-minute break he spoke to him.

"Mr. Bird, do we have a problem?"

"I think you and Pavel have a problem. There were three of you and now there are only two. One minute I hear an argument between the others and now I can't see him anywhere. I want out now. Don't order me an Uber. I'll walk to Carlton and get a taxi. Do not contact me again and make sure

Antonov doesn't. I wasn't here, understand? I have never met you. Money wise I am happy to walk away breaking even. Don't say anything, I'm leaving," the very scared sounding politician said quietly so as not to be overheard by Antonov who he now looked on as the Devil himself.

Bobrov couldn't do anything but stand aside as Bird took his money and walked out of the back door and subsequently the side gate, but not before stopping and taking a long look towards the shed. Once in the alleyway, he disappeared into the early morning darkness.

Bobrov looked at the quick striding Minister realising that what had started as a high stake albeit one-sided money-making card game had suddenly and irretrievably turned into something much more sinister.

Back inside, Antonov was counting out the money from the last hand. The only person who really wanted to keep going past four was the Australian cricketer with money to burn.

He was down twenty thousand dollars, which wasn't a problem except for his ego which was telling him to keep punting. His ego needed soothing. He was annoyed that others didn't mind finishing up even though their winnings were down also. The doctor was shy fifteen thousand and the news reader the same, the others a bit less. He did realise though that if they all wanted to stop, it was useless to just keep playing against Antonov and keep bleeding money to him.

Bobrov had the phone numbers of the Uber drivers for the night who he quickly rang-minus one. By four fifteen the remaining punters had all been sent on their way, oblivious to what had taken place in the back yard. Pavel Antonov had shaken them all by the hand and promised there would be more card nights, to which they all responded positively. Losing money did not deter any of them from what had been a 'dangerous' night out. Bobrov turned a deaf ear to the banter. He didn't know what to do but there was one thing for sure.

From now on it was the horses only. He would put all this behind him and move on. At least that was what he hoped.

Everything was put back in place and the rear patio cleaned of any cigar and cigarette butts. The area of concern was down the back yard and as far as Bobrov was concerned it was Antonov's responsibility. He was not going anywhere near it.

Antonov took the rubbish bag from Bobrov and spoke to him.

"My car is three streets away. I'll get rid of it. My cleaners will be here shortly and they have been briefed. I think we should both go. My boys will lock the gate after they have sanitised down the back. No need for you to worry Ricky. Toscano is no loss, just an accident. No one knows about him. The punters didn't know his name and he has no connections over this way. He was a western suburbs boy who hasn't really been a name over there for a long time. That's why he was trying to get into business over here. He tried and failed. He had a big mouth for a little guy, and I warned him to shut up about Bratva business. If I hadn't disposed of him, my colleagues would have. I won't lose sleep over him."

"I suppose so, but that politician, Bird got out of here quick. He suspects something," Bobrov said quickly. "He overheard you and Marco talking about your begging scheme."

"No matter, Ricky. He didn't see anything, and he won't go to the police. Be happy, mate. You can have Toscano's share. I've taken twenty on top of the bank. It's all good."

As Antonov headed down the alley way he slowed, then turned back to face Bobrov and spoke.

"I know you won't do a thing Ricky because you'll have to charge yourself as an accessory to murder and I don't think you would last too long in Barwon State prison as an ex-cop."

Neither Pavel Antonov nor Ricky Bobrov knew that they were being filmed by the DRU. As they stood facing each other in the bluestone lane, a black Toyota van drove slowly along

Faraday Street in answer to Antonov's phone call for a 'cleaning' team to attend.

As Bobrov came out of the alleyway, it stopped at the side gate of number forty-two.

Chapter Twenty-Five

"DRU to Command," Mick York said with a tired voice into his portable radio.

Tony Signorotto looked across at Kate McLaren.

"You're closest, Kate. Grab that will you?" An equally tired sounding voice said to his Sergeant.

Kate picked up the handset as she looked around the office at the other members. Phil Stone was signing off on some previous paperwork. Tony and Max Tyler had been quietly discussing what was happening with a minor turf drug war centring around the northern end of Carlton where it met the City of Melbourne proper. Detective Inspector Conlon was pouring himself another cup of coffee. Kate thought that she had never seen anyone drink so much of the stuff, especially given that it was about four o'clock in the morning. She pressed the transmit button and spoke.

"Sergeant Kate McLaren here, Mick. How goes it down there?"

"All the punters have gone, Kate. Bird went about half an hour ago on foot and at quite a trot. Don't know why he didn't go by car. Just up and walked with Bobrov staying at his back as he went. Probably lost a packet and decided to call it a night. The others have all been packed into Ubers and sent off. Bobrov and Antonov have closed the side gate and are going their separate ways, but there is no sign of Toscano, and we've had our eyes on the whole area. We haven't spotted him. I think we are about to pack up here, Command."

"Stand by, Mick and I'll let the boss know," Kate said as she walked over to Stone who was holding his glasses in one hand and rubbing his tired eyes with the other.

"Boss, Mick York is..."

Suddenly, York's urgent voice cut over the radio in a tone that made them all sit up and take notice.

"Stand by all units. We have a black Toyota van pulling up to the side gate of number forty-two."

Silence engulfed the Command Post. No one dared speak until the DRU said something more. Thirty seconds passed before the air waves were broken with York's voice again.

"Okay people, we have two heavy set looking dudes in black who got out of the van, one with what looked like a type of large black body bag or similar, gone into the open back gate and are now loading that body bag into the back of the van, but this time it looks weighed down. I've got some close-up shots of them both. Let's all remember that we can't find Toscano anywhere."

Stone grabbed the radio hand set as the nervous energy of the group started to roll through the room.

"Have you got a number of the van, Mick?"

"Yep. One Oscar Tango Seven Uniform Papa. Black Toyota van."

"You in a position for a closer look or even a very careful tail?" Stone said as he cast a look around the others as Tony Signorotto grabbed Max Tyler by the sleeve and propelled him out of the door towards the change room.

"Onto it, Boss. Going to dog them as soon as they move. Johnny and I are on the way in the van to the end of the alley."

"Good. Don't know what they're up to but at this time of the morning the only other thing they could be doing is delivering the morning papers, but they sound a bit old for that. Keep up the sit reps."

"Will do, Boss, game on for us," came the now fully awake voice from Mick York.

Stone spun around and yelled out to Tony Signorotto. "You doing what I think you're doing, Tony?"

"For sure, Phil. Max and I are getting into our scruffies and will link up with the DRU down the track. I'll grab my own car from the yard so it's not obvious. I reckon this might be bigger than a card game, people."

Heads slowly nodded in agreement around the room.

Chapter Twenty-Six

A third member of the DRU team drove the old Nissan van slowly, with its lights off, down the laneway, following the black Toyota van from a safe distance. Mick York stayed on the radio in the back while Johnny Petran kept eyes on their quarry as best he could in the dark streets.

"Just keep your headlights off as long as you can, mate," Petran said to their wheelman who nodded in response.

With little traffic at that time of the morning, both vehicles got through Carlton and were headed down Flinders Street in very quick time.

"What's your bet, Johnny?" Mick York said to his laid-back colleague.

"Well, they might be tempted to do a quick pit stop on top of the West Gate bridge and heave whatever it is they are carrying over the side," Petran said with a grin on his weary but experienced face.

"Have to be a quick Formula One type though if they don't want to be spotted giving the heave-ho to the bag," York replied as both vehicles drove past the old Victoria Police headquarters towards the entrance to the bridge.

He spoke into the radio handpiece. "DRU to Command."

Kate McLaren replied. "Command receiving."

"Looks like we are heading over the West Gate. I take it you want us to keep dogging them even though we are heading into someone else's patch?" York queried.

Both Stone and Conlon nodded their approval immediately.

"Tell them Tony and Max are on their way as back up and they'll contact them in case they want to swap over with the tailing," Stone said.

Kate relayed the message.

Max Tyler's voice suddenly came over the air. "Got you on the channel, Mick. We aren't too far back. When you get to wherever you are going let us know."

"All good, Max," York said. "We're over the bridge now and heading towards Altona."

Minutes later he was back on the radio again.

"Okay listeners. We've pulled off the freeway onto Millers Road then onto Marion Street. They've stopped at a very ominous sounding factory people.

"Why ominous, Mick?" Phil Stone cut in.

"Well boss, if you combine Toscano's disappearing act together with these boys and a body bag and their destination, it doesn't look too promising. The factory is called KORM Pet Meat Supplies. Think someone should get onto this place and find out who owns it. We are going to get some long-distance photos of what's going on. If they're in there too long we'll need Tony and Max up here to back us up. It doesn't look like it's operating at night, but we don't want them offering up a sacrifice to a sausage factory, do we?"

"Get up real close, boys," the sudden request came over the radio. "We have to presume that is Toscano in that bag and we'll need the body autopsied, not minced up. We don't know how far Bobrov is in on this, but we need everything going our way including what's in that body bag."

"Gotcha boss. Tony, can you back us up quick if we need you?" York asked quickly.

"Just down the road boys. Yell out if you need us," Signorotto replied.

"Thanks boys. Johnny has just got shots of them hauling the bag into a side door," York said quietly before coming up suddenly on the radio again.

"Stand by Tony. They've come straight back out. Must have dumped it just inside."

Back in the Command Post, Stone and Conlon gave each other a quick look before the Commander spoke.

"Photos only, fellas. We're going to let them go on their way. We can deal with them later. We want that body if that's what's inside the place, before they turn it into dog food. We want a comprehensive photo shoot of the room it's in and anything else you may think is important, but you'll have to be quick before the sun comes up and workers arrive. We'll make inquiries back here as to who owns the place."

"They're back in the van and leaving now. Got a heap of photos so we'll move in. Just in case there is someone inside though Tony, can you two come up? Between us all, we can do a good sweep of the place while we also get photos and deal with the body," York said.

"Right behind you," Max Tyler said as Tony gunned his car to a sliding stop on the gravel behind the DRU van.

They all approached the darkened meat works with guns drawn even though the two suspects had driven off. At the door where they had seen the two men enter carrying the body bag, Tony and Max took one side and Johnny and Mick the other. Petran yelled loudly. "Police. Drop your weapons."

Mick York turned the doorknob slowly, fully expecting it to be locked, but it wasn't, so he quickly turned the handle and pushed the door wide open so the others could immediately enter, fan out and with torches and scour the room for any suspects.

Inside and with the sweep of the room done, the only objects they saw were a desk, a chair and the black body bag they were looking for. Johnny Petran knelt down beside the bag and slowly unzipped the cover to reveal a male body. He got out his mobile phone and held it up next to the head in the bag. The photo on his phone and the body were the same. It was Marco Toscano.

"Boss, Tony here. Come in Command."

"Command receiving," Stone said.

"It's Toscano in the bag. I'd say they dropped him off to be part of today's shipment of pet meat. No one else around. The boys have done a quick sweep of the factory but luckily none of the day shift have arrived yet."

'Here's the plan, Tony," Stone said. We reckon that place will be crawling with workers soon. Kate's been on their website and done a Wikipedia search. KORM pet food supplies is owned by a group of Russian business men. KORM is Russian for pet food. One of the owners is Pavel Antonov. Get the body into the DRU van and bring it back to the coroner's office. Kate's organised a Forensics team who are heading over as we speak to Faraday Street. We have two members from Collingwood standing guard on the place. Don't want anyone from Carlton in case Bobrov finds out. The registration on that van comes up to the Russian Ethnic Representation Committee, which is in Greaves Street, Fitzroy. I'm going to get Kate over there later today to speak to them about the van. Command in town are letting Bobrov have a bit of space at the moment until we get an emergency autopsy done. It's almost light now so get out of there. DRU to the Coroner's and Tony, you and Max back here. We are all going to get some shut-eye and we'll be back in this Command post at six tonight. All understand?"

"DRU received," Mick York said.

"Carlton 265 received," Tony Signorotto replied.

"The Deputy Commissioner from the Crime Department will be here tonight. This has become a top-level priority one job now the Russians are involved. We know where Antonov and Bobrov live. DRU from Northern Metro have been briefed and will do surveillance on them till midnight. At this stage neither of them knows we are onto them. Let's keep it that way. See you all in a few hours," Stone said as he slumped back in his chair looking from Conlon to McLaren.

Chapter Twenty-Seven

Everyone from the morning's operation was now back at the Carlton Police Station, sitting around in the upstairs office talking quietly and drinking coffee.

Phil Stone had made sure the upstairs room was secured. Members who were working downstairs had been told under no circumstances were they to enter the room unless it was of the utmost importance and then only with a quick phone call from below saying they were coming up.

He had entered the room with the epaulettes denoting his new rank of Commander as this was now Sunday and his first official day of being promoted. There had been a few quick handshakes from his team, but they all knew the top priority was what had happened during the previous morning and night. He waited for a short break in the murmur of conversations around the office before taking the lead.

"Okay, listen up. The Deputy Commissioner from the Crime Department is on his way over and will be here soon, so let's just get each other up to speed. First things first. I called in a big favour with the ME at the Coroner's office, and they have already come back with a partial autopsy. It appears that Marco Toscano was killed by a blow to the head with what appears to be a terracotta pot. The crime scene boys that we got down to the address in Faraday Street found some blood and broken pieces from the pot at the crime scene. It was a very hard blow from a powerful person because it ruptured part of his brain. The ME won't sign off on it yet until he is finished, probably by late tomorrow, but he certainly indicated that we have a murder on our hands."

A desk phone rang loudly and was answered immediately by Max Tyler.

"D C's downstairs. I'll bring him up," he said.

"Thanks Max," Stone replied before continuing. "To save some time, I have already spoken to him this morning and given him the preliminary report from the ME, so we can keep going when he comes up." Thirty seconds passed before Max entered the door and showed in Deputy Commissioner Craig Stewart, who immediately took over the meeting with his presence.

"Okay, folks. I'm across everything that happened last night and this morning and may I say I am proud of what you have all done and what you will accomplish going forward and I'll speak about a few things when the newly promoted Commander finishes. Carry on, Mr. Stone," he said with a beaming smile and a mouth full of very white teeth.

Another headquarters, ladder climbing politician, Tony Signorotto thought, staring back at the figure in the new suit and crisp white shirt.

Phil Stone nodded and continued with a slightly questioning look towards Stewart.

"We knew that this was most likely going to be a card game we would be monitoring knowing Bobrov's history. It looked like one crooked member with hopefully a good lead on Antonov coming out of it. Even the slightest thing on Antonov would help the Department with knowledge of the Russian mafia." Stone stopped to sip his coffee then continued. "I know it all took us by surprise with the standard of high roller that arrived at the Faraday Street address. T.V. personalities together with the medical, sporting and political elite. It... "

Stewart suddenly cut in. "I want everyone here to forget the politician, understood?" he said forcefully. Stone looked at Stewart and shook his head slowly before continuing.

"As I was saying, it then became a big stakes game being held in an empty house for which we had the nod of the owner to continue our sting. A couple of strange things then happened as far as I could tell, and please jump in if any of you have other thoughts. First off is that these type of high roller games go all night through to sunrise. This one stopped at about four in the morning and I don't think it stopped because of money. Secondly, one of the punters, and here I have no choice but to mention the Right Honourable Steve Bird, who left via the side gate in a real hurry on foot just after four with Bobrov following down the alley. The DRU said that he was almost running. No Uber, no taxi. Why? You take over now Tony," Stone said deliberately ignoring Stewart who was about to interrupt. Tony could sense the hammer was about to come down on any more talk involving the politician so he spoke immediately.

"My guess is that he knows something the other punters don't. They all left with a handshake and an Uber ride, but not him. He flew the coop as soon as he could. The fact that we now have preliminary evidence that Toscano was murdered in the backyard I'd say we have a State MP scared out of his wits that he may be embroiled in whatever happened. What we have with the other punters is just circumstantial in that they have gone to a high stakes card game for some excitement and the possibility of winning or losing some cash. I think we have a big leverage factor though with Bird, and we have to speak to him."

Stewart coughed loudly and stepped forward, but Tony Signorotto was old school and, on a roll, and he wasn't going to be stopped by Departmental or political interference.

"First thing tomorrow morning, Max, you and Chloe Schaeffer, now that she's back from leave, are going down to the Russian Ethnic Representative Committee headquarters in Greaves Street, Fitzroy to find out about that van which was registered to that address. We need to know who had it and who has the use of it. It's a secondary crime scene because it transported Toscano' body, so if you get any kick back impound it. With this Russian connection it's odds on that Antonov has control of it or arranged it to do the bodysnatching. What we have to work on is the connection between Bobrov and Antonov in relation to Toscano's murder. We will also have to sit off Antonov's place. Bobrov is down for a seven a.m. shift tomorrow and if he turns up it must be work as normal. Neither of them knows we have been on to them from the get-go." Signorotto noticed Stewart getting very close to him so he spun around to him and spoke.

"Mr. Stewart. Do you want to add something?"

A clearly agitated Deputy Commissioner began tersely.

"Not add, Senior Sergeant. Take away. There will be no talk here or anywhere else about the involvement of any politician being in this. He will not be interviewed by anyone in this room. Is that clear? He is a State Member of Parliament and if he is spoken to by anybody it will be up to the Chief Commissioner."

To everyone's surprise, Detective Inspector Conlon from Internal Investigations spoke up.

"Why does that not surprise me, Sir? I suppose the fact that the state election is upon us and the Chief wants to continue as Chief wouldn't have anything to do with this would it?"

The silence in the room was palpable. There was sudden respect for the Toecutters Inspector from everyone bar the Deputy Commissioner. The look that passed from Stewart to Conlon could have cut through steel. Stewart pressed on.

"I know that we all want to catch who murdered Toscano, but from a Command position there's been a development. The Chief makes the call on this, not me. Don't shoot the messenger. He is also across the situation and the possible, albeit remote possible involvement of a Member of Parliament and he wishes to emphasise that nobody from this room even speak to any of the night's participants about this situation."

Tony Signorotto stood to speak, but Stewart got in first.

"Senior Sergeant, this is not open for discussion."

"With all due respect, Sir. That cuts out any possible witnesses to the crime of murder. All we have left to interview are two people and one of them is the obvious offender. Maybe we wouldn't get much out of the others, but I and other members in this room know that Bird knows something. What's the reasoning behind it?"

"That's enough, Tony," Stone cut in knowing that Stewart did not have to give any sort of explanation to a sub-officer, but he certainly had to give one to a fellow high-ranking officer. "Orders are orders, but I think an explanation as to why our hands are being tied behind our backs is due." Stewart knew that he had to say something. Stone had him cornered. Stewart walked over to a side office and motioned for Stone, Signorotto and Conlon to follow. Once inside he closed the door.

"I know getting Antonov will lead nowhere without a witness. That's why you have to concentrate on Bobrov to do that. Approaching the Russian Consulate who I know would like to see Antonov gone can't be done unless the approach comes from the Chief or a Member of Parliament of this State. The Chief won't because he wants to remain as Chief after the election. On that point you are right Mr. Conlon. No one is willing to upset the good ship SS State Government.

"Sir, even if we got Bobrov as a witness, he would be cut to shreds in court because he would have already been up on gambling charges with Antonov. He's a co-conspirator," Conlon said. "We have a bent copper in this, and we don't want to be seen at some future court date that we put a murder on the back burner for the sake of anyone's career be it in the Department or Parliament House. Let's lay it on the line here. If it came down to public opinion, I think dealing with a suspect politician with something to hide would be paramount. Hiding him till after the election stinks to high heaven."

"This can't turn into a police or political shit show, fellas!" Stewart said angrily. "We can't be dragging in a polly just to question him over something he may or may not know about which really started off at a card game. He would lawyer up and we would be told to fuck off."

Phil Stone took a chance.

"How about this. I approach him and talk to him over a coffee without lawyers, cameras or the threat of coming into a police station. Could even be done on the quiet at his place. For him telling us what he saw we promise that the night of gambling will go away if he is the one to approach the Russian Consulate and tell them all about Antonov and Toscano but probably more important to them is that we can guarantee that if they ship Pavel Antonov back to Minsk or some other Godforsaken frozen tundra it will shut down the entire illegal street begging operation in Melbourne. It would be a win win situation. I'm not fussed about ending my career as a Commander. This is about murder, not careers!"

Stewart paced up and down the office before answering.

"I won't be approaching him. If you want to put an end to your rise through the ranks then so be it. Just leave me right out of this. I know nothing. If it blows up in your face then you're on your own, Commander," Stewart said as he walked out of the office door, past Kate McLaren, Max Tyler, Johnny Petran and Mick York.

Stone, Conlon and Signorotto walked out of the meeting and stood by the others.

"I'm not going to brush any murder on my patch under the carpet just because some high-ranking police are too scared to make tough decisions. This happened here and will be dealt with by us. I stick by my crew," Stone said fiercely.

Conlon took a step forward and put out his hand to shake that of Phil Stone. Stone smiled and offered his in return. "Never thought I'd be shaking hands with one of the Toecutters," he said with a laugh.

Conlon spoke. "Members may hate Ethical Standards, but I bet ninety-nine per cent of them would want Bobrov dealt with. We need to get him in and we need to speak to Bird. I'm with Commander Stone here, guys. Regarding Stewart, I will tell you something."

Suddenly all eyes were on him.

"I won't say what side of politics he's on but if the Government stays in after the next election, the present Chief will remain. If the Opposition become Government, I can tell you that the good Deputy Commissioner will be the new Chief. Politics dictates their lives and a murder or two will always take second place if it looks like blocking their paths. Working in Ethical Standards you get to know who's who in the zoo, let me tell you."

"What a circus," Mick York said virtually spitting out his words.

"Where do we start with Bobrov?" Kate McLaren asked. Conlon continued.

"I say we threaten him with everything from gambling offences right up to being an accessory to murder, but we offer him an out by taping him and getting him in closer with Antonov while you, Commander, work on Bird. It will take a bit of time to get to see someone at the Consulate and in the meantime, we get Bobrov to cosy up to him and work on another card night all the while telling him he wants to quit the Force and move onto to bigger things if Antonov can take him under his wing. I think Pavel's ego would like that. Bobrov either helps us get more on Antonov and his Bratva mates or we hang him out to dry on charges. If he goes down in court for illegal gaming stuff and is sacked then he loses all his superannuation that the Government has put in. If he does what we want, we let him resign and he keeps all his dough. What do you think, Commander?"

"Worth a try," Stone said with a tired voice. "You're the investigator, Detective Inspector, how should we split it up?"

"Sir, you run the Bird part with Kate. He will want a shoulder to cry on so you can do the good cop bad cop routine. Tony and I will work Bobrov around while he still works here. I would work Max on just about every shift with Bobrov to stop him getting the jitters and keep a close eye on him. I think I might just have to base myself here for a while as a uniform

Inspector that has come in to do a two month or so audit of the station. That will be okay. We work both of them over slowly. Bobrov wants to stay out of gaol and keep his superannuation and Bird wants to keep his parliamentary pension intact. We have to convince both of them that what they are doing will save themselves. Tell Bird that the other punters have been left out of everything. One talkative celebrity will be enough. We should end up with one bent copper out of the Force, one Russian back in the land of the permafrost and a clean-up of Melbourne streets. Leaves us with a politician who could be quite useful to us in the future.

"No wonder they call your office the Toecutters, Mr. Conlon. By the time we slice and dice these two they will probably only be left with their toes," Max Tyler said with a grin on his face.

Chapter Twenty-Eight

"How was your leave?" Max said to Chloe Schaeffer as they drove slowly along Greaves Street, Fitzroy, looking for the Russian Ethnic Representation Committee premises.

"Yeah, great. Two weeks in Bali. Sun, sand and sea. You should have come, too," the young Constable said.

"Would have loved to, but with the upgrading to Sergeant with this Bobrov business I couldn't."

"Everyone knows we are going out together so I hope we can arrange our next lot of leave and both get away," Chloe said softly before pointing across at the address they were looking for.

Max slowed the car outside what looked like a small factory with a concrete front yard and three-metre-high cyclone wire front fence. Behind the fence and in plain view was the black Nissan van that featured the day before in the snatching of Marco Toscano's body.

To not alienate any occupants of the premises, both members were in plain clothes and parked the unmarked police vehicle on the opposite side of the street and a few doors down.

Max Tyler pressed the intercom by the front door and after introducing themselves as police officers, the main door opened, and they were met by an elderly bearded male.

"What can I do for you, officers?" the obviously wary person said.

"Sir, we are making inquiries in relation to an incident in Carlton where the van parked in your yard was involved," Tyler said indicating the black Nissan. "Can you tell me who had the van on Saturday night?"

After what seemed like an eternity, the man answered very quietly. "Is there somewhere we can talk besides here?"

Chloe smiled and spoke quietly. "We have a plain car down the road a little if you'd like to talk there?" The man nodded slowly and replied.

"Please wait for me outside. I'll see you there in a minute," he said as he quickly shut the door.

The two members walked across the road to their car. Max got inside while Chloe waited until she saw the man step out onto the footpath and waved him to the car. He looked around nervously while he walked to her and very quickly climbed into the rear seat. Max Tyler spoke to him.

"You seem worried about us being here. Is there a problem?"

The old man replied slowly.

"You must understand. The Russian Ethnic Committee House is just a meeting place for members of our community. Nothing more. We are all immigrants to Australia, and we do not want any trouble."

"There's no trouble," Max replied. We just want to know who had the van on Saturday night."

"The van is only used very occasionally by any member of the community. We never wanted it. It was a gift from the Russian Embassy and is taken from time to time by people we do not want to be associated with. To you it would be the Russian mafia but to us it is known as the Bratva. The van must be available to them at all times on short notice and is registered to the Committee here at this address, I think to cover their own business dealings. Sunday afternoon there were about fifteen of us playing cards. It was late and we always play through the night. No real money but it is a tradition we carry on with from the old country. I had noticed that the van was gone but two men brought it back while we were here. I know it had been here on Saturday afternoon because I came in to do some cleaning."

"So, you can positively say that you saw it here on Saturday afternoon and then saw two men bring it back in on Sunday afternoon?" Chloe said.

"Yes. After they left, I went and had a look at it because it looked as though it had been cleaned, and I was right. Surprisingly though, the boot area and the inside had been thoroughly cleaned as well. The keys were still in the ignition. They are still there. No one has touched it. They left with another man who was parked outside in a big black Mercedes. They are bad men. That is why I talk to you here and not at the house. We are old Russians who just want peace. We don't want to know about young Russians in dark suits. We have come here for a new life of peace."

"If I show you some pictures, would you be able to recognise them?" Chloe said reaching for the photos from the stakeout.

"Yes, but no trouble. No courts., No more police questions. You two are nice, but show pictures and then I go."

Chloe handed the man three pictures. Two of the van men and one of Pavel Antonov.

On taking the photos, the old man's hands began to shake, and tears formed in his eyes. Chloe held his arm gently.

"These two," he said indicating the van men who had been photographed outside the Carlton address. "They brought the van back. They have taken the van on several occasions. They work at the Russian Consulate."

"That's something the boss will want to know," Chloe said.

"And the other man?" Tyler said indicating Antonov.

"He was the one in the Mercedes," the man said as he quickly handed back the photos. "What are they carrying in the photo?" he asked.

Max looked kindly at the old man. "You really don't want to know the answer to that. Thank you so much for your help and I can tell you something that I think will make you happy."

"What is that?" the old man said.

"We were never here, and you won't see us again. Go back and enjoy your card games."

The old man smiled weakly, climbed out of the back seat and shuffled quickly away.

Chapter Twenty-Nine

A very scared and worried looking Ricky Bobrov fronted up for work on Tuesday morning. He didn't know that the DRU had been keeping his flat under observation since early on Sunday. The reason he didn't know, was because since getting back home early on Sunday morning, he hadn't ventured outside. He had closed the blinds and become a virtual recluse.

All through Sunday and Monday there had been no contact between himself and Pavel Antonov. What kept going through his mind was that he was covering up a murder, and for every minute that went by he was not only getting himself deeper and deeper into trouble, but he was becoming more and more under the invisible control of the big Russian. Unbeknown to himself though was that his world as he knew it was about to come crashing down around him.

"Good morning, Sergeant," Tony Signorotto said, striding into the Sergeant's office, which at the early hour of eight a.m. was empty save for Bobrov. The nervous Sergeant looked up from his desk like a startled rabbit caught in the headlights of an approaching vehicle. His mouth opened and closed a few times.

"Morning boss," was the sum of his reply.

Signorotto gave him a long hard stare which Bobrov seemed to wilt under very quickly.

"Right. Need you to help me bring a few files back from the old cop shop in Drummond Street. All the troops on today are tied up with their own paperwork so you're it I'm afraid," Signorotto said as he noticed a distinct sheen of sweat on his nervous Sergeant's face.

"When?" came the monosyllabic reply.

"Right now, Sergeant. See you downstairs in five minutes," Signorotto stated emphatically as he turned and walked out the door.

Bobrov never thought to ask why there would still be files at the old station when even he knew that the old police station in Drummond Street had been closed for over a year. His brain was only concerned with his immediate future.

On the short drive to Drummond Street, neither Signorotto nor Bobrov spoke a word. The Senior Sergeant pulled into the driveway of the old red brick building, got out, unlocked a side door and indicated to Bobrov to go in before him. It took all of Tony Signorotto's self-control to restrain himself from slamming the disgrace of a Sergeant up against the dusty paint peeled walls. Walls that were very used to that happening in times gone by.

"Where are these files?" Bobrov said as he looked around at the barren interior of the old police station.

"In here," Signorotto signalled, indicating the room to his left. Tony didn't walk directly behind Bobrov, knowing that if he did, he would walk directly into the now statue like figure that was in the doorway staring at two males at the other side of a table, which combined with four chairs, was the only furniture in the windowless room. Both males were in suits.

Tony Signorotto closed the door behind Bobrov with a resounding slam.

A now hyped-up Ricky Bobrov turned around to see that his way out was barred by the imposing cross-armed figure of Signorotto. He spun around to face the other two.

"Who the fuck are you?" he stammered.

"I am Commander Stone from Regional Command, and this is Detective Inspector Conlon from Ethical Standards. You already know Senior Sergeant Signorotto. Together, we are the people who are going to decide your future, but first we must make up our minds, depending on you, as to whether you will even have a future. Now sit down, shut up and listen."

Bobrov's mind was now exploding in directions that were all bad, but he did what he was told, which spoke reams in relation to his burden of guilt.

Stone placed both hands on the table, leant forward and spoke in a menacing voice to Bobrov.

"I'm not going to fuck around, Ricky. We know all about Saturday night at the house in Faraday Street. Everything down to and including the disappearance of Marco Toscano."

Bobrov attempted to interrupt Stone. "I've got no idea what…"

Stone spoke over the top of him. "The DRU were watching, photographing and filming everything right through the night. I won't bore you with the facts, Ricky, but suffice to say you are facing accessory charges to Toscano's death."

Bobrov's head snapped upwards. "I didn't murder him," he blurted.

"Jumping a bit, aren't you? I didn't mention the word murder. Are you saying someone murdered him?"

Bobrov looked at the two officers but couldn't control the tremor that was running through his body and down his arms. It was obvious to everyone in the room.

Conlon stepped forward suddenly, throwing a picture onto the table in front of Bobrov.

"Who's that lying on the morgue trolley?" he said with a raised voice acting out the bad cop routine to perfection. Bobrov stared at the corpse of Marco Toscano.

"Now, we'll give you about ten seconds to realise you are completely fucked and another ten until we start asking questions. Do you understand me, Sergeant Bobrov? I use that rank only in the present situation because once we are finished here, you'll be wishing you'd never joined the Force," Conlon said angrily.

Ricky Bobrov knew he had only one choice. It was obvious that these three knew everything. It was now just a matter of trying to get some damage control going forward. His career was over. Now it was survival. He looked up slowly at the three men before him.

"I just wanted to make some quick money. I'm hooked on the horses. I had nothing to do with this," he said pointing at the photo of Marco Toscano.

Tony Signorotto stepped forward like an ogre into Bobrov's eye space.

"Tell us what we want to know. Answers to every question. No lies, no dodging. Then we will decide your fate, Bobrov. Everything about your association with Pavel Antonov also."

Up to that point, Ricky Bobrov had been hoping he could palm the whole thing off to Antonov but the mention of his name by Signorotto meant they knew much more than they had said so far. He was trapped. It was time to save his own skin.

Two nerve wracking hours later, Ricky Bobrov had no more to tell. He was a broken, sobbing wreck.

Chapter Thirty

"Let's go over it again," a tired Phil Stone said in a weary and patronising voice to an equally exhausted Ricky Bobrov.

Bobrov had been questioned for over two hours by Stone, Conlon and Signorotto. They had all peppered him with questions one after the other about not only the gambling night but even more so about his involvement with Pavel Antonov. Everything had been recorded which Stone had emphasised at the very start. There would be no backtracking for Bobrov.

Signorotto had returned to the old police station with enough sandwiches and coffee from the local delicatessen to last them well into the night. He placed everything down onto the old Formica table, so Bobrov was fully aware that they weren't anywhere near finished with him. Stone kept the dialogue going.

"You say you didn't see Antonov strike Toscano but that Antonov was still standing over him with the broken terracotta pot in his hand and blood coming from Toscano's head. Is that correct?"

"Yeah."

"You are an experienced police officer. What on earth do you think happened to Toscano? He fell and hit his head on a pot? The truth Bobrov, and the absolute truth. If you want any shred of help from us at all!" a furious sounding Conlon said.

"Okay, okay, I know he hit him. Marco had been going on at Antonov about the begging scheme the Russians had going on in the city and he wanted in on the action. It was and still is bringing in a lot of money. Probably not huge by Russian mafia standards but certainly by Marco's standards. Antonov warned him to stop talking about it because it was run by the Russian mafia, the *Bratva* he called it. Marco was really getting under his skin. He was like a dog with a bone: just wouldn't let it be."

"So, what happened after Toscano was struck?" Conlon continued.

"That politician that was there. He obviously heard the argument between Marco and Antonov. He wanted out of the game real quick when he saw that Marco didn't come back inside."

"What did he say that gave you that impression?"

"That three of us were outside during a break in the game and that he heard an argument and only me and Antonov returned. He just up and left."

"What then?"

"Antonov was really laid back about Marco being dead. I didn't know what to do so I basically put a stop to the game early. The punters didn't mind. The politician had left and they packed up soon afterwards. They'd had their fun. Some won, some lost but the bank had won overall and that was all that mattered. Antonov wanted to make some phone calls and he was running the actual game, so it came to a stop anyhow."

Conlon looked at Stone and Signorotto. They all knew the key question was about to be asked. Conlon leant over the desk right at Bobrov.

"Okay Ricky. Think about your answer to the next question and don't stuff us around on this. Your whole future for what it's worth depends on your answer."

Ricky Bobrov knew what was coming. He nodded his head and waited.

"What was your reason for stopping the game early?"

Bobrov looked across the table at the three staring faces. He answered slowly and deliberately. He could only try and regain remnants of his future at this point.

"Because I knew Antonov had killed Marco and was phoning some of his associates to come and get rid of the body."

"Are you guessing this or did Antonov tell you?"

"He told me that I had nothing to worry about and that he would get some associates to get to the address and remove the body. He said Toscano was no loss and that I needn't worry about anything because the 'cleaners', as he called them were coming."

"Who were the 'cleaners' do you think?" Conlon said with a raised eyebrow.

"People who would get rid of Marco's body. As I left, I saw a black van coming into the alley. I just kept going. I wish I had never got involved with Antonov. I didn't know he was Russian mafia.

"So, what you're saying to us is that you believe Pavel Antonov struck Marco Toscano with a terracotta pot, killing him. Then he arranged for the body to disappear?"

Bobrov looked at the floor and answered with one word.

"Yes."

Phil Stone leant over in front of Ricky Bobrov and spoke directly at him.

"Sergeant Bobrov. You know you are now implicated in a murder which we will have to investigate by interviewing other witnesses. If you want to save any part of your miserable hide, you will go along with what we have planned."

Bobrov's head suddenly snapped upwards and swung from side to side looking at the three police officers.

"What plan? What are you trying to get me into?" a suddenly panicked Bobrov blurted.

"We are going to need more than the word of a self-confessed crooked copper to nail Antonov. That member of Parliament will have to be interviewed, but more importantly you are going to go back into the lion's den and front up to your new best friend, Pavel Antonov. You are going to tell him that you want to earn some real money by setting up more card games. You are going to remind him quietly about going along with Marco's death. He won't touch you because you are still police. The last thing he wants is to attract attention to his Russian mafia mates."

"How is this going to help you nab him for murder?" a confused Bobrov said quietly.

"Because from now on, Ricky, you are going to be miked up and wired for sound twenty-four hours a day. We now own you, Sergeant Bobrov.

Chapter Thirty-One

It had been many a long year since Phil Stone had stood on the steps of Parliament House in Spring Street. In fact, the last time he had been on the steps, he had been sat firmly on his arse by a big trade unionist who was taking part in a mass rally in support of the building trade. The unionist had taken umbrage at the fact that some young Constable had dared block his way up the same steps that Stone now stood on. After all, it was the people's Parliament and said unionist wanted to not only go up the steps, but right through the front door. Stone was unfortunately standing in his way. Subsequently, the big man had been led away by two other officers towards the nearby Police brawler van for incarceration. The unionist hadn't liked the idea of being placed in the back of the van and with a shrug of both shoulders had released himself from their grip and was last seen bolting through Treasury Gardens towards the Melbourne Cricket Ground, never to be seen again.

Stone strode up the first five steps onto the driveway section and looked at the old circular brass markers that were inlaid in the bitumen to signify the stopping place for all vehicles carrying either politicians or VIP's that had been invited up to the historic building which had been opened in the 1850's to serve the people of Victoria. Alas, in later years to the present day, there was no looking west along Bourke Street for any guest alighting on the driveway because both ends of the roadway had been blocked with bollards. The days of both international terrorism and urban terrorism had arrived in Melbourne. The VIPs had to be satisfied with being unloaded in the rear car park. The Government had even installed 10-millimetre-thick bullet proof glass in the lower windows facing the steps after one fateful day in the early nineties when a student protest had been grossly misread by the Police

Department hierarchy and the front doors of the famous building had nearly been breached by a crowd demanding free education for university students. From then on, upon advice from police specialists in demonstrations, the Government had quickly upgraded security measures. Stone quietly lamented the changes in social attitudes both to people and property.

The meeting with the Minister for Licensing and Gaming, the Right Honourable Steve Bird had been arranged by Phil Stone under the guise of discussing several new amendments to the Liquor Control Act which were about to be introduced into Parliament in the next few weeks. As the new Commander in charge of the CBD, Stone thought it would be appropriate to meet the Minister in person—but not necessarily for the reason he had originally suggested to Bird's secretary. The other thing that Bird didn't know was that Stone was bringing his 'attack dog' with him—Detective Inspector Ted Conlon.

Stone and Conlon waited in the vestibule just inside the main entrance after being put through a thorough scanning process. They both had their fully charged mobile phones in their pockets, ready for the moment the Minister would agree to their request. Yes, it was a form of blackmail, but they would make the Minister realise that he could do a great service for law and order in the community—and himself if he went along with their plans.

After the usual fifteen minutes of waiting just to make sure of where they stood as police officers in the great 'pecking order' line, the Minister for Licensing and Gaming, Steve Bird stepped quickly into the waiting area of the beautiful old building and walked quickly towards them.

Steve Bird knew all about Phil Stone's promotion and had studied his file before greeting the newly promoted Commander.

"Phil, congratulations on the new rank. Well deserved," Bird said as a matter of course as he put his right hand out to shake hands with Stone. The handshake was given in the normal politician style that meant he was 'on top' of any situation he came across. His hand outstretched palm down on top of Stone's, which therefore was palm up. Phil Stone knew all about power handshakes as he had worked his way up through the ranks and corridors of power at Police Headquarters. It was always a source of amusement to him because power was always defeated by people who had all the facts in front of them and Steve Bird didn't.

He and Conlon had videos and black and white photos of the Minister at the House of Cards in Faraday Street.

As Stone greeted the Minister, he felt Bird's left hand on his right shoulder with a slight directional push to start him walking away with him. Phil Stone stopped dead in his tracks.

Now I seize the day, Minister.

"Oh, sorry, Minister. I forgot to introduce you to my associate. Steve Bird, this is Detective Inspector Ted Conlon."

The handshake forthcoming from Bird was more of a dead fish one as he looked back and forth between the two officers.

"Sorry, Phil. Have I misread something? I thought this was going to be more of a chat between us to discuss some clarifications to liquor licensing laws."

"Yes, it should have been Minister, but I took the liberty to bring Ted along as he is our expert on the investigation of corrupt police officers."

"I don't understand," Bird replied with a quizzical look on his face. "What has that got to do with licensing matters?"

Conlon removed a foolscap size black and white photograph from his leather, police engraved folder and held it up in front of the Minister's face. It showed a clear picture of Sergeant Ricky Bobrov talking to the Right Honourable Minister for Licensing and Gaming, Mr. Steve Bird in the side alley off Faraday Street as he left the illegal card night. It came fully 'loaded' with its own date and time stamp in the bottom right-hand corner. Stone continued.

"The one on the left is a very corrupt Police Sergeant by the name of Ricky Bobrov and the other figure I believe is you, Minister."

Bird's face started to sweat profusely and turn very white. He stammered as he spoke.

"I didn't know he was police," Conlon jumped straight onto the comment.

"So, you admit being at an illegal card night?"

"I just happened to be outside talking to him. I said nothing about being inside anywhere with him," Bird retorted quickly. Conlon pulled out a swathe of black and white photos before he said. "We have videos as well, Sir." Bird looked around the vestibule furtively.

"Just a boy's night out. No harm really. Not something that has to go further than here, really. Everyone had a good night."

Stone placed his hand on Bird's shoulder this time and started to direct him back from the way he had come.

"Well Steve, I think we need to have a little chat about that," Stone said as he lowered his head and spoke quietly into Bird's left ear.

"We have one person in the morgue who, if he could talk, might disagree with you on that subject."

Chapter Thirty-Two

Steve Bird walked into his Parliamentary Office in front of the two police officers. With a perfunctory wave of his hand, he dismissed his secretary.

"Take a long coffee break, please. I will text you when I've finished. Close the door."

The look from his secretary at the stern duo standing next to her boss helped her exit the room post haste. Bird indicated for them to sit.

"You had better remember that I am a Member of Parliament before you go making any sort of accusations."

Conlon fired a salvo back. "You are the one that needs to remember that fact, sir."

A still sweating Steve Bird stared silently at the pair in front of him before speaking.

"Go on. What is it you have to say?"

Phil Stone crossed one leg over the other and spoke.

"Mr. Bird. Let's cut to the chase. It concerns something very serious, and I don't think it comes more serious than murder. We know that you had nothing to do with it, but we need your assistance and cooperation."

"Murder?" Bird spluttered. "What are you talking about? Assistance and cooperation with what? A card game which I admit I was at. There were other people there, also. People of standing in the community I'll have you know. I admit I was there, but I won't be telling the names of others."

Conlon took over very quickly. "Sir, we know the who's who from famous cricketers to well-known television, media personalities and the medical world. We don't want to go to them and tell them it was you that ratted them out. That would put you in a very bad place in many circles, don't you think?

We want your singular assistance regarding one person who was at the card night. We can do this the nice and tidy way or the very messy public way. You either talk to us and we work together, or we walk you out of here in handcuffs for being a possible accessory to murder. Mark my words Mr. Bird, I don't give a damn about who or what you are. If we must march you out of here, it won't be via the rear carpark where only the gardeners will see you. I will make sure you are dragged kicking and screaming through the vestibule and onto the front steps of Parliament House in full view of the public and MPs from both sides. Oh, and I can guarantee you that the press will be there from every television channel, radio station and print media. So, let's cut the crap about being a protected species because you're a politician and hear us out. Which is it to be?"

Phil Stone had been standing back letting Conlon take charge and was secretly in awe of the way he blew Bird and his inflated ego out the window. No bullshit, no prisoners.

Silence engulfed the office before both police officers noticed that Bird was blinking rapidly and his eyes were filled with tears.

Stone spoke quietly, coming in as the good cop. They had planned this over many meetings back at Carlton in the previous days.

"Steve. We don't want you or the others in that game. We, like you, want that to go away. What we want from you is a statement about what happened in the backyard between the Russian, Antonov and one of his partners. You know something happened because you insisted on leaving early. We have already interviewed one of the three running the game. He is a corrupt police officer, which you probably didn't know. He has told us everything about the night and that you probably knew or guessed what happened in the yard. You then became scared and wanted to leave. We just want evidence on the Russian who invited you to the game. Help us and we'll help you."

Chapter Thirty-Two

Bird sat behind his desk wringing his hands and blinking rapidly.

"I knew this would come back to bite me," he stammered.

"Doesn't have to be too hard a bite Steve. First off, who invited you to the night?"

"It was the Russian."

"What is his name and how long have you known him?" Conlon said, taking over as he and Stone laid their phone on Bird's desk with the recording devices on.

Bird looked at the two phones as if they were ticking time bombs, which in fact they probably were. He did not object to them though.

His name is Pavel Antonov. A Russian I was introduced to at a card night in the northern suburbs some time ago.

Conlon continued. "Do you have his name and phone number stored in your phone?"

"Yes, why."

"Obviously then he has been in contact with you or vice versa. We want Antonov, not just for this murder but for other things which we think will lead back to the Russian Consulate here in Melbourne."

Bird's eyes grew even wider with the Consulate connection.

"Okay. I'm one of his VIP contacts if there is a big game going on. He contacted me about this one. You've got to understand the stress of my job. Cards are my relief valve. My wife knows, so what's the big deal?"

"Your wife might know, but I bet the public of Victoria don't know that the games you are attending are illegal ones with a banker skimming the pool," Conlon spat.

"We all play the percentages in life, Inspector. What's the difference between that game and the TAB?"

"Easily answered. One is in line with the laws of this state and the other, the one you attended, is not. You are breaking the law attending them and you know it. Everything's fun until something goes wrong and that something went wrong the other night and the reason you didn't report anything was that you knew you'd be caught up in a scandal."

"Okay, Steve," Stone said quietly. "What happened for you to leave this card game so quickly. They are usually an all night stand. You left very early. Bear in mind we had plain clothes police filming and photographing the night from the moment you arrived till your early exit. Without any lies, we want your version."

"It was just another card night with good, like-minded people. We all know that we get scammed through the night here and there. It's not so much about the money, God knows we can all afford it. We play because we all just want to be out of the limelight and playing the darker side for a while. Walter Mitty stuff, you know. We go for the buzz to get away from people's expectations. If we all went to a casino or such, we'd have cameras and paparazzi in our faces all night."

"What happened to wreck your night, Steve?" an impatient Ted Conlon replied.

Bird took a big breath before he spoke.

"Hours in we took a break in the yard. Antonov was down the back behind a brush fence and was yelling at someone. I presumed it was one of his people because all the players were accounted for. That other organiser, who I swear I didn't know was a cop, was down the back also. I walked down the yard having a whisky and suddenly there was a loud smashing sound and the arguing stopped. All I heard was something about a scamming thing involving Asians. The other players were up under the back patio so didn't hear anything. I just froze because I didn't know what had happened. All the other games had been great nights but suddenly this one became scary. I didn't move until that guy you said is a cop came back up suddenly and said we were starting again. We all went back inside but Pavel didn't appear for quite a while. The third guy, Mario or Marco or whoever never surfaced again. It didn't take

Einstein to figure what happened. I swear though, I didn't have anything to do with it."

Conlon placed a picture of Marco Toscano under Bird's nose. "That the one you call Mario or Marco?"

"Yeah, that's him. What happened to him? I mean I presume Pavel did something."

Conlon looked directly at Bird as he spoke.

"He was, and I repeat was, a two-bit organiser from the western suburbs by the name of Marco Toscano. He is now lying in the morgue, and we have our corrupt cop as a witness to the fact that Pavel Antonov struck Toscano with a terracotta pot which subsequently killed him. Later that morning just after you left, two of Antonov's associates who we think work out of the Russian Consulate came and took Toscano away in a body bag."

"I didn't see anything though," a relieved Bird said very quickly.

"No, but you knew there had been a serious assault and you did nothing about it. You just wanted to get yourself out of there because you knew you shouldn't have been there in the first place. You're a witness to the argument between them and the sudden cessation of same. Tell the truth, Steve. What do you think happened?"

"All I'll say is this. Pavel obviously stopped him from talking-permanently, from what you have told me. I couldn't do anything about the argument. What happens now?"

"Well Steve," Stone said quickly. "You've admitted being at an illegal card game as well as admitting that you witnessed a serious crime which you didn't report. That assault resulting in the death of Marco Toscano. Your reputation as Gaming Minister is shot completely, but as we said, we want Antonov not only for the murder, but stuff Russian Consulate staff know about regarding running a huge scamming syndicate involving illegal Asian immigrants. We are not saying the Consul General knows, but when you tell him about Antonov, we know he and his mates will be cut adrift. Then we will step in and blow the whole operation apart leaving the Consul General out of it.

"You think that I'll tell the Consul General? Are you serious?" a now frightened Steve Bird said. Conlon took over.

"You are going to meet with the Russian Consul General and inform him of what Antonov has been up to regarding the illegal card games and give him information on the street scamming which we will brief you on. We will give you the photos of two of his staff members, which are the same two that picked up Toscano's body. That will allow him to distance himself from them. All links to the Consulate will cease between them. The two body snatchers will be in their own diplomatic pouch on the way back to fight in some war for their mother Russia and Antonov will be left to us."

"What do I get out of this?" a nervous Bird said.

"You will be left alone to sit the next State election and then if you win, you will resign a few months later citing health reasons and you can slide into oblivion. You will be doing this as an upstanding Member of Parliament because you have it on very good authority about the scamming. If you are questioned at all you don't have to say anything if you say it from inside Parliament. Right now, you are going to be our fizz. No arguments."

"So, all I have to do is give Antonov and his mates up to the Russian Consul General?"

"Yes, but also give us a detailed statement about the night which we will keep locked away. We have our crooked police officer, who has sung like a bird."

"Fuck, you don't want much, do you?" a sweating Steve Bird said loudly.

Stone replied quietly. "What I really want is justice for Marco Toscano and all those poor immigrants who are probably being kept under lock and key somewhere and only being let out to work for the likes of that prick Antonov."

Chapter Thirty-Three

The days since his grilling from Stone, Conlon and Signorotto had been a living nightmare for Ricky Bobrov.

He had fronted up for work every day and had been assigned meaningless filing jobs by Signorotto, and to add insult to injury, he had been overseen at every turn by Max Tyler. Even the most junior clerk in the station must have realised there was something amiss. He had been put on a continuing day shift roster and the only difference between the scrutiny that felt like prison was the realisation that unless he cooperated, there was a far worse prison awaiting him. He was wondering when Signorotto would drop the axe on him when Max Tyler walked into the dingy little filing room in the basement.

"Boss wants you upstairs now," Tyler said.

"Fuck you, Tyler," Bobrov snapped as he stood up suddenly. "You just came here to Carlton to spy on me, didn't you? You weren't upgraded for any other reason than to get beside me. You're just an Ethical Standards stooge, you prick."

Tyler stood his ground as Bobrov closed the short distance between them until their faces were only inches apart. He was about to tell Bobrov exactly what he thought of him when Chloe Schaeffer suddenly pushed him back and stepped between the two, facing Bobrov.

"I'm calling you out Sergeant Bobrov because at the moment I have to, but don't think I wouldn't kneecap you with a Smith and Wesson from the safe in a heartbeat if I had half a chance, you lowlife. The powers to be must have big plans for you if they are allowing you to keep that uniform on. This is all a pretence now, and you don't have any choice but to go along with whatever the boss's plans are for you, so I'd suggest you get upstairs real quick."

Ricky Bobrov stood motionless during the ferocious verbal attack and didn't put up a defence.

Max Tyler knew that if it wasn't for Chloe's appearance in the office, he would have been trading blows with Bobrov. Taking a big breath, he stepped aside as Bobrov barged past him towards the door as he headed downstairs to Signorotto's office.

"Thanks, Chloe," a relieved Tyler said. "If it wasn't for you stepping in, I was going to belt him. I just hope the bosses are doing the right thing with this prick."

Bobrov was still fuming as he entered Signorotto's office to not only find the Senior Sergeant there but also Phil Stone and Ted Conlon.

"Close the door and sit down," a gruff sounding Signorotto said.

Bobrov knew he couldn't go up against these three. They had him by the balls. All he could possibly hope for was to resign from the Force and save his superannuation.

The three senior police had decided that as Signorotto had been controlling Bobrov since his arrival at Carlton right through to his confession about the gambling house, that he might as well continue with the disgraced member. Stone and Conlon would run with Steve Bird while Signorotto together with Max Tyler would pull the strings of their new puppet— Ricky Bobrov. Signorotto started the proceedings.

"Bobrov, we haven't at this stage arrested or questioned Pavel Antonov. We all know that he is responsible for the murder of Marco Toscano. That's a given. You are being monitored twenty-four seven by the Divisional Response Unit and we have taken telecommunications warrants out to tap your mobile phones. In other words, we are all over both of you like a cheap suit. Only difference is that he doesn't know it.

We want you to understand this because now we are going into another phase of this operation. With us so far?"

"We haven't contacted each other for over a week now. I'm not stupid but I know he will contact me just to find out if there's been anything pop up about Toscano, even though he wouldn't give a rat's arse about him. He will just want to make sure he can keep circulating and making money."

"Okay, then it's about time you took the initiative, Ricky," Signorotto said. "You're going to contact him with some news."

"Why would I want to contact him? I'm cooked any way I turn in the oven. He won't want to be hitting up any of those punters again, not for a while anyway. He has his city stuff to keep him busy. That begging scam I told you all about."

"We've thought long and hard about that, Ricky," a serious sounding Ted Conlon said. We may want you to set up another card night, but at this stage we want you to make contact to give him the news that because you've seen how much one card game netted you, that you've decided to chuck your day job as a copper and team up with him as his right-hand man."

"Why on earth would he want me? He has his close Russian contacts who help him out with anything he wants. You saw those two goons who snatched Toscano. He won't need my help," Bobrov said incredulously.

Phil Stone leant forward to Bobrov and spoke directly into his face.

"He will when he realises that those two goons are no longer contactable."

Bobrov looked from one member to the next before he spoke.

"What do you mean? What's happened?"

"Let's just say they will soon be returning to their homeland upon recommendation from the Russian Consulate. Antonov won't have the muscle to help him with his city scam anymore and you telling him that you have resigned from the Force may be perfect timing. You want to hang with him on a permanent basis and help him with the logistics side of things. After all, Ricky, you did do a good organising that Carlton night, but I think you may have had plenty of practice at it over the years. He wouldn't have gone along with your last plan unless he thought you were up to it. This way, he can cut his losses if he has been giving his share to the Consulate boys and take you on. Timing is everything. You just leave the Russian Consul General to us," Stone said.

Ricky Bobrov's mind was racing back and forward, switching between thoughts of what he could salvage from this train wreck and what could happen to him if Antonov found out he was being asked to be some sort of double agent. Tony Signorotto de-railed his train of thought after about ten seconds.

"Bobrov, our way will let you resign officially when this is over, and your superannuation will be safe. Basically, the Force just wants you gone, but we want our pound of flesh first. The other way, the Police Association will give you no legal help if you decide to fight the gambling and misconduct charges that we can slap on you and when, not if, you lose in court, the Department will apply to the Government to have the State's contribution to your superannuation fund re-directed back into Government coffers. You end up with a record as well as a legal bill and only half your superannuation. On top of all that, your reputation will be shot when you go for another job. I will make sure of that, mark my words."

Bobrov stared at Signorotto with a look of venom. Signorotto stared back with a look of 'fuck you.'

"Let's cut to the chase. You're saying go with you lot or I'm possibly screwed?"

"No possible to it. You will be screwed. Both by the court and the Department. I really don't know what I want more, you being done over or catching Antonov for more crimes than murder," Signorotto said through gritted teeth moments before Phil Stone stepped in.

Chapter Thirty-Three

"What's it to be, Ricky? To me it's a complete no-brainer."

"Alright, I'll go along with you, but convincing Antonov he needs a new business partner won't be easy."

"Life wasn't meant to be easy, sunshine," Signorotto replied. "We will have control of you all day and night. Max Tyler will be your handler and will be reporting back to us. You are our main witness to Antonov killing Toscano and we have your signed statement to that effect. Yes, we can charge him with that today or in six months. The body's in the morgue with the autopsy report sitting on the Coroner's desk. It can all rise like Lazarus from the dead at any time, but we want to wipe out this begging scam of his. Just buddy up to him and see what he comes up with. He'll soon realise his associates at the Consulate have frozen over like their snow-covered motherland. He may just want another high roller game because of the profit he made from the last one, which reminds me Ricky, Max Tyler will be collecting all your profits from that last game. It will be going through our property book and when this is over, I will show you the receipt of it being turned over to the government. It is known as proceeds of crime."

"Let's face it, Ricky," Ted Conlon chipped in. "If he is interested, there are plenty more games that you could organise and as an informant you will be exempt from any prosecution that we may throw at him. If needs be, we can organise another card house which you can let him know you arranged. Just keep him going and keep us informed about his other business. We want to know how this illegal line of immigrants is being arranged. We reckon the Russians are involved but how high up the chain we don't know."

"Alright. How are we doing this?" a beaten Ricky Bobrov said with bowed head.

"First thing tomorrow Max and I will sit down with you and go through the hoops. By the time we finish, you will be, for want of a better phrase, an ex-member of the Victoria Police Force," Tony Signorotto said with a smile on his face.

Chapter Thirty-Four

A very tired looking Johnny Petran from the Divisional Response Unit walked into the mess room of the Carlton Police Station. Seated at the table were Tony Signorotto and Kate McLaren. Before Petran could say a word, Signorotto called out to him.

"Look what the cat dragged in, Kate. Looks like one of the DRU's own down and out clients has wandered in."

The big undercover police officer sat down quickly at the table.

"Bloody look and feel like one, Tony. We're all burning the midnight oil on this job at the office at the moment. That's what I've come to see you about."

Signorotto pointed at his own cup of coffee.

"Looks like you could do with a brew. Want one?" he said, starting to stand.

"Thanks," Petran said as Kate McLaren pushed Signorotto down by the shoulder back into his chair. "I'll get it. Looks like he needs a chat with you. How do you take it?"

"Black, one sugar, thanks Kate," Petran replied as she grabbed the big jar of Nescafe from above the fridge.

"What's up mate? Seriously, you look about stuffed," Signorotto said with a look of concern on his face.

"Tony, we can't keep tags on Bobrov all the time without some more help. My boys have been pulling twelve-hour shifts and although the overtime is great, I have a duty of care to them, so I'm going to have to give them a break real soon. I don't want to keep going and miss something with him like a hook up with Antonov, which is the main reason for this whole exercise. Mick York, myself and two others have been at this solidly for a fair few days now. What I need are some more bodies."

"Johnny, Phil Stone is calling a meeting of this Task Force very soon because we have had our little sit down with Bobrov yesterday. He's been told he is being watched twenty-four seven and he has been given the ultimatum of either co-operating with us or taking his chances. Hopefully it won't be much longer before he teams up with Antonov and we see some real progress. If you like you can cut out sitting off him outside the station here during work hours. He won't be slipping off anywhere. Just keep up his house and any shopping trips. He's agreed to our plans to get Antonov, but I'm a bit old school mate. Still wouldn't trust him as far as I could kick him."

"That's good Tony, but I still have to knock off at least one crew for some rest days." Petran replied.

Kate McLaren sat down opposite the two men and pushed a cup of coffee towards Petran.

"I can see where you're coming from," Signorotto continued. "Max Tyler and I are responsible for all to do with Bobrov, so I'll guess I'll have to look at our roster. I'd rather keep everything in house, but I can't spare Kate or any of the other sergeants. They've got too much on their plates here, especially since we have a new batch of trainees that have just arrived. How many members do you need?"

"Ideally four, but I know you couldn't do that. Can you give me two who know the area just in case Bobrov has to meet up with Antonov quickly? I can't trust this to newbies who may end up running around like headless chooks."

"Got any ideas, Kate? You know the roster better than I do," Signorotto said to his sergeant as she reached for a copy of the station roster that was hanging on the wall behind her.

"We've got a new arrival from Melbourne North Highway Patrol. Wanted a six-month change from traffic work. I've given Eddie Downes at the Highway Patrol one of our young

Constables who is traffic mad. He gave us a Leading Senior Constable Paul Romano," she said pointing to the name on the roster.

"That's one. What about the other two?" A smiling Johnny Petran said, tongue in cheek.

"Don't push your luck pal. One more is all you get. I seriously can't spare any others. We have a big operation coming up, the annual Lygon Street Festival."

"Okay," one more and I'll team them together and I'll even write up some good reports on them for their profiles."

Kate McLaren chipped in. "Chloe Schaeffer has done some good work recently and is looking for plain clothes experience, no doubt because she wants to get into town to be closer to Max. I can spare her. She did great work on that pistol hijack case a while back."

"Yeah, okay. I want them both briefed here first though. No going in cold when there's somebody like Antonov involved. I know it's only a sit off job for a while. Shouldn't be anything too dangerous in that," Signorotto said.

Crooked coppers and Russians…mmm, don't know about that, Kate thought as she felt a finger of fear walk its way up her spine.

Chapter Thirty-Five

It had been a few days since the visit of Phil Stone and Ted Conlon to Steve Bird's Parliamentary office. Time though had not diminished any of the anxiety or fear of what he had to do next.

He sat at his large desk clutching several black and white photos of that night in Faraday Street. The images of himself in the laneway talking to a person he now knew as Sergeant Ricky Bobrov, combined with photos of what appeared to be a body bag being loaded into a van by two burly looking thugs was doing nothing to calm his nerves. He quickly put the photos away upon hearing a knock at his office door.

"Come in, Mandy," he said, knowing the type of knock that he and his secretary had devised between themselves to give him notice that his polite conversation time with one of his constituents was up. It was normally a ten-minute gig only but there was the occasional time that he had to press the button under his desk to get her to rescue him in a hurry. Mandy entered immediately.

"Mr. Bird, you have a meeting with the Russian Consul General in half an hour. Shall I call your driver around?" she said quietly.

"Yes, I'd better not keep him waiting," he replied nervously.

"Sir, under Parliamentary guidelines recently introduced by the Premier I am obliged to enter the details of any visit a delegation makes to a foreign consulate. Basically, I must record why you are going to see the Russians," Mandy said without batting an eyelid.

Bird also spoke in a quiet tone as he looked at her.

"Besides you and me, who looks through my electronic diary, Mandy?"

Bird's secretary had been in her position for over three years and would openly admit that beside the very generous salary package she received, there were also fringe benefits that she didn't want to give up. She handled all his day-to-day affairs including his private finances which were all transacted in cash. Some large deposits and some even larger withdrawals that she would never question or tell his wife about. Mandy had convinced Bird's wife, rather than make a call to her husband's mobile phone, which could interrupt an important meeting, it would be better to come through her desk. She believed to have an ongoing well-paid job you needed control, and she was not about to let her guard down now. She returned his look as she placed both her hands, palm down on his desk so that Bird lowered his eyes, taking in her well-endowed figure and low-cut dress. After turning to make sure there were no eavesdroppers about, she continued in an even lower voice.

"Steve, put it this way. The Premier does take an interest in his Minister's affairs, albeit only the work-related ones, regarding what and where they are, but if I have read the fine print of his latest manifesto correctly, which I'm sure I have, it only talks about recording delegations that are visiting foreign dignitaries, and seeing that talks about two or more people attending. I figured you certainly don't want me coming along as your secretary today. Let's just put this down to an impromptu getting together over a cup of Russian Caravan tea. Nothing to see, nothing to report."

She didn't know exactly why he was seeing the Russian Consul General, but she would bet a month's wages that it had something to do with the police visit days before. Bird had been on tenterhooks ever since.

"Thank you, Mandy. You are a very loyal staffer and it's good to know we have each other's backs," Bird said as he stood, walked around his desk and left the office.

Mmm. Your back, my back and a lot of other body parts. If only the walls of Room 201 of the Mayfair Hotel further down Spring

Street could talk after some so-called late night Parliamentary sittings, she thought as she rearranged her dress back to good secretary mode.

Steve Bird meanwhile stepped into the front passenger seat of his official white BMW car and nodded to the driver, who reached over to the Sat Nav device before asking his destination. Bird reached across and removed the driver's hand. The driver had been told by Mandy of the destination, but he wanted to double check the quickest route for his passenger.

"Just drop me off in St. Kilda Road near Domain Road. I'll walk from there. You can take the car home as I won't be needing it again today. Have the rest of the day off. I'll make my own way home, thanks."

The driver, a retired Leading Senior Constable, nodded and exited the rear gates of Parliament House, turning towards Spring Street. What he didn't say to his Ministerial passenger was that he still had to fill in the details of the trip given to him by Mandy, and he wasn't about to ignore that. He knew all about blow backs from not filling out police logbooks from his forty years in the Force. Time, date, pick up and drop off location together with any instructions would be recorded. He, like the Minister's secretary, valued his job. Ammunition was sometimes more valuable stored than fired, was an old police saying.

Bird got out of his car and walked towards the Consulate trying to form in his own mind how he could tell the Consul General that he believed people who were connected with the Consulate were engaged in not only the disposal of a body but were also highly likely connected with an illegal Chinese immigration scheme which was used for street scamming between states of Australia. He was sure that with a little digging, the Consulate would discover that some of their staff had their fingers into fake passports as well.

The reception area of the Consulate was as austere and cold as the greeting he received from the man behind the desk.

"You have appointment?" he said in broken but still rather derogatory English that implied Bird would not get one step further without one.

"Yes, State Minister for Liquor and Gaming, Steve Bird to see the Consul General Dimitry Lebedev."

"Are you a representative of your Premier?"

Bird had become even less impressed with the tone and manner of the man. He had bigger things to think about than bow to this glorified goon whom he recognised as one of the body snatchers from the photos Stone had given him. The photos that were in his jacket pocket.

"Just do your job and inform Mr. Lebedev that I am here," he said snapping back with authority.

The duly chastened hired help scuttled away, returning after a few minutes.

"Mr. Lebedev will see you now. Follow me."

Steve Bird deliberately walked beside the man, not behind him. This was about confidence. As they turned into an open doorway which was obviously a greeting room, Bird brushed aside the man's arm, put out his own hand in a greeting and spoke.

"Mr. Lebedev, so good to see you." The Consul General waved away the lackey, indicating for him to close the door.

As he quickly returned to his desk, the goon pressed the speed dial on his mobile phone. The number quickly came up with the name Antonov. Rather than ring him, he sent a text.

#You talked other night about politician being at card game. There is politician seeing Lebedev now. Gambling talks. Might want to see him leave. Same one? #

After a few minutes without a reply he decided to ring the number.

Chapter Thirty-Six

"Strange that I have not been contacted by the Premier's office, Mr. Bird. Is this an official visit or are you just here to, as you Aussies say, 'pass the time of day'. I think not, eh?" the experienced diplomat said.

"Ah, no, Mr. Lebedev. Or may I call you Dimitry?"

"Please. Unofficial visits call for first names and Russian tea, Steven. Please make yourself a cup," Lebedev said, indicating the large antique sideboard by the wall. "There are several types of tea there, but if you are in Russia, please enjoy some Caravan tea. Delicious. Hot water is in the Samovar."

Bird took what was an expensive Lomonosov cup and saucer and poured himself a cup of the dark looking tea and returned to sit in one of the large lounge chairs.

"Please tell me why you are visiting."

"Dimitry, it has unfortunately been brought to my attention by a senior police officer connected with Melbourne City command that two of your people who we believe work here at the Consulate have been engaged in the disappearance of the body of a person from an illegal card game days ago. The card game was the subject of a police investigation and all people who were connected with it were caught on video as well. I am telling you this as we wish to get to the bottom of this and another situation without making it a diplomatic problem. By no means are the Police or myself accusing either of these two individuals of being involved in the death of this person, just the transporting of his body. The body was recovered unbeknown to these two or anyone else for that matter. It is now in the morgue awaiting further investigation. They simply removed and transported the body upon instruction of a third party who we believe is responsible for the killing."

Lebedev had raised his cup of tea to his lips but had not taken a sip. The cup and saucer were slowly placed onto the coffee table in front of him. Lebedev's eyes bored into those of his guest.

"I cannot believe this, Steven. My staff here are very loyal."

"Unfortunately, I have a picture here of the two individuals loading what appears to be a body bag into a van that belongs to the Russian Ethnic Committee House," Bird said as he removed one photo from his jacket and placed it in front of Lebedev. He had no intention of producing the photo of himself talking to Ricky Bobrov. Lebedev picked the photo up, slowly examining it closely. Bird could see his eyes widen and his face go a deep shade of crimson. He was one angry Russian.

Bird had been involved in politics long enough to judge people's faces and their reactions to situations they had been put in suddenly and unexpectedly. After the initial look of anger, Lebedev's face took on an ashen appearance and his jaw dropped. He was now also shocked. Bird was always going to let Lebedev speak first. After another minute of examining the photo, he did.

"Steven, these two men work here. In fact, one of them was the person who escorted you into the room. The other is my driver. What is going on here and who is this third person you talk about. Why are your police not coming to me about this, why you?"

Because they've got me over a barrel and are screwing me. That's fucking why! Bird thought but couldn't say.

"The third man is Pavel Antonov, another Russian. The Police can pick him up now and charge him with the murder, but they want to play the long game and remove him from what they think is an Australia wide begging scam that involves the import of Asian migrants from China. As you can see, with your country and China involved, it could get messy. That's why I am dealing with it and not the State or Federal Police. We want to keep it as low key as possible. There's much more to the story, Dimitry. The Police believe that this Antonov is a member of the Russian mafia, the *Bratva* and is possibly laundering money through the Consulate. They want this illegal immigration scheme stopped first. The Federal Police can then come in and clean up what is left, but my police want to charge Antonov with murder from this card night and what we would like you to do is assist the them in stopping this scheme by removing his assistants. The Police want to squeeze Antonov after he realises that his assistants have been gagged. What you do with them is your business, but they want to deal with Antonov. At the end of the day, I don't think you want to involve the Consulate with the *Bratva,* do you? Even the Premier does not know about this because if our press ever got hold of it, the consequences for trade and whatever else could be damaged irreparably."

Lebedev slumped back in his chair, shaking his head.

"I will be removed from my post and sent home," he said quietly.

"No Dimitry. This can be handled discreetly by a small police task force and with instructions there will be no headlines, press or anything. It is of benefit to us both that this is treated carefully. We just want to remove the head from the snake. I will be the only person you deal with. You let me know that these two in the photo are no longer capable of contacting Antonov and the Police will move in. I will make sure you are kept out of this. These two along with Antonov are discrediting your country."

"You promise me that you can keep this to ourselves? Why would you worry? It would have no consequences for you, Steven?"

"We don't want diplomatic headlines," was all the reply Bird could think of as Lebedev stared at him, stood, walked to the sideboard and poured a fresh cup of tea.

"Maybe there is something that you are keeping to yourself here, Steven, but let me assure you that I also know what a short life people like ourselves can have in politics and I will do my utmost to assist you, not just for my country, but for the fact that I much prefer the climate here as I'm sure you would understand. What you don't tell me is of no consequence as I am thinking that you may have a shadow lurking in your background. We scratch each other's backs, eh?" Lebedev said as he smirked like a true political animal.

Bird knew that he was now 'on the books' not only with the Victoria Police but also with the Russian Consulate. He returned a sheepish grin and could feel the sweat running down his back.

"Steven, you have my guarantee that the two in the photo will not be heard of again. We have two cells in the basement here. Something left over from the Cold War I believe. They will be occupying them from before sunset. Their days of working with this Antonov are over and I can see by the look on your face that we will be firm friends whenever I, or should I say we, need each other again. You never know, trade between our countries might be the beneficiary from this which would be good for both our careers."

Bird, by this time was mentally and physically exhausted. He just wanted to get home and make a call to Phil Stone to let him know he had kept up his end of the arrangement. Like Dimitry Lebedev, he wished to continue his way of life, but he couldn't help feeling he was now the puppet with two masters who could pull his strings anytime they wanted. Now he knew exactly why he had to deal with Lebedev instead of Stone. He got the appointment because of his political connections. To the Russians, no police department would get inside the Consulate. They were of no political gain to them, where this Bird was definitely now 'in hand.'

Chapter Thirty-Seven

"Pavel, you wanted me to keep you informed about anything unusual or special that happens here at the Consulate. There is a State Government Minister here now talking to Lebedev," the Consulate minion said hurriedly from behind his desk.

Antonov had just parked his Mercedes in St. Kilda Road and was about to embark on another cash pick up from his Asian immigrants. Getting out of his car, he answered in a bored sounding voice.

"So, what's unusual? Lebedev would see lots of the Government officials."

"They never come here by themselves. It's always a delegation of at least three. This must be personal."

"Okay then, surprise me. Who is it?" Antonov said as he was mentally planning the day in front of him.

"It's the State Minister for Gaming, Steve Bird," the lackey answered.

The answer brought Antonov to a sudden stop. At the same time his brain went into overdrive.

"What's he doing there? What's the appointment for?" Antonov blurted into his phone.

"I don't know, Pavel. It's a private meeting of some sort. I think Lebedev is not knowing what for," the agitated helper replied just before Antonov cut the call off and began pacing up and down the footpath near his car before stopping suddenly and re-dialling the last number.

"I'm coming over there. You let me know if he leaves, you hear?"

"I will immediately, Pavel," came the timid reply.

Antonov stepped quickly back to his Mercedes and took off hurriedly in the direction of the Consulate, which was only a few kilometres along St. Kilda Road. He didn't really know what he was going to do when he got there, but in his mind, he had to double check that this Steve Bird was the same one that was at the card night in Carlton. He had a bad feeling about this.

Fifteen minutes later he was nervously standing in the shade under a tree almost directly opposite his destination. Two things struck him as odd. His contact inside the Consulate had not rung him back so he presumed Bird was still inside with Lebedev. He just waited and watched. If this was just a private meeting, then he thought he could control anything that came out of it. Violence crossed his mind. The other thing that was out of sorts was that, if Bird was inside talking to Lebedev about anything of an official nature, he would have his Ministerial car and driver waiting for him outside. There was no sign of either, which in one way was bad, but again, controllable. Deciding to take a chance, he crossed the road to outside the Consulate. He knew the layout of the entire premises both inside and out because he had paid a princely sum for the plans to his two contacts for a 'just in case' day— and that day might be today! Knowing the blind spots of the CCTV, he managed to slip between some large bushes and the window which showed the interior of the reception area. From here, he could also keep a slight view of the front door.

Minutes passed before suddenly Lebedev and Steve Bird appeared and shook hands before Bird walked out of sight, presumably towards the front door. Antonov was about to make his way back to the footpath when, out of the corner of his eye, he saw his contact inside the Consulate being spoken to at some length by an obviously enraged Lebedev. Suddenly his other contact was escorted into the same foyer and was also spoken to by Lebedev. The next thing he saw were both walking to a side door with three other large men. *What is going on here?*

After getting back to his car, Antonov grabbed a burner phone and rang both his contacts at the Consulate. No answer.

This is not good. What did they discuss in the meeting?

He concentrated on getting back to picking up the daily takings along Swanston Street. He was thinking of trying again later with his contacts when he felt the vibration of his mobile phone in his pocket.

"I was getting a little concerned because neither of you were answering your phones, Antonov said."

There was an uncomfortable gap of silence before the person ringing in spoke.

"Pavel, it's me, Ricky. Ricky Bobrov."

A surprised but disappointed Pavel Antonov took his time to reply.

"What is it you want, Ricky?"

"Just to give you some news, Pavel. I've resigned from the Force. I've had enough of the bullshit. Can we meet up for a coffee?"

A suspicious Antonov replied very slowly.

"Yes, Ricky. Let's meet. Tomorrow morning, ten o'clock, Argyle Square in Lygon Street," he said as he watched Steve Bird walking away from the Consulate on the opposite footpath.

"Yes, fine," Bobrov replied.

Antonov's brain was working overtime formulating some sort of safety plan. His money collection could wait one more day. Those Asians would not dare rip him off. The only one that did try was feeding the fishes at the bottom of Port Phillip Bay.

Antonov knew Bobrov's address and slowly started to make his way there. A connection was niggling away at him, and it wasn't a good one. Was it that Bobrov was trying to set him up in some way? Was Bobrov really out of the Force? After all, it was Bobrov that approached him in the first place about the gambling house. He thought that he would just surprise him at his house and tackle him with what he had seen.

Heading back through the city and out into Flemington he felt bad about everything by the time he got near to Bobrov's house. Parking a few streets away, he took an old baseball cap from the back seat, jammed it down on his head, crossed the road and just like at the Consulate, propped himself some distance away but still within sight of Ricky's house.

Antonov was always keeping an eye out for the police. He could spot an unmarked police car a mile away—and there was one parked just up from his house. His antennae were now on high alert, especially as minutes later a young plain clothes female got out of the car just as Bobrov came out of the front door and talked animatedly to her. From his hand gestures it looked as though Bobrov was holding an imaginary phone. The female put both hands out and waved downwards in a calming fashion and after a minute or two, Bobrov returned inside.

Ricky, Ricky. You talk to the police, Bird talks to Lebedev and suddenly I can't get hold of my contacts. I have plans for you, Ricky!

Chapter Thirty-Eight

"I told Schaeffer yesterday that Antonov wanted to meet me this morning. I want to be sure though that someone is covering me. After I show him my discharge papers, I don't know what he will want from me," a very nervous Ricky Bobrov said to Tony Signorotto and Max Tyler in the backroom of the Carlton Police station. "You're my supposed 'handlers'" he said indicating with two raised fingers on each hand and making quote marks in the air. "What are your plans to keep me safe?"

"Okay Ricky, settle down. We've got two hours before you meet up with him. I'm going to have Schaffer and Romano covering you from the Cardigan Street side and myself and Max will be quietly having a coffee in Dom's restaurant. You won't see us, but we'll see you. Now, what are you going to say to him?"

"First off, I need to show him my discharge papers. Have you got them?"

Max Tyler produced the fake papers from a folder he was holding and passed them to Signorotto, who in turn held them up in front of Bobrov's face.

"As genuine as the real thing," Signorotto said as Bobrov took hold of the form and examined it minutely. "It's the real deal parchment paper."

"Now that you have the papers what are you going to offer him?" Tyler chipped in.

"That I'm still available to hunt for houses for gambling nights as I've got a mate in the Real Estate business that can find me places, no questions asked, cash deals only. If he asks for a name, it is Carlo Genessi from Genessi Real Estate."

"Commander Stone and I have talked to Carlo, and he knows the complete story about the Faraday Street house because he owns it and gave us permission to keep your game going so we could film you. He will give the correct story if by some chance Antonov wants to check up on you. He will say he knows you from years back."

Bobrov stared at Signorotto without speaking.

"Yes, Ricky, we know Carlo very well. He is a pillar of the Carlton Community, so don't kick yourself too much. You don't know Carlton and its people like I do," Signorotto said with a sly grin. "You were never going to do any good that night. You picked the wrong house in the wrong suburb."

"I'm not wearing any sort of wire," Bobrov said.

"That's okay. We just want you to show him your papers and offer to work in with him. The two bullet heads that were helping him out have now been, how shall we say, eliminated from the equation. When Antonov realises he can't get in touch with them any more after a few days of trying then he'll move on with his money from the begging and most likely find another source to launder it through. You may want to offer up a few names from your track days to string him along. We really want you to concentrate though on the begging scam. We want to pass onto the Feds where these people are coming from and how they are being shipped around the country from city to city. Now, let's get something to eat and get you down to Lygon Street. You've got work to do."

"You've got me by the balls, haven't you Signorotto?"

"We do, Ricky, but at the same time as I reckon you are an absolute blight on the Force, I still have a duty of care to look after you until this is over and I'll do all within my power to facilitate that," Signorotto said, staring back at Bobrov with eyes of steel.

"Don't worry about the breakfast. Couldn't eat a thing. I'm just going for a walk, grab a coffee and head down to Argyle Square," Bobrov said as he stood and headed out the door.

Chapter Thirty-Eight

"Take care," Tyler said to his back before Bobrov turned.

"You really couldn't give a fuck, Tyler. It's just promotion for you."

"You've got a chance to try to redeem something here, Ricky. Don't blow it," Tyler said.

Ricky Bobrov left the station by the back entrance and headed over to Humble Ray's café in Bouverie Street. It would take him a good twenty minutes to get there but he just wanted to walk, think and to calm his nerves.

After spending a fair time in the café, he got up and walked out towards the well-known meeting place between Cardigan Street and Lygon Street. He got there about five to ten but couldn't see any sign of Antonov. He could swear though that he was being watched, and not necessarily by his minders.

He looked to his right as he lowered himself onto the step area of the piazza and nearly jumped out of his skin when he felt the presence of someone next to him. Spinning his head around quickly he was looking directly into the cold eyes of Pavel Antonov.

"Nice to see you, Ricky. You wanted to talk to me?"

Chapter Thirty-Nine

"So, you give the Police the boot, eh?" Antonov said as he examined the certificate Bobrov had passed to him minutes before. Bobrov replied nervously.

"I don't care about what happened at that last card game, Pavel. I know one thing though and that is beside the fact that we made a decent haul from it, my adrenalin was pumping all night. I'm sick of taking orders from idiots above me. I'd rather learn about making money from people like you rather than working for them."

"What makes you think you could work for me? I have my contacts and they help me with my city business. You would be handy getting a few card games, but you have nothing set up for that. Why should I take a risk with you?" Antonov said.

"The fact that I resigned lets me keep a lot of contacts I have. If I had been kicked out, no-one would talk to me. I think, with a little bit of planning we could set up an ongoing card business. At the same time though I could help you out with the city stuff and I would learn very quickly. Who do you have helping you now? Some heavies maybe?"

"Why would you be kicked out. Are you not telling me something?" Antonov said, playing Bobrov along.

"No, no. I just wanted out because I think I can earn more money and I like how you do things," Bobrov said as sweat ran down his back.

"I have work to do today, Ricky, but I will think about it. The card games are good. Maybe we could get back some of our punters from Faraday Street for a reunion game. Maybe that Minister could get us some more players," Antonov said, staring at Bobrov, trying to gauge a reaction.

"How about we start new and get ourselves some fresh punters?" Bobrov replied, far too quickly for Antonov's liking.

"I will think about the future for you and me, Ricky. I will get back to you. You never know, you may be of some assistance to me in my city business. Maybe it's time I got away from my Russian roots."

With that, Antonov stood and headed towards Cardigan Street where he had parked his car. Bobrov stood on shaky legs and walked towards Lygon Street. The short meeting had stressed him no end.

Pavel Antonov smiled to himself as he quickly strode across the grass area of Argyle Square. He walked deliberately past a young man and woman who were sitting on one of the benches while they looked at their phones. Antonov immediately recognised the girl as the same undercover Police officer who had been outside Bobrov's house the day before. To doubly confirm his suspicions, he saw the same plain Police car parked in the centre parking area of Cardigan Street. Climbing into his car, he headed slowly north, out of sight of Argyle Square then turned right into Grattan Street and then right again into Lygon Street where he drove under the speed limit southwards and began looking to see if Ricky Bobrov was still around. Bingo! He was just on the eastern footpath talking animatedly to a couple of males outside a restaurant called Dom's. He drove past and parked so he could see them in his rear vision mirror. The younger of the two strangers was waving his hand in the direction of Argyle Square. The young male and female from the bench walked across Lygon Street and joined the other three. After a quick chat, an agitated looking Bobrov walked into the restaurant, followed quickly by the others.

So, Ricky. You have resigned from the Politsiya, but you are still surrounded by them. You take me for a fool at your own expense.

Antonov had plans to make as he headed into the city to pick up his earnings from his street scam. He thought to himself that if Bobrov was onside with the police and working with them, then he was most likely being pressured. It was obvious now that either he or the Minister had told all. But why? It had been a private visit by the Minister to Lebedev, so things were being put in place quietly against him. Both Lebedev and Bobrov were being used and it was a fair guess that the police knew about the body. Suddenly, his cohorts are being removed and he is being spied on. They could drag him in anytime for the murder, so why not now? There must be something more important than the murder.

The penny suddenly dropped with Bobrov. It must be to do with the money scheme. Just the money? No, more than that. If Lebedev had been warned of something it wasn't just about money, it must be to do with the whole Asian illegal migrant situation and how I am connected. They are wanting more information and that is why Bobrov wants in with me.

They won't touch me until they have a lot more information.

As Antonov got out of his car and after two more unsuccessful calls to his Consulate contacts he knew things had changed dramatically. Both calls had come back with the replies that the numbers were no longer in use. Then he realised that he needed to put plans in place. The begging scheme had been running for a long time now and his money had been constantly put into offshore accounts. He wanted to keep it that way. Right now, it was time to play with the rats.

Chapter Forty

Ricky Bobrov was sitting in his flat late the next morning thinking that he really had no control over anything. That had all been taken away by Phil Stone, Tony Signorotto and even more alarmingly by Pavel Antonov. Thoughts were criss-crossing his mind when his mobile phone rang. It was a silent number. Not knowing who it was, he answered with one word.

"Yeah."

"Pavel here, Ricky. You come with me today and we talk more. Outside Arts Centre in one hour. If you do not show, then forget any plans you might have had. Understand?"

A stunned Bobrov knew he had only seconds to reply.

"I'll be there." He was about to add his thanks, but the line had already gone dead.

Must be a burner phone. Quick and no number. Why?

Heading hurriedly out to his car he realised that the techs at Ethical Standards would have already passed on information about the call to Stone and his crew, so he didn't bother doing anything about it because he would undoubtedly be contacted very soon. Sure enough, as he was attempting to find a car park close to the Arts Centre, his phone rang. He got in first.

"Be quick. I'm trying to find a park," he said without giving away whether he was talking to the Russian or to the police.

"Tony Signorotto. What's going on?"

"Antonov's called me in to the city for a walk and talk. I've got to be there soon so don't bother with the tail because I don't know where we will be going, and I don't want him to suspect anything. I'm meeting him outside the Arts Centre, that's all I know."

Signorotto replied with a decision he knew would haunt him.

"Okay. Be careful and keep in contact. We will be tracking your phone, but we won't be ringing you. Get back to us as soon as your done with him, understand?"

Bobrov gave Signorotto a dismissive reply.

"Whatever." *Christ, he actually said to be careful.*

He parked his car on the opposite side to the Arts Centre in Linlithgow Avenue and walked past the Police Memorial, crossing the busy road at Southbank Boulevard. Passing the waterfall at the main door of the Arts Centre, he saw Antonov just moving away from the pop-up coffee stand situated on the forecourt. Bobrov walked up to him and noticed that the Russian looked very relaxed as he sipped his takeaway purchase. He was dressed in old jeans and a T shirt.

"Good to see you are on time, Ricky," a smiling Antonov said.

"Shows I take you seriously, Pavel," Bobrov said as he looked at the coffee in Antonov's hand.

"Get yourself one my friend and then we'll walk and have a quiet word as I show you something."

A strong coffee was just what Bobrov needed at this moment, so he went over to the small shop and ordered a flat white and was just about to put his hand into his pocket for some change when Antonov reached past him and placed a five dollar note on the counter.

"On me today, Ricky." Bobrov said nothing.

A few minutes later, coffees in hand, Antonov spoke.

"I have given it a lot of thought overnight, Ricky and I think you may be right. Some new blood may be a good thing. However, if I take you on board with my city business it will be a sign of trust, so I hope this will flow both ways. While I will show you the operational side of things, I expect you to also concentrate on more premises for card games. There are days here in the city where I don't operate because I may be changing my personnel around. There is a saying that I truly believe, Ricky and that is, *'softly, softly catchee monkey'.*

As they walked along St. Kilda Road towards the actual city, Bobrov saw that Antonov was carrying a large but seemingly empty backpack over his left shoulder. They crossed Princes Bridge and then over into Federation Square. Bobrov had hardly said a word on the walk as he didn't want to be seen as some sort of junior apprentice keen to impress his so-called boss. Once they had walked up to the stage area, Antonov indicated to Bobrov to stop. Near the stage there was an elderly Chinese man kneeling on what looked like a prayer mat. The male was bowing towards the ground and then raising his head. This procedure went on constantly. Beside him was a large begging bowl which looked mainly empty except for what appeared to be some small change and one folded ten dollar note. The male had a large cloth bag across his shoulder, swung in front of his chest.

As Bobrov stood still, Antonov sat down next to the beggar who unclipped the cloth bag from around his shoulder and let it fall between them. Antonov did not immediately pick up the bag but waited while a middle-aged female had finished putting a handful of coins in the bowl and walked off. When there was no-one around, he quickly picked up the bag, stood and walked to the side of the stage and out of sight of any passers-by. He motioned to Bobrov to follow him while the Asian beggar resumed his constant begging and bowing.

Bobrov was amazed as Antonov removed what looked like several hundred dollars in notes and put them in his backpack. Antonov left all the coins in the man's bag, walked up behind him and placed it around his shoulder. There was no break in the begging routine. Walking back behind the stage, he turned to Bobrov.

"Okay Ricky. This is what it's about. Mind you, I didn't do a pickup yesterday as most times my assistants do that. However, for some unknown reason I haven't been able to get hold of them the last day or so. If a pickup's done every day, by this time of the morning each of my people would normally have roundabout one hundred dollars in their bags."

"How many pickups are there?"

"I have ten working the city. They all start about seven thirty in the morning and work their mark till one in the afternoon. By that time, the lunch crowds have gone back to work. After that they know to move to the next point, so this one will change over in a couple of hours and move on up Swanston Street to outside the Town Hall. He changes his dress and changes how he begs. I have a couple who look like tramps in Bourke Street. They are set up with mattresses and such and they rake in the money and food for themselves. You will see as we make our way up Swanston Street."

Bobrov was not surprised by the amount of money one beggar had taken but when he multiplied it by ten, he realised how much Bobrov was taking in.

"Mate, how much is this worth?"

"About five thousand to six thousand a week in the city but I also have a young university student who works Southern Cross station. He approaches young females and gives them a story about how he must get to a new job somewhere up country, has lost his wallet and doesn't have the fare. I run him and one other with varying stories. On a good day they take in about two thousand dollars. They work their arses off and get paid in drugs of their choice which they otherwise couldn't afford. You wouldn't believe how gullible some people are, Ricky. People will hand over fifty dollars sometimes if they think the story is good enough."

Bobrov stared at Antonov in disbelief.

"Why do the street beggars do it? What do they get out of it?" he said with a tone of incredulity in his voice

"I won't go into the behind the scenes of this, but all you have to know is that I work loosely for the *Bratva*. These people originally were smuggled in here thinking their families would follow them and this is their way of getting them here. They are driven between here and Sydney and Adelaide. None of the state police forces have the manpower to deal with it and the

Feds won't do anything unless it gets handed to them on a plate by the state police. It's a begging circle and has been like this for years."

"What happens to them when they realise they aren't getting their families out here?" Bobrov said.

"Does not present a problem if they complain. We always have more where they come from. Some find their way into Port Phillip Bay and Sydney harbour, if you know what I mean," a laughing Antonov said.

"This is good money, Pavel," Bobrov said hoping to glean some more information.

"I am kept very well by my brothers in the *Bratva*. Anything else I do, like what you are going to arrange with some card nights is all mine. I live very, very well Ricky," Antonov replied.

"What do you do with these people after they finish each day?"

"We control their minds and movements with the thought of their families. They make their way to some houses we own and are run by other Chinese. They are fed and kept well, and they never wear the same clothes too often. They are transported to the city outskirts within walking distance of their starting points every morning. We sometimes work them on evenings near Federation Square after a big football match which always has those winning supporters giving plenty."

"Am I allowed to ask where most of the money goes?"

"Of course you can ask, but would you believe me if I told you a lot of it goes into political donations in various states so there are always doors kept open for influence by other countries of our choice. Now let's do some collecting, my friend. Oh, there is one little thing if I am telling you all this."

"What's that?" a nervous Bobrov replied.

"You will be staying with me for the next few days. If you want in on this then we need to make sure you are across everything from the pickup, the people, the money transfers, everything. We will be up early and working till late because I also need to look at some houses with you that we can use for card games. If we are going to do this, let's get into it. If my other contacts come back online then I'll tell them to have some time off. They are only muscle anyway. Good for lifting heavy weights, eh?" Antonov said slowly as he winked at Bobrov.

"I haven't got any clothes or anything, Pavel. I'll need to pick some things up from my place."

"No need, Ricky. If I want you as a new business partner I will buy you some. We'll drop into Myers on the way. You need some new jeans and a change of shirts. My money."

"What about my car?" Bobrov said feeling that he was becoming trapped.

"Leave it. The parking tickets will be on me. We'll use mine. Pick yours up in a couple of days."

Bobrov didn't know what to say next in case he overplayed his hand, so as they passed Bourke Street after pickup number three had been relieved of his money, Antonov indicated towards Myer's. After picking out some new clothes, Bobrov headed toward the change rooms but before he could open the door, Antonov spoke.

"Give me your phone and wallet, Ricky. You don't know what thieves there are around here."

Bobrov reluctantly handed over his wallet and his only means of contacting Signorotto before closing the door behind him.

Antonov removed a paper clip from his pocket, bent it so one end could enter the SIM card holder on Bobrov's phone, removed the SIM card and lightly scratched the gold-coloured computer chip. He then quickly placed the same SIM card back into the phone. It would have been too obvious to just get rid of the phone. This way Bobrov would feel safe enough with it back in his hand. He wouldn't realise that there would be no outgoing or incoming calls. The phone would look okay but that was all it would do. More importantly, no one could 'ping' it for its location.

Minutes later, Bobrov emerged from the change room with the jeans and shirts that he had picked and quickly put out his hand to a bored looking Antonov, who in turn gave back his phone and wallet.

Bobrov placed the items on the sale counter and Antonov handed over a stolen credit card to pay for the items. There was no way the card would be missed before he paid for Bobrov's new clothes. He wanted nothing traced back to himself.

Once they had walked out of the store, Antonov flicked the stolen card into the nearest rubbish bin.

"Okay, let's get all the traps done and get to the house so we can start training you, Ricky. Tomorrow, as well as doing another run, I want to show you a place in Carlton that may be the place where we can expand our enterprise. I want to get your opinion on it."

"Fine by me, Pavel," Ricky thought. *Don't like the idea of staying with him but as long as Stone and Signorotto are tracking me they'll know I'll be at Antonov's house.*

An hour and a half later, Antonov pulled his Mercedes into the back alley of the *Melbourne Carlton Central Apartment Complex* in Finlay Place. Antonov could see the look of apprehension on Bobrov's face.

"Why are we coming here?" he said.

"Just got to pick something up from a guy. Come and give us a hand," Antonov said quickly.

By the time Bobrov had got out of the passenger side, Antonov had rounded the corner by a garage and disappeared. Bobrov ran to keep up with him.

As he went around the same corner, he suddenly saw Antonov standing and facing him, hands on hips. Before he could speak, he felt a heavy impact to his head, and he dropped to the ground. Groggily shaking his head, he realised that it wasn't Antonov that had hit him. There were two black shrouded figures holding him on the ground.

Attempting to move only brought more pain as his head was pressed into the bitumen. A low guttural scream emitted from his mouth as a needle was roughly jabbed into his arm. He vaguely heard Antonov say something about Sydney associates before he was rolled into a body bag. Darkness descended on his world.

"Where do you want us to dispose of him? A bullet now would make it quick," a Russian accent said.

"No. No bullet. Load him into the boot of my car. I want him alive. I have a place to take him where he will learn over the next few days that he should not have crossed me. A big empty house nearby that has been forgotten. There is one more person who I wish to take alive also, but I will handle him. You two know the play in this city for the next few days until the *Bratva* have hierarchy in place that will take over down here while I disappear.

Minutes after Bobrov had been dumped into the boot of the Mercedes, Antonov headed on the short drive to Rathdowne Street.

Chapter Forty-One

"What the hell happened?" a furious Tony Signorotto said over the phone to the Technical Department. "Are you telling me that his phone is out of order or what? I was talking to him this afternoon, and everything was cool just before he was going to meet Antonov. What's going on?" he yelled into the handpiece.

The air in the upstairs office of the Carlton police station was blue with expletives not only from Signorotto but also from Johnny Petran from the DRU. Suddenly from keeping tabs on Bobrov they now had nothing. Phil Stone was waiting for Signorotto to get off the phone while Max Tyler, Chloe Schaeffer, Paul Romano and even Kate McLaren stood nervously around the room talking quietly. A clearly frustrated Signorotto eventually got off the phone, held his hand up for silence and spoke.

"I'm taking all the blame here. I was last to speak to Ricky and he told me to keep the dogs off him in case he got sprung. Foolishly I went along with that which left him one out with Antonov and now we have lost him. The Techs have come across this before where one minute they have the person tracked and the next they just get occasional blips. Apparently, it is an old trick to take out the SIM card, lightly scratch it and then replace it," a clearly frustrated Signorotto said to those around him.

"What does that do to the phone?" Kate McLaren said from the back of the room.

"The screen on the phone isn't affected and your contact list is okay, but you can't make or take a call and all the tracker gets is an intermittent blip here and there. They reckon whoever did it knew what they were doing. It's also an old Mafia trick, which doesn't go down well in my thinking."

"So, are you saying that Antonov has done it after somehow getting Ricky's phone off him?" a concerned Phil Stone added.

"Appears that way," a dejected Tony Signorotto said to no one in particular. "I shouldn't have let him get rid of Chloe and Paul."

"Well, he's either gotten rid of Ricky because he's smelled a rat, or he's taken him hostage. Either way we must find him," a now quieter Johnny Petran said. "I'll get Mick York to get onto the Melbourne City Council and go through their Safe City camera feeds along St. Kilda Road and Swanston Street," he said walking away and punching the speed dial on his mobile phone.

"I don't think we are giving Antonov enough credit. He's no fool and has obviously twigged to something. It's not your fault Tony," Phil Stone said. "Anyone in here would have let Bobrov off the leash, especially when it was all done in such a hurry. Let's get out there and shake a few trees."

Max Tyler clicked his fingers loudly making Tony Signorotto hurriedly turn around.

"Any idea will be a good one at this stage," Signorotto said quickly looking directly at his offsider.

"We know Ricky met Antonov and the next thing is that Ricky's phone is offline, so we can take it that he has got him offline too, right?"

"What's your point, Max?" a puzzled looking Kate McLaren said.

"Then if he shows up at his city begging points then we could grab him. My bet is he won't. We have eliminated his helpers from the Consulate, so my guess is he'll have a ring in working his rounds. We split up and sit off as many of the beggars as we can and if a bagman turns up then we grab him and shake his fucking tree!" Tyler said looking around the group for support.

"That's a bloody good idea, Max," Signorotto replied quietly. "What do you reckon, Phil?"

"Could work but we'll all have to take a point," Stone said going through a head count of the office. "There's eight of us if you include Mick York. Tony, you and I'll have to do one each, too."

Fifteen minutes later after figuring out where each of them would observe from, Johnny Petran came running back into the office.

"Got Antonov and Ricky on CCTV in the Bourke Street mall. Both went into Myer's and then a while later they came out with Ricky holding onto a big shopping bag."

"Where did they go after that?" Stone said.

"Tracked them further north up Swanston Street and then they disappear near Victoria Parade after a few more bag jobs."

"You're right, Max. Looks like Antonov was the last person with Ricky but he won't want to give up his daily takings," a slightly happier Tony Signorotto said. "Chloe, can you get down to Radio Electronics in Collingwood and pick up about ten portable radios. I want everyone to have one tomorrow morning. Paul, get onto D24 communications and get us a channel to work on for this. I want everyone back here at six in the morning. I want Antonov, but at the end of the day, I want Bobrov safe first off. We know he's a crook, but he is doing what we want. He's actually shown a lot of guts doing this."

Chapter Forty-Two

Ricky Bobrov was in a world of pain. His hands and feet were bound, and he could feel the rope that connected the ties on his feet to the ties on his hands because every time he went to move either his feet or his hands it pulled painfully. His head was thumping, and he could smell the mouldy floor he was lying on. The only part of him that was functioning without hindrance were his eyes-and he wished they weren't. They were now focussed on a very large rat sitting in the middle of a heap of discarded syringes. The rodent was staring back at him with jet black eyes from about one metre away. Bobrov shuddered as it bared its teeth.

He didn't know how long he had been here. The last thing he remembered was going around a corner and seeing Pavel Antonov standing still looking at him. After that it was a blank. He tried to focus on what was around him by slowly rolling from one side to another, albeit very painfully. Besides the rat that was now scurrying away because of his movements, he could see that he was in a dilapidated room. The walls were full of holes where they had been kicked in and he could see the old lathe and plaster that had once held the room together. This method of plastering was a long-forgotten art, so he was in a house that was either being renovated or one that had been the home to rats and drug addicts for quite a while. He was thinking that the answer had to be the latter, just as a nearby door swung open on very rusty hinges. He could only see a large figure silhouetted in the frame of the doorway.

"Ah, Ricky. You are awake at last."

Ricky Bobrov's worst nightmare was being realised. The voice belonged to Pavel Antonov. Bobrov attempted a shot at bravado.

"What the fuck are you playing at Pavel?" he said with an indignant voice.

"What the fuck am I playing at?" Antonov spat back. "Do you and those hopeless undercover cops take me for a fool? I have got into and out of more trouble than you lot could ever hope to know about. I saw all your police friends with you the other day outside that restaurant in Lygon Street. Do you think I am giving you all the inside information on my jobs so that you can step in neatly and arrest me? I told you everything to get you in. There is only one thing left to do now and that is to kill you. You haven't just taken on me, you stupid, pathetic little fool, you are dealing with the Russian *Bratva*. You mean nothing, as do your so-called friends. Now that we are alone and out of sight and somewhere you won't be heard, I will be leaving you here for a while so I can pick up a friend for you. You know each other well but I don't think you will be playing cards together."

"What have I done to you, Pavel? I thought we were going to be business partners."

"Ricky, Ricky, Ricky. The Russian Mafia doesn't do business partners very well. I couldn't take you on even if I wanted to. What I find very strange is why you are going along with the police? What do they have on you?"

Ricky Bobrov was not feeling at all brave at this point in time. He knew that if he fucked Antonov around now, he wasn't in a very good place to defend himself.

"They've got me over a fucking barrel, Pavel. If I don't help them get you then I'm going to the can for being an accessory to murder. What would you do? I don't have a fucking choice," he screamed from the dirt strewn floor. "They filmed the whole night back at that house in Faraday Street. They've got witnesses. You're on your own."

Ricky Bobrov never saw the kick coming, but when Antonov's boot sunk deep into his unprotected gut, it took all the strength and breath out of him. Antonov began to scream down at him.

"I knew something was going on when my associates at the Consulate disappeared into thin air. You and one other are the only two who could go up to court against me for that piece of shit, Toscano. You and that politician, Bird," Antonov said as he began to laugh.

Bobrov gradually regained his breath as he watched Antonov pace around the filthy room. He knew he had probably signed his own death warrant by talking, but Antonov would have beaten it out of him eventually. He was waiting for the next outburst from the now incensed Russian when suddenly he was grabbed by his pinned arms, dragged across the floor and pulled painfully down a flight of wooden steps then thrown on the floor in what appeared to be some sort of cellar.

"No one will hear you in here, Ricky. This is a solid brick wine cellar with a steel door. You will get air in here but that is all. You are going to get a bullet in the head but not until I execute your friend. It might take a day or two to get him here, but I'll give you an extra minute of life while you watch his brains splatter all over the walls. Once I have gotten rid of both of you, there will be no more of your so-called fucking witnesses. Wait with the rats."

"If you are talking about Bird, you won't get anywhere near him. They are covering him the whole time," Bobrov said as he tried unsuccessfully to sit upright on the brick floor.

"Not when he gets an invite back to a Russian morning tea. That's a solo trip, Ricky. See you in a couple of days after the rats have had a nibble on you."

Chapter Forty-Three

Tony Signorotto was leaving nothing to chance in trying to find Ricky Bobrov. The next day he had the members from the previous meeting out along Swanston Street keeping an eye on all the street beggars. Phil Stone had given him extra patrols, and everyone had been briefed at Carlton early that morning. Now it was just a matter of waiting, and that was where the veteran police officer had little patience. It was a matter of hurry up and wait, the mantra of every police officer world-wide. Stone and Signorotto realised it would be a late afternoon pick up because the amount of money wouldn't be worth it till then.

They knew they were taking a risk because any of the crews that jumped on some person or persons that were getting close with any of the beggars would cause the operation to be shut down if they didn't get the right man. The beggars would know the type of person who would be doing the daily pick-ups, so the members really had to keep an open mind in case they didn't grab some poor fool who had sat down with one of the scammers just to 'feel his lifestyle' or some such woke crap.

The one thing they all knew was that Bobrov and Antonov had started from the south end of the city on their last walk, so Stone and Signorotto had decided that most likely whoever it would be that did the pick-up, they probably weren't going to come quietly, therefore they would put two teams on the first beggar. Mick York and Johnny Petran were a given duo for this because they were both big, strong and very good undercover officers. As a backup, Chloe Schaeffer and Paul Romano would be there.

Shortly after eight in the morning, Schaeffer and Romano had noticed an Asian male taking up a seated position on the bricks in Federation Square in a perfect location to scam anyone coming up from the river walk who was headed through Federation Square to the city centre. Within minutes he had started his routine of bowing towards his begging bowl and offering a nodding head in thanks. An hour later, the scam artist was transferring all the money from the bowl into a large hessian carry bag that he kept around his shoulder with the bag itself in his lap. Schaeffer got on the radio to Signorotto. They had all been given radio call signs and she used her given one of Carlton 230.

"Carlton 230 to Carlton 210." Signorotto replied immediately.

"210 here Chloe, what is it?"

"Boss, we all think the pick-ups will be much later in the day but our beggar here in Fed Square has already taken a heap of money and transferred it into his bag. If ours is like the others, this is one big money taking scheme over a day."

"210, you are right, but I'd expect it to slow down a bit after about nine when all the office workers are at work. Probably kick off again around twelve and then again about five for an hour. Stand by and I'll talk to everyone." Schaeffer acknowledged.

"Carlton 210 to all units. If your targets are taking in a fair bit, I can't see any of these beggars just getting up and leaving, at least not till after the lunch crowds have gone. I reckon there will probably be a second shift or some kind of rotation going on. Even these guys must eat and go to the toilet. They can't sit in the same place all day. The punters are stupid but not that stupid that they'll give more money to the same person on their way home. Keep your eyes peeled because I think it will be a long day, folks."

As the day wore on and all the begging locations had been spotted, it became obvious to the members working that this was indeed a huge money taking racket. The Command team of Stone, Signorotto and McLaren had been told by Schaeffer and Romano that after about two hours, a new beggar had taken over the Federation Square position and Chloe had followed the first one to where he took over at the second location outside the Town Hall. This swap-over was repeated right up through the city until the last beggar up near Melbourne University had left his bag with his replacement and walked off to where he caught a tram.

All the members gave back the same information that the beggars went to toilets and food places on their link up walks. This was a well-run scheme that was obviously taking in thousands of dollars.

Stone, Signorotto and McLaren grabbed a bite to eat at The Quarter Cafe in Degraves Street near Flinders Street station and discussed the day so far. Kate led the conversation.

"Antonov must have something over all these little beggars. They're like little robots. Beg, take money, beg, take money. On and on for hours and the only break you get is a quick bowl of rice or such and then repeat everything in a new location. I think you're right, Tony, this will go on till about six, so the money pick up won't be till at least five thirty. What do you think?"

Between mouthfuls of smokey bacon, Cypriot haloumi, sheftalies and field mushrooms, Signorotto managed to reply.

"I've been thinking about this operation all day, Kate. If Antonov is lying low and we take his collectors in, he won't get any report back from them at the end of the day unless we force their hand back at the station. We've got to get one of his collectors to let him know how much they've taken. He will already have told them what to do with the money. If we grab them, say at the first beggar, we create the situation of not collecting the other beggars' takings. What we must do is be right on our toes so that when it happens at the last beggar, we pounce after the bag man walks away. That way the beggars will go about whatever they do, we have the money and whoever picks it up." Stone held up his hand to interrupt.

"Yes, but we risk the situation of the beggars coming back tomorrow and having no-one to pick up from them. I know this may put Bobrov at risk but as the Commander, I have to look at a much bigger picture. What I'm saying is that we are going to have to grab each one of these beggars after they finish. To my mind I reckon they must all live in some sort of commune somewhere. With the last one though, we follow him to wherever they live. Tony, get Johnny Petran onto that. At the end of the day, and I know it's going to be a long one, we need the whole Dog and Pony show back at Carlton. Kate, get onto headquarters and arrange for a Chinese interpreter to be at Carlton tonight. I reckon these poor beggars have a big axe over their heads and I think Antonov, or his group, are holding it and they're threatening them with it. I know you feel bad about Bobrov Tony, but I am at the pointy end of the ship, and we must move on this in a bigger way than just him."

Tony Signorotto looked at his good friend and slowly pushed his plate away without finishing what was on it.

"I know you're right, Phil but I am determined to find Ricky alive. It's all very well having this business sanctioned with the top floor, but all of us at Carlton live in the valley and the shit will flow downhill at a fast pace if anything happens to Bobrov. You and I both know it."

The three members rose from the table and made their way back to the room they had borrowed from the long-time lessee of the Princes Bridge hotel, which was known more to Melbournians as Young and Jackson's. From up there they had a view north along Swanston Street past Federation Square and to the north down to the Melbourne Town Hall.

It was now coming down to the wire. Antonov had to make some sort of move.

The day wore on.

Chapter Forty-Four

The crews that were out looking for the scammer's bagmen were tired and getting more tired. Even Tony Signorotto and Phil Stone were becoming disillusioned as the clock passed five-thirty in the afternoon. Kate McLaren had radioed through to all the patrols and had got a negative result from them all regarding the sighting of any money pick-ups. In the last hour, she had swapped some of the members around in an effort to keep them on their toes. Even the keenest sets of eyes were getting tired. She turned to Signorotto.

"Even with the overtime at the moment, boss, I think we're running on fumes with a few members. What time do you want to run them through to?"

Signorotto and Stone had been discussing this point between themselves and had decided that six-thirty would be the cut off point. After that, the bulk of the working crowd would have already been on their trains and trams and well on their way home, if not there already.

"We won't go past six-thirty, Kate. Jump on the radio and tell everyone that will be stumps time," a disappointed sounding Signorotto said.

Kate picked up the portable radio and was just about to hit the transmit button when Max Tyler's urgent sounding voice cut over the airwaves.

"Carlton 215 urgent."

"Go ahead 215," McLaren said immediately.

"We've got movement at Fed Square. Two salty looking dudes in black have just walked up and started emptying Number One's bag into a big backpack. Where are our DRU boys?"

Kate knew she didn't have to reply. Johnny Petran and Mick York would be all over this. They were about to be let off their prospective leashes.

"Carlton 220. We've got them in sight walking towards us. Carlton 230, your location for backup?"

"Carlton 230, we're coming into Fed Square from Flinders Street. We have a visual on you and those two serious looking boys in black."

"Roger that, 230. We aren't mucking about here. These two are going down on the bricks. Need you quickly to grab the bag and then grab the scammer."

Phil Stone and Tony Signorotto both had binoculars on Fed Square. They watched as the two dudes realised that they were in trouble. Both tried to dodge past Petran and York without any success. Mick York grabbed one in a headlock as the crook tried to outmanoeuvre him. Dude One's legs flew up parallel to the bricks and then he suddenly came crashing to the earth with a thud. York flipped him over like a rag doll and had handcuffs on him before he knew what hit him. Dude Two didn't have much more luck with a dodging move, although he was a bit quicker than his partner in crime. He was not to know that the Johnny Petran had played a lot of Australian Rules football in his time. Petran simply planted his left foot on the bricks and dropped the left shoulder of his big frame as the second one tried to brush him aside. It was never going to be a success for the boy in black. Running into Petran's shoulder was like running flat out into a brick wall. He crumpled to the ground, dropping the bag full of cash in an effort to grab his possible shirt full of broken ribs. Paul Romano arrived and did the honours this time and turned Number two over, cuffed him and left him lying face down on the bricks face to face with his groaning partner. Vic Pol 1: Russians nil.

Both Stone and Signorotto put down their binoculars and smiled at each other.

"Just the way I would have handled the situation, Phil," a beaming Signorotto said to a totally shocked looking Phil Stone who managed to give the classic reply.

"In your dreams, mate. You're getting your past mixed up with today's reality. They would have kicked your arse and laughed about it all the way up Swanston Street. Now let's get everyone rounded up, Kate."

"On it, boss," Kate said grabbing the radio handpiece. "Carlton 100 to all units. Message from Commander Stone. All units to move in immediately on your targets. All to be cuffed and taken to nearest Police car and transported back to Carlton. Carlton 220, Johnny Petran. You hearing me?" Kate said anxiously.

"Loud and clear. Let's get them all back to the station but first I want all mobile phones taken from them. Confiscate them and keep the beggars away from the two goons we got. The interpreter will be there so let's get started," an excited Petran said.

Stone and Signorotto couldn't see it, but there were police cars pulling to the kerb right up Swanston Street with members getting out, speaking to all the beggars and quietly ushering them into the rear of the cars after being thoroughly searched and cuffed.

Kate McLaren raced downstairs to the exit of Young and Jackson's, fired up their car and headed off quickly after Stone and Signorotto climbed aboard.

"Kate, when we get back, hop on the phone to Dom Santino at his restaurant and organise for meal packs to be delivered to the station for the troops as soon as he can. Get him to go to the Malaysian place up in Grattan Street and get a heap of food for the Asians. We are going to feed them and look after them. I know we're tired but let's nail these pricks that have been preying on them."

Chapter Forty-Five

Three hours later, Max Tyler walked out of the interview room where he had been interrogating one of the two Russians that had been taken from Federation Square. He looked angry and tired.

"Don't know about how you went with the other one boss, but this one is a brick wall. Name rank and serial number only. Obviously ex-Russian military or something. He is quite happy to be done for possession of the money from the first Asian scammer but that isn't going to faze him. He's as hard as nails."

"Might have got a bit further with the second one," Ted Conlon replied. "This boy wants to stay in Australia at any cost. He just wants immunity from any prosecution and a new identity because he is Russian mafia. I'll have to make a few phone calls, but I think if we give him what he wants we could end up helping the Feds big time."

Phil Stone, Tony Signorotto and Kate McLaren were all listening intently to what Conlon was saying.

"What's he going to give up that the Feds will want that we can't give them? After all, we have them on the money and the Asian scammers. We've shut down the operation here in Melbourne," Kate said.

"Yes, but these two goons are from Sydney. My guy is singing like a bird and will also give up all he knows on the same operation they are running in up there. Apparently, it's even bigger than this one. The Feds will have it handed it to them on a platter. Even they couldn't stuff this up," Conlon said with a smile on his face.

Tony Signorotto jumped into the conversation.

"That's all good Ted, but I want information on Ricky first up. Has he said anything about Bobrov or Antonov?"

"I thought I'd leave that to you, Tony. With the uniform it will be a bit more intimidating. Go and have a crack at him but remember the big picture, too."

Signorotto got up immediately, walked over to the interview room door and threw it open. It banged loudly on the wall inside causing the young Russian's head to snap upwards.

"The suits are interested in what you have to say about this scamming set up, but I am more interested in why you came down to Melbourne," Signorotto said as he placed his two beefy hands on the interview table and stood towering over the prisoner.

"I told the detective everything. I was sent down here with Boris to take over the money collection. I was looking for a way out of everything, but I was just doing it till I had a chance to disappear. What else can I tell you?"

"Let's start with who called you down here?"

"The Sydney bosses told us to meet up with a Pavel Antonov and give him any help he wanted. What he wanted was to grab the person he was with outside some address. Boris and I thought it would be a hit job. We grabbed him and we thought he wanted us to knock him and dump the body but when it came to it, we just gave him a needle to knock him out and then he wanted him put in the boot of his car. He didn't want him killed at all, not by us anyhow. We did that and then he told us the bosses wanted us to take over the money collections in Melbourne for a few days until we got orders from Sydney."

Signorotto desperately wanted an answer to his next question.

"The guy you put in the boot, what did he look like? How was he dressed?"

The description he got was identical to Ricky right down to the clothes he was wearing on the CCTV footage from the Bourke Street mall.

Chapter Forty-Five

"Think real hard here, son. Where did he take him?"

"Do I get what I want out of this?" the handcuffed male said.

"You give me what I want right now you lowlife little prick or you'll not only go down for the charges from Federation Square, but I'll also make sure that when you hit gaol, your Russian *Bratva* associates will know exactly what cell and bunk you will be hiding in. I've got no hesitation about throwing you to the wolves for this, so you tell me where the man in the boot is or you are fucked," a savage sounding Tony Signorotto said to the now sweating face of the prisoner.

"All I know is that he said he was taking him to some house nearby that had been forgotten."

"Nearby? Where did you meet him?"

"Some apartment block in Carlton."

Signorotto's patience snapped at that point. He lifted the prisoner out of his seat and slammed him up against the concrete wall of the interview room.

"One last fucking chance. Where in Carlton?"

A now terrified prisoner stammered an answer.

"It was a street like Windley, Dinley, I don't know. Boris got us there."

"Finley! Was it Finley?" Signorotto shouted as his brain did a Goggle search of similar sounding Carlton streets.

"Yeah, yeah. That's it. A big brick apartment block. We met him around the back."

Signorotto threw the prisoner back into his chair as he turned towards the door.

"Do I get a deal from this?" the blubbering, handcuffed figure said loudly.

"I never promised you anything. Some suit might have, but not me, and you won't get the chance to give him any more information because I have what I want so he'll probably never speak to you again. He was a Detective Inspector, but you will now spill your guts to a Detective Sergeant. You'd better tell him everything about everything if you hope that he will mention your little deal back to his boss. Personally, I hope you do time, because while you're doing that, some of those poor migrants that your mob has been treating like slaves will be getting their own lives back. I'm sure our government would rather help them than you. But then, I'm only a street cop who detests stand-over blokes like you. I'd think the best you could hope for is a single cell," Signorotto said, knowing full well that the little piece of shit would be handed everything by the Feds so they could wrap it all up with a nice big bow.

Chapter Forty-Six

Pavel Antonov's mind was made up. The only way for him not to be charged with the murder of Marco Toscano was to eliminate the witnesses. Simple. Brutal, but simple. After all, what was another body or two? Antonov had been raised by parents who dished out punishment for any misdemeanour whatsoever. The worst was not picking enough pockets in his Russian hometown of Myshkin on the Volga River. Severe beatings were given out by both his mother and father to himself and his five siblings if the day's pickings were too lean.

He remembered well the day he turned fifteen and decided to spend it with some of his friends doing nothing but fooling around smoking stolen Troika cigarettes and drinking cheap homemade vodka. Hang the consequences. Those consequences were a brutal beating from his alcoholic father that was so bad that Antonov junior vowed revenge if and when he got out of the hospital. His mother had dumped him in with the story that he had been beaten up in the local park.

Three weeks later, Pavel Antonov stood over the snoring prostrate figure of his father in the front room of the hovel they called home. He made sure he partially woke the drunken figure, so he knew what was about to happen. His fathers' eyes bulged in horror as Pavel yanked his head back and proceed to slice his throat open from ear to ear with his own cheap cutthroat razor. As his father tried to stem the never-ending flow of blood from his throat with dirty, shaking hands, Pavel stepped in front of him and smiled. After wiping the blade on his father's shirt and listening to the last gurgling attempts of his breathing, Antonov junior picked up an old backpack with some clothes in it and walked out the back door never to be seen again.

He knew the local police would never try and hunt him down for two good reasons, the first being that Pavel had the names of many officers he was giving kickbacks to so he could continue to steal, pickpocket and sell drugs in his town. The second reason was that his father was a well-known and unpopular peasant whose reputation as a bully preceded him. In death all you got was a pauper's grave and little else, let alone a real investigation by a Police Force that was corrupt and undermanned.

With that memory pushed aside, Antonov sat in the driver's seat of an old Saab he had stolen the day after leaving Ricky Bobrov in the cellar of the rundown and forgotten house.

He was in the act of following the government car of Steve Bird from one meeting to another. Bird had a white BMW at his disposal because he was a Minister of the State. He also had a full-time driver who would take the car home at night, which was in one way convenient, but it meant that he was on-call twenty-four hours a day.

It had been easy to find out where Bird was going on his daily drives because through a contact inside Parliament House who liked the occasional party pack of drugs, he got access to his daily schedule. It wasn't where he was going that interested Antonov, he wanted to see the routine of his driver. Like most chauffer drivers, he presumed he would probably lock the car up and head off to a nearby café or TAB to sip a latte and have a quick punt on the horses.

Antonov knew that the third meeting Bird was attending was at the very top of the skyscraper he was entering. It was a routine monthly meeting of the State Gaming Board that was, according to his schedule, meant to take approximately one hour. As Antonov looked at the government car, the driver got in and did a U-turn into a side alley where it was quiet. Antonov smiled to himself as he knew the driver stood no risk of getting a parking ticket as all the parking wardens in the city had a list of government cars that were impervious to infringement notices. Bird's was one. The driver got out and without turning, held the remote backwards, hitting the lock button. The next hour was his, as Antonov, who had parked in a legal zone, lifted a small set of binoculars and saw a copy of the daily horse racing form guide. Little did the driver know what a rude shock he was in for on his return.

Overriding the lock code was a piece of cake for Antonov as he already had the small piece of illegal equipment in his pocket. The Black Market was alive and well. He gave the driver a good fifteen minutes before he got out of the stolen car and walked up to the nearside door of Bird's car, hitting the silent button of the override lock opener causing the indicator lights to flash on three times instead of the usual two. With unusual manoeuvrability for a man of his size, he slipped into the back door, closed it and waited behind the darkened windows for the return of the driver.

Twenty-five minutes passed before his victim returned, completely unaware of the fate that was awaiting him. Antonov heard the double beep of the alarm followed very quickly by the opening of the driver's door. When it closed he went to work.

Chapter Forty-Seven

Antonov quickly reached over the driver's seat and looped the leather garotte over the unsuspecting driver's head, causing several fifty-dollar notes along with the Form Guide to jump out of his hand in surprise.

Pity you won't enjoy your last win, Antonov thought as he tightened his grip around the man's neck. He knew exactly how much pressure to apply and for how long. This job had to be quick as he looked at the driver's eyes bulge in their sockets and his fingers try their hardest to get under the leather thong. When it was over, Antonov climbed through between the front seats and propped the driver up straight before going through his pockets for his phone then quickly removing his jacket and putting it on himself. The fit wasn't perfect, but it would be good enough to fool someone approaching the car as the security shaded windows kept visibility coming in to a minimum. He let the dead man slump across to the console and then with a mighty effort manoeuvred him into the rear of the vehicle and lay him on the floor. It had only taken a few minutes all up.

He pressed the ignition button and did a U-turn in the tight alleyway before taking up a park outside the building Bird had entered earlier. Antonov spent the next minute picking up the murdered man's money, folding it neatly and placing it in his top pocket. Death meant nothing to him, but money did.

He didn't have to wait too long for the politician to emerge from the building. Bird hesitated for a fraction of a second as he neared the front of the car, then with an angry look, grabbed hold of the front passenger handle, threw the door open and spoke loudly as he sat in it with his back to the driver and slammed the door.

"One of your jobs as a driver is to make sure you open the car door for me. After all, I am the Minister, not the hired help. You understand?" Bird said before turning to look at his driver.

"What's going…" he managed to say before staring down at the body behind the front seats. As he looked up, all he could see was the blue metallic end of the barrel of a pistol pointed between his legs. As the gun was drawn back ever so slightly, Bird's vision ran from the pistol, along the arm of the holder and focussed on the face of the gunman. He realised two things straightway. The first was that he knew exactly who was holding the gun. It was the big Russian from the card night, Antonov! The second thing was that he knew he was in deep shit. He opened his mouth to speak, but the gun barrel was suddenly jammed into his mouth, causing him to gag at the same time as one of his bottom front teeth was flattened like a headstone in an old cemetery. He was forced into the front passenger foot well by the force of Antonov. He knew people on the outside of the car couldn't see through the specially darkened five-millimetre-thick security glass that had been installed on all the Ministerial cars. He waited. He waited and shook. He waited and shook and felt a warm sensation soaking through the crotch of his expensive suit pants. He had pissed himself.

"We are going for a drive, Mr. Bird. Do not move from that position. Understand?" a quiet Antonov said.

Bird tried to answer but nothing came out of his mouth. He was literally about to pass out with fear. By the look of his official driver's twisted body, he knew he was dead. The only thing that kept him from slumping down any further was the pistol, as he saw the driver flip the gun backwards as the butt suddenly collected him on the side of his head. Blood flowed freely down onto his white shirt.

"Mr. Politician man. You should have walked away from that night and forgotten me. Now because you have poked the bear, you will have to pay the price," the smiling Russian said as he restarted the car and drove off slowly, holding the steering wheel with one hand while he aimed the snout of the Makarov nine-millimetre pistol at Bird's head as he shook and sweated in the passenger foot well.

"What have I got to do with anything, Pavel?"

"You would have had a better argument if you hadn't visited Dimitry Lebedev, my friend. There are two things I now must do."

Bird hesitated as he tried to stem the blood flowing from his pounding head.

"What?" he said hesitantly.

"Get rid of two witnesses. Excuse my sense of humour but I now can kill two birds with one stone."

Bird made a feeble attempt at rising himself from the floor but was blown backwards by another blow to his already injured head.

"A short drive and we will have a nice reunion with the other witness. Sadly, for you both it will be a very short reunion."

Chapter Forty-Eight

Phil Stone and Tony Signorotto stared at the grid map that Chloe Schaeffer had put on the notice board in the upstairs office. All they could go on was what the prisoner downstairs had told them and that was Ricky Bobrov had been taken to an 'empty forgotten house'.

The rest of the crew consisting of Max Tyler, Paul Romano, Johnny Petran and Mick York were hunched over the main table looking at a much larger laminated version of the Melways map that had been rolled out. Stone turned to the entire office. Beside him was Ted Conlon.

"I know we all have our own ideas about Bobrov's location, but I have called in a favour with one person who I think may be able to help us out. Kate is bringing him upstairs now."

Just as he finished speaking, Kate McLaren walked through the door with an Italian looking man in his sixties dressed in a very expensive suit. His smile lit up the room when he saw his old friends Phil Stone and Tony Signorotto.

"Phil, Tony. So great to see you," the happy looking individual said as the others looked on a little bemused. Phil Stone spoke.

"Okay everyone. This man knows every nook and cranny of the housing market in Carlton. This is Carlo Genessi, owner of Genessi Real Estate. You may know him as the man who so generously gave us permission to keep using his house in Faraday Street for the sting involving Ricky Bobrov. I've taken the liberty of telling Carlo what's going on and the fact that we need to pinpoint this house that our boy downstairs says Antonov has him in. I'll hand over to you Carlo."

A much more business-like and serious Carlo Genessi stood near the grid map on the wall.

"Thanks Phil. Thanks Tony. If this individual said that your friend is in a house that has been forgotten, then it will be a house that first off is not for sale and secondly, I would say that it is a house that has been partly renovated and not finished or a house that has been partly renovated and funds have run out because of the downturn in the economy. There are quite a few of these, but apparently, he also indicated that it was a big, empty and forgotten house. I know all the old big empty houses in Carlton, and I don't forget any of them. I've narrowed it down to three," he said as he took a Sharpie pen from Chloe Schaefer and made three circles on the laminated map before continuing.

"The first is a house called Manresa which is in Loyola Avenue. Not quite Carlton but just off Glenlyon Road in Brunswick. Has had work done on it up until about a month ago but is presently under a court order because some of the guys working on it haven't been paid for months. The CFMEU have basically shut it down until the money flows again. A possibility. The second is a place near here called Krinclafold House. The address is 875 Rathdowne Street. Renovations stopped more than a year ago and it has fallen into disrepair. Pity, because it could be magnificent. Has an underground wine cellar that you could park a car in. Builder by the name of Perkins went bust and there are a lot of people interested in it. I'm hovering around because it would sell for a fortune with the right renovations done. The third has been renovated but it is empty at the moment. Price is way too high even for Carlton. It's up at 105 Pigdon Street. Looks like crap on the outside but has been done up beautifully on the inside. Been empty except for show furniture for about three months. I think the neighbours would have known though if there was activity at it."

"Nowhere else that stand out, Carlo?" Phil Stone said.

"No, nothing else that falls into the old and forgotten bracket, sorry Phil."

"No need for an apology, Carlo. This might narrow it down completely. Thanks for coming in on such short notice."

"Pleasure my friends. Having a bit of a function up at Dom's in a few weeks. Opening another shop which will cover Brunswick. Hopefully you can all come along. We'll talk later, Phil," Carlo said as he headed out the door. Stone and Signorotto waved back in appreciation.

Ted Conlon indicated for everyone to come over to the rolled-out map with the three circles on it as Signorotto spoke.

"Look crew, I know it is late but if we don't jump on this now it may be too late for Ricky. I am splitting you into three crews so we can hit the three premises at once. I want you, Johnny, along with Mick and anyone else you have to go to that Manresa House in Loyola Avenue. Go right over it. Talk to the neighbours and check it out. Max, you, Chloe and I will get over to that one in Rathdowne Street, Krinclafold House and check out that cellar. That leaves the one in Pigdon Street. Kate, if I could ask you to go with Inspector Conlon. Probably won't be any good but you never know. I know what a nose Carlo has for the area because his family comes from around here like mine did. He knows everything there is to know about property in Carlton. Paul, if you could stay here and maintain a radio call sign log and assist Commander Stone with anything he needs. All of you tool up and make sure you have comms with you and be careful. Right, let's go," Signorotto said loudly as he headed towards the gun safe.

Chapter Forty-Nine

The first unit to call in the all clear on one of the premises was Kate McLaren and Ted Conlon.

It was obvious when they arrived that one thing Carlo had forgotten to mention or didn't realise that at night, the inside of the premises was lit up like a Christmas tree for advertising reasons. They did a U-turn and headed back to the station.

Meanwhile, Tony Signorotto and his young team were approaching their targeted premises.

"Bit like a needle in a haystack," Chloe Schaeffer said from the rear seat.

"Yes, Chloe but we might just get lucky. We'd be searching Carlton on a grid pattern for days otherwise. Remember, this Russian prick is dangerous. We are taking no chances, so that is why I brought an extra friend with me," Signorotto said as he pulled out a short double-barrelled shot gun from under his seat. Attached to the butt was a leather strap holding six shotgun cartridges. The barrel gave off a mean looking blue tint as Max drove under each streetlight. "I owe it to Ricky to sort this out and if it means using resources that aren't in the Department's arsenal then so be it." Max Tyler looked sideways at his old boss and could see the hard-set jaw. This man meant business.

Max Tyler pulled up near the house in Rathdowne Street. It certainly had an abandoned look to it. The front yard was a monument to rusty scaffolding which was surrounded by large weed patches and knocked over rubbish bins. There were also two big mounds of hard-set concrete on wooden pallets in the yard near the gate.

"Looks like it was abandoned in a hurry," Max said to no-one in particular.

"I would say, after months of wages haggling, the CFMEU have hit the site and told everyone to down tools, even if it was in the middle of a concrete pour," Signorotto said quietly. Max, you and Chloe take a look down the alleyway and see if there is any sort of backyard with this place. I'm going to have a look up the street."

Tony Signorotto had got less than fifty metres from the building when his phone lit up. It was Max calling him.

"Yes Max, what is it?" a surprised Signorotto replied.

"Boss, there's a State Government BMW down here in the yard and there's a body in it."

Signorotto stopped dead in his tracks.

"A what?" Signorotto replied.

"We have it here in the back yard of the address we've been given. Can't see much else but the bonnet is warm. Registered number is 1ZP 656. The driver's licence comes up to a Michael Declan. Looks like he's been strangled or garrotted. How do you want to do this?"

"Is there any way in through the back?"

"There's a lot of entry points where the brickwork has only been partially started, but I can't tell where the openings lead to."

"Okay, stay there but keep out of sight. I'm jumping on the radio to get some help."

Signorotto had walked back quickly to the front of the house and was reaching for his portable radio when he saw an elderly man standing in the front yard of the house next door yelling out to him.

"About time the police did something about all the kids playing next door," he screamed, indicating the suspect house. "They get in there and smoke pot and all sorts of things. There's someone in there now in the cellar getting up to who knows what."

Chapter Forty-Nine

Signorotto jumped the front fence and dragged the man back to his front door.

"I want you to be quiet. Get back inside and stay there. They aren't kids in there, understand?" he said as he pressed the transmit button on the radio.

"Carlton 250 to Phil Stone. Come in. Urgent."

Seconds passed and he was about to transmit again when Stone answered.

"What's happening over there? I've been listening. I'm getting Paul to ring through to the Parliament House garage and find out who the car should be allotted to."

"Roger that. I need an answer ASAP, Phil, and get the SOG rolled out. Carlton 250 to the DRU. Get over to our house quick as you can. This is going to go pear-shaped real quick I think."

Johnny Petran didn't mince words. "ETA less than five minutes. We've got two shotties with us."

A shiver went down Signorotto's spine. It was a while since he had been on the front line with the troops.

"Max, stay out of sight and let me know if you see anything. Got the DRU on the way with some heavy shooters. Get back to you when they get here."

"Thanks, boss," the quiet reply came back. "Standing by."

Less than a minute later, Signorotto's radio blared. It was Phil Stone.

"Tony, Steve Bird hasn't turned up at Parliament and his car and driver can't be found. That registration is locked out to him. The SOG are rolling so just stay where you are.

Chapter Fifty

Pavel Antonov had both Ricky Bobrov and Steve Bird on their knees in the basement of Krinclafold House in Faraday Street. His mind was made up about one thing and that was that he had to eliminate any witnesses to the death of Marco Toscano. An old-fashioned style bullet between the eyes seemed the right way to accomplish that.

"I think maybe you can go first," he said to the beaten Bobrov as Bird began to cry as he knelt next to the crooked cop. The only light coming into the basement was from the stairwell which led up to the first floor and the front door which was illuminated by a street light.

"Why me Pavel? I want to join you. I want to work with you," the dishevelled Bobrov pleaded.

Bobrov had been tied up and lying in the dirt of the old basement with rats running over him. They had nibbled at his face and hands which were covered in bites and congealed blood.

"I saw you with those undercover cops, Ricky. No way have you left the Force. You were just trying to set me up. For that you die," Antonov said as he pointed an automatic pistol at the bowed head of Bobrov. Bird started to yell.

"I was just a player at the card night, Pavel. We've played cards together at these nights for a long time. What have I done?" Bird pleaded.

"My associates just disappeared after you visited Dimitry Lebedev. Do you think that I believe you are not in on a plan to frame me also?" the ranting Russian exploded. "You will be just another politician that no-one will miss."

Neither hostage said anything as Antonov stepped up and put the barrel of the pistol against the back of Bobrov's head.

As quickly as he put it there, he lowered the firearm and looked quickly to his right as he heard a man yelling from next door. He lashed out with his foot and kicked both Bobrov and Bird backwards onto the rubbish strewn floor, then he quickly ran over to a partially bricked up window and peered through just in time to see two armed people, one male and one female retreat behind a low brick wall. Antonov spun around and flattened himself against a wall.

Fucking police. How the fuck?

He then crept up and looked out of the filthy front room window. There was no-one there, but he knew an unmarked Police car when he saw one.

Police front and back!

His only possibility of escape was to get rid of one hostage. Question was, who was more valuable as a hostage, a cop or a politician. He didn't know how he had been found but that was unimportant now. He had got out of Russia as a cold-blooded killer, so he just had to apply the same process now. He quickly retreated down to the basement and picked up Bird by the arm.

"You and I are taking a drive but first I must get rid of some unwanted baggage," Antonov said as he stood to one side, grabbed hold of Bobrov and threw him into a corner. Bending down he grabbed a large bunch of rags that had been left on the floor, wrapped the barrel of the pistol in them and held it against Bobrov's chest. The sound that the gun made was muffled completely. Bobrov's eyes widened as he slumped backwards, hands tied behind him. He lay still with blood trickling out of his chest. Bird immediately vomited.

Antonov held the pistol between Bird's shoulder blades and shoved him out of the basement and up to the ground floor. He dragged him around to where he could get a glimpse of the two police in the backyard. It was now or never. The darkened back yard helped.

He kicked open the flimsy entrance from what was the rear kitchen into the backyard and as he did, he yelled loudly as the two officers spun in his direction. They could immediately see a gun being held to the hostage's head in the beam of their torches.

"Put both your pistols down and get your hands in the air away from your radios. Do it fucking now or Bird dies."

Max Tyler and Chloe Schaeffer knew there was no alternative. They didn't know who or how many people there were in the building.

"Antonov, don't be stupid. That's a Government Minister you've got at gunpoint. You won't get away with it," Tyler said loudly all the while thinking of what had possibly happened to Ricky Bobrov.

"I want you to throw your guns behind the brick wall along with both your radios and torches now. Do anything stupid and Bird dies right here."

Both members did as they were told and then stepped away from the white BMW.

"Lie on the ground with your arms out."

Not having any other option, they both spreadeagled themselves but faced each other.

"There is already one dead cop in the house so if you two want to live just lie there and do nothing while we drive away."

The two members looked directly at each other taking in the words Antonov had just spoken. He had to be referring to Bobrov.

Antonov backed Bird up to the passenger door, opened it and shoved his hostage into the front seat after coldclocking him with his gun. Bird slumped unconscious into the footwell as Antonov raced around and got in behind the driver's seat before firing up the white vehicle.

Spinning the car around, he aimed it at the entrance to the alleyway just as he saw the business end of the short-barrelled shot gun pointing at the front windscreen from only about three metres away. At the trigger end was Tony Signorotto.

"Stop right there. I will have no hesitation in pulling the trigger," an enraged Tony Signorotto said from the narrow entrance to the rear of the site.

Antonov took no notice and gunned the car. He closed the distance to Signorotto. The last thing Antonov or Signorotto remembered was that neither Italian nor Russian blood would back down.

Chapter Fifty-One

As Antonov hit the accelerator and the car lurched forward, Signorotto leapt to the driver's side and fired both barrels at the side window. He had loaded the shotgun with full penetrating cartridges, but the blast only had the effect of basically sandblasting the windows. Signorotto lay on the ground as the BMW fishtailed out of the backyard entrance and turned left at full speed. He hauled himself off the ground, shotgun in one hand and stared at the back of the car as it disappeared up alongside the building and then turned left into Faraday Street. Tyler and Schaeffer ran to him. Signorotto gasped out some words.

"Those shells should have punched right through his window. What the fuck?"

"That's Bird's government car, boss. If it's a Minister's car, it'll have thickened bullet proof glass. All those Beamers are built around protecting the principal occupant," Tyler said.

"Christ yes," Signorotto said as he stood and brushed dirt off him. "Just wish the DRU boys were here. They could have blocked him in."

Just as Signorotto finished speaking, A frantic radio call came over the airways.

"DRU to anyone. In pursuit of that white BMW. Headed south along Rathdowne Street towards the city. Don't think we'll be able to keep up with him at this stage. Way too dangerous."

Phil Stone came up on the air immediately.

"Call it off everyone. No night chases. That car will have a tracker in it. I'll get onto the appropriate parties from here. I want everyone back here ASAP."

Both the DRU and Signorotto replied in the affirmative before continuing.

"Phil, we are going inside this building. Max has said that Antonov only came out with Bird and that the body in the car was the driver. That leaves Ricky Bobrov unaccounted for."

"I want updates, Tony."

"Roger that."

Signorotto led Tyler and Schaeffer through the opening that Antonov had escaped through. "Do the ground floor you two and I'll get down to the basement."

Moments later, Max and Chloe heard their boss scream from the basement.

"Get on the radio now and get an ambulance here. Bobrov's here and just alive. Tell them it's a member been shot. Sucking chest wound and bad."

"We'll do it from here, Tony," Stone replied urgently.

Max Tyler and Chloe Schaeffer hurried down to the basement where they saw Signorotto cradling the head of Ricky Bobrov. Blood was spreading across the chest of the prone figure.

Max Tyler immediately ripped his shirt off and pressed it down hard on Bobrov's chest to stem the flow of blood. Signorotto called to Schaeffer.

"Chloe, get outside and wait for the ambulance. We've given it over as a member down so they'll drop everything and send at least two. Get them in here quick."

Schaeffer raced outside through to the alleyway and sprinted up to the front of the house.

Minutes passed like hours before she heard the wail of multiple sirens as two ambulances tore down the street. She waved at them and then ran back down the alley and pointed them inside the back yard. Both crews jumped out as one of the ambulance crew called to her.

"What have we got?"

"Male, mid-thirties. Bullet wound to chest. Bad one. Have two members trying to stop the bleeding. Just follow me."

Laden with all their gear, the four ambulance officers hurried as quickly as they could through the debris strewn building, eventually arriving at the scene.

"Thanks guys. One of mine will take over the chest area, if you could step back now and leave us to it. Looks as though you've done as much as can at this stage. Let's hope it's enough," the lead ambulance member said as he and his colleagues went to work on the unconscious figure of Ricky Bobrov. All the police members stumbled back into the yard and sat down in the dark.

"You look like shit boss. How are you doing?" Chloe said.

Tony Signorotto looked around slowly at his two subordinate members.

"You didn't hear me say this, but I have unfinished business with Pavel Antonov. I need to make this right for Ricky. He's a dishonest cop alright but this Antonov is just an animal."

"Because he shot Ricky?" she said quietly.

"Not just because he shot him, Chloe, but because he shot him after tying his hands behind him. He wanted to execute Ricky. It's game on as far as I'm concerned," a dishevelled and angry Tony Signorotto replied through gritted teeth.

Chapter Fifty-Two

Phil Stone was fighting his hardest at Police Headquarters to try to stay in charge of the hunt for Pavel Antonov and his hostage Steve Bird. He knew without doubt that all the specialist groups from the SOG to the Anti-Terrorism Squad were champing at the bit to take over the situation and cover themselves in glory. The thing was that he wasn't interested in the kudos and the glory, just the job at hand trying to find them. After a tense stand-off in the Deputy Commissioner's office, he managed to keep control of the situation by stating they had been across the whole situation from the beginning. The Deputy Commissioner, an old associate of Stone eventually calmed the meeting of all the Department heads when he spoke.

"I'm leaving it with Commander Stone at this stage. Whatever he wants, he will get from all of you, no questions asked. Now let's all work together to resolve this. We have a state minister missing and a mad Russian holding him somewhere. All of you get your people out on the ground and get this done. No bitching, backstabbing or grandstanding. Just damn well do your jobs. Everyone's head is on the chopping block here and not just because a state election is coming up, but I can tell you, if this isn't fixed then we'll probably all be looking for new occupations. We all know this job is run by politics so get out there."

One by one various Superintendents, Inspectors and such filed out of the office. The Deputy Commissioner called out to Phil Stone.

"You stay, Commander. I have a few questions for you."

Phil Stone closed the door behind the last member, turned and slumped in the chair opposite the Deputy Commissioner and reached out with his right hand to receive the crystal tumbler of Glenfiddich scotch that his old friend was passing to him.

"Hope it's a double, mate," Stone said wearily.

Deputy Commissioner John Galbraith looked at Sone and spoke.

"First up, how is Ricky Bobrov doing?"

"It's been twenty-four hours now, but they reckon he'll pull through. Bullet went straight through, but he'll live."

"One big compensation payment coming his way. More if he sues. Don't know if it was the right decision sending him out as bait for Antonov. Could backfire badly, Phil."

"Yeah, I know John. Whatever way it goes with Bobrov, I'm taking the hit. This was my idea in the first place."

"You know the rules of the game, Phil. I'll back you all the way, but with an election…well, either political party will be trying to score points on this."

"That six-month road trip around Australia on long service leave and then a consultancy gig in the private sector is looming large."

Both men finished their drinks and Stone rose from his chair to leave. Galbraith spoke quietly. "Let's get this done first before we talk retirement, okay?"

Chapter Fifty-Three

Pavel Antonov had wasted no time in dumping the government BMW. He had kept to the back streets for hours with the terrified Steve Bird in the front passenger footwell. Eventually he hid the car in bushland in the eastern suburb of Warrandyte. He didn't care about the body of the driver in the back of the car, but he wasn't going to let go of his captive. He waited for daylight before making his next move.

Dragging and pushing the scared politician through a nature reserve in the early dawn he saw a Ford F350 utility on the side of the road with the front door open. Crouching down with Bird on the ground, he could see who he thought was the owner about seventy metres away brush cutting an overgrown paddock. Time to move. He pushed Bird over to the passenger side of the big ute, slowly opened the door and shoved him inside then ran around to the driver's side and jumped in. He was about to lean down and hot-wire the vehicle when to his amazement he saw the keys in the ignition. Looking back at the man brush cutting he could hear the loud noise that the machine was making, so he had no hesitation firing up the V8 beast, slamming the door and taking off. In the mirror, the man still had his back to his ute, so he would only realise later that his stupidity had cost him his wheels.

"Now to get out of this country," he said looking down at Bird.

"How? What will you do with me?"

"You will sky dive, but without a parachute," he said as he pulled into a side street and picked up his phone. "I have an associate who has a light plane at Lilydale airport. He will take us wherever I want to go. Well, he will take me, but you will be disposed of during the flight. Now shut up while I make the call."

Bird began to shake violently. His hands and wrists had turned numb hours ago from being tied. He was a gibbering wreck of a man. Antonov's phone call went through.

"Ah, Viktor. Pavel Antonov. I need you and your plane for a little journey. I need to…"

"What? What are you saying? You must assist me. We are *Bratva*. Brothers. What papers? No-one? What do you mean no-one? I am *Bratva*. What do you mean the network has cut me off? Viktor, Viktor," Antonov said before he stared at his phone with a look of disbelief on his face. He immediately tried another number. It did not answer. After trying several more calls he realised that what Viktor had said was true. He had been abandoned. He threw the phone on the seat, turned the big vehicle onto the road and stopped at the next small set of shops where there was a newsagent. Keeping his head down he walked quickly into the shop, leaving Bird lying in the ute. A minute later he reappeared with a newspaper in his hand.

"Fuck, fuck, fuck," he yelled before throwing the paper down next to Bird. On the front page was the story about Bird's abduction together with two large pictures, one of Bird and the other of Pavel Antonov. It had only been a bit more than twenty-four hours since they had escaped from the house in Carlton, but it was obvious as to why the story was big. Bird took a chance.

"Pavel, I am a state minister, everyone in the land will be looking for me and you. It sounds as though all your contacts have abandoned you. What now?" Bird said as he realised he could be signing his own death warrant.

"Shut up and let me think. Keep talking and I will put a bullet in you," a now distressed Antonov said as he gripped the steering wheel and drove without knowing where he was going. Eventually he pulled into an empty shopping centre car park, stopped the car and slumped back in his seat. Bird said nothing. Minutes passed before suddenly, Antonov looked down at his captive.

Chapter Fifty-Three

"Looks like I will have to return to my homeland."

"How on earth are you going to do that?" Bird said very quietly

"Your good friend Dimitry Lebedev must give me refuge. After all, I am Russian. But first we will stay out of the way until tomorrow," Antonov said as he looked in the back seat of the twin cab Ford and saw a large Esky. Throwing the top off he saw a mixture of sandwiches, fruit and drinks. He laughed out loud and then spoke.

"Not only does he lose his transport, but he loses his lunch. Things are looking up for us, Stephen. We will find a nice place in the bush so we can eat and rest. Tomorrow, everything will be alright."

Bird looked up at Antonov and just shook his head. He knew he would be lucky to get out of this alive.

Chapter Fifty-Four

Antonov had not only tied Steve Bird's hands behind his back, he also found a piece of rope in the back of the utility and secured his ankles by tying them together and running the rope outside the passenger window to where he knotted the rope around the massive bull bar. Bird was going nowhere. He had parked the big car in an empty shed on what looked like a run down, overgrown hobby farm only a few kilometres from where he had stolen it. It was a long day.

When daylight came, Bird had only dozed for minutes at a time the whole night and was totally distraught about his situation. Antonov on the other hand had slept well on the long bench seat in the big utility. He woke and untied Bird's wrists so he could eat some of the food that had been left in the vehicle by the owner. Antonov's calmness worried Bird to the extent that he had to say something.

"What are you going to do with me, Pavel? I have a wife and children so please don't kill me."

"You are disposable like all politicians. If I make a phone call and get what I want, you may live. Do not make a sound while I am on the phone."

Bird shook his head rapidly from side to side. He had no intention of upsetting this madman. Antonov punched a number into his burner phone and waited.

"I want to speak to the Consul General. Tell him it is Pavel Antonov."

There was no answer from the person who first answered but seconds later, Dimitry Lebedev spoke.

"Are you mad, Antonov? First you cause two of my staff to be shipped back to Moscow, then you are all over the paper because you have kidnapped a state minister and now you ring here. What are you doing?" a distressed Lebedev said.

"I am going to claim diplomatic status, my friend. I am coming to the consulate, and you will ship me back to Moscow though diplomatic channels. I will take my chances back home."

"Why would I even let you come in here. You are insane."

"Dimitry, I have run card houses all around the city. Illegal ones where several members of your staff and other well know members of the Russian community have come along to and enjoyed the nights pleasures. I will go public with names and even photos of some of your closest associates if you don't let me in."

"I do not believe you, Antonov. Give me names. You are trying to save your own skin."

"Yes, I am, and this is now the only way I can do it. If I get back to Moscow, I will disappear into the *Bratva* and I will say nothing. I will give you two names from memory, but I also have a little black book. Some of your wife's friends are in it. It wasn't just a boy's club, Dimitry. The girls liked to play also, and not just cards. These are the two names. The first is Anya Fedorov and the second is Georgy Semenov. I will hold the phone and give you sixty seconds to place them in your world," Antonov said before putting the phone on the car seat and lighting a cigarette.

Dimitry Lebedev didn't have to think for even ten seconds let alone sixty seconds. Anya Fedorov was the Cultural Affairs attaché who was based in Canberra but spent a lot of time in Melbourne because it was the artistic home for the arts in Australia. A beautiful woman whom he had met on many occasions and one he considered too close to many westerners and had a love for French champagne. The second was Georgy Semenov who worked in his own consulate whom he knew had a habit of frequenting racecourses and brothels around the city. He shuddered as he waited for Antonov to pick up the phone. The sixty seconds passed.

"Dimitry. Let's cut it short. Fedorov has been sleeping with the lovely lady who is the Shadow Attorney General whom we both know has a lot of American connections. Mud sticks when it gets thrown, Dimitry. As for your own man Semenov, he owes several of my connections many thousands of dollars. He has been whoring around Melbourne since he arrived here three years ago. Trouble is when he drinks, he talks. Do you want me to talk, Dimitry?"

Lebedev couldn't have cared less about Fedorov's sexual preferences or her connections because it was a problem for the Embassy in Canberra. Semenov was another matter altogether and could cause him problems. He thought quickly before replying.

"If you come in, it must be this afternoon. I will be gone for three days after today," he lied to Antonov. "Ring me later and only come via the back gate. Do you understand? I will help you as much as I can. I presume you have other names, and I will want them."

"You have a deal, Dimitry. I have my little black book with me, and I will be coming through the back gate at three o'clock. I do not want trouble."

"I will make sure I am here. I want this done quietly. You and your two associates will be shipped back within forty-eight hours. You can take your chances with the authorities."

"I will sleep well on the flight, Dimitry."

You will Pavel. You will sleep like the dead!

Chapter Fifty-Five

It was early morning at the Carlton Police Station. Phil Stone and Tony Signorotto were in the upstairs conference room, coffees in hand and worried looks on their faces. Ted Conlon was also in early. They hadn't called any of the others in because they didn't know where they were headed with the search. They were relying totally on public calls and luck at this stage. Signorotto looked up as Kate McLaren walked in quickly with a piece of paper in her hand.

"Kate, there's no need for you all to…" McLaren talked over the top of him.

"Boss, they've found Bird's car out in the bush at Warrandyte. Bird's driver was found in the back, dead. Looks like an execution style strangulation with a garotte or similar. If there's any good news to come out of this is that a local farmer reported his Ford ute stolen from the same location. It must be Antonov. I've put out a KALOF along with the usual not to be approached tag."

By the time Kate had finished telling her bosses the story, the rest of the Task Force had walked in. Max Tyler had a large picture of the same model Ford ute that had been stolen and was pinning it up on the notice board.

"Just a matter of time before he gets spotted. Hope Bird hasn't gone the same way as his driver," Johnny Petran said as he made himself a coffee.

"Where do you reckon he could get to in that?" Chloe Schaffer said as she stood looking at the photo.

"He won't be able to stop at many places if he has a live or dead politician in it," Mick York quipped.

Phil Stone turned to Paul Romano. "Senior, get onto the Assistant Commissioner for Traffic's office and talk to his Staff

Officer. I want a photo of that big ute in front of every Highway Patrol member. If Antonov gets more desperate than he already is he will give us a run for our money." Stone called Signorotto and Conlon aside to talk to them in private.

"Simple truth is fellas, that if this isn't brought under control today, I'm handing in my resignation tomorrow. It all started with me, so I am taking all the responsibility of it going pear shaped. It's bad enough at the moment with Bobrov in hospital and not looking good. I'm the one who let him loose at Carlton and before you say anything, Tony, you are more valuable to this place than I am. There will always be someone snapping at my heels for my job. At my level it is dog eat dog and to be honest, I'm tired of it all."

A shocked looking Tony Signorotto looked from Conlon to Stone and back again before speaking.

"That's bullshit, Phil. I should have had people watching him that day when he disappeared with Antonov. If anyone is going down for this, I'm taking my share also."

Ted Conlon, who up to this point, hadn't said anything about the situation turned to them both.

"From an Ethical Standards point of view, neither of you have done anything that you shouldn't have. Phil, your first move in bringing Bobrov to Carlton was something that had been forced upon you by headquarters. As for you, Tony, you had to make a quick decision based on the intel at the time, and don't forget that Ricky himself told you not to tag him. What has happened after that is all up to Antonov. The hierarchy know I am working with you and will want my opinion when it is all finished. I'll back both of you to the hilt, don't worry about that."

"As may be, Ted, but at the end of the day, it's down to me. The trouble with going up the ladder in the Department is that you lose too much contact with where you started in the bloody job, catching crooks. It's all set in policies and favours now. If it wasn't for the fact that this involves a politician, there wouldn't be nearly the fuss being made. I think I'm just tired of fighting on different fronts. You are trying to do the job on the outside, and the knives are being sharpened behind your own doors," a despondent Phil Stone said.

For once in his life, Tony Signorotto was speechless. It made him feel old when he thought about Stone pulling the pin on the job. They had gone through so much together, right from the Academy onwards. Where had the time gone? He was standing still with his mind in a void when the desk phone next to him rang. Picking it up he answered in a flat monotone sounding voice.

"Senior Sergeant Signorotto."

"Boss, front counter here. We have a phone call for Commander Stone."

"Take a message from whoever it is, thanks. We're a bit tied up here at the moment."

"This guy said it's urgent. Foreign sounding name. Dimitry Lebedev. Says he's the ringing from the Russian Consulate in St. Kilda Road."

Tony Signorotto's eyes widened as he spun around at the same time as putting his hand over the mouthpiece of the phone.

"Phil, it's Dimitry Lebedev on the phone, the Russian Consul General. Wants to speak to you urgently."

Stone grabbed the handpiece quickly and spoke.

"Mr. Lebedev. What can I do for you?"

"I tried ringing you at your headquarters, but never mind. I take it you are still looking for Pavel Antonov?"

Stone didn't quite know how to tell the man that they had really no clue at this stage of the fugitive's whereabouts. As he was about to give an answer of sorts, Lebedev took up the conversation again.

"He will be coming to the Russian Consulate this afternoon. He wants asylum and transport back to Russia."

Stone put his hand up and silenced the room immediately. His next move was to hit the speaker button on the desk phone so the Task Force could hear the conversation.

"I've put you on speaker phone for my colleagues here if you don't mind, Consul General?"

"Not at all, Commander. Anything to bring this situation to a mutual low-key ending. I have said he can drive in through the back entrance of the Consulate, and I have told him I will assist with his repatriation to Russia."

"We cannot stop you from that…"

"Turn the speaker off please, Commander. Just a quick word and then we can resume the open communications with your colleagues." Stone immediately turned off the speaker. Members of the Task Force glanced at each other with quizzical looks.

"I didn't say the gate would be open for him, Commander. I'm sure your men would like to speak to him outside my premises. The gates are old and rusty and are a very low item on our maintenance list. It could take several minutes for the security detail to open them." Stone was quick on the uptake as he hit the speaker button again.

"What time will he be arriving?"

"He said three o'clock this afternoon. I don't know what he will be driving, though."

"We do Mr. Lebedev. My team and myself will be there well before three o'clock."

"Little fuss please, Commander, and if by any chance he steps on Consular property in any form of aggressive state, then my own security detail will handle things. Is that clear?"

"A pleasure to speak to you, Consul General," Stone said hanging up as he turned to speak with his troops. "Tool up people."

Chapter Fifty-Six

Pavel Antonov was in a dilemma. He could see two problems with his plan to keep his life intact. The first was that even though Dimitri Lebedev had agreed to him coming into the Consulate for asylum, he didn't trust him to keep good on his word. Also, he knew he had to do something with his captive, Steve Bird. The last thing that Lebedev would want was a politician being dumped on his doorstep, dead or alive. He had to off load him, but where?

Antonov had driven to the Westfield Doncaster shopping centre and, riding his luck, had found a reasonably similar vehicle to the one he had stolen. He could have just stolen this one and dumped the big Ford, but what he wanted as part of his contingency plan was something that his present vehicle had and the one at Doncaster didn't and that was a large bull bar. He had made sure that he was out of sight as he swapped the registration plates over and made a hasty exit down the ramp from the car park and headed to the to the Eastern freeway. It was decision time though as regards to Steve Bird. When he thought of the big picture, his brain said that he had to off load him, but as he drove at the speed limit down the freeway towards the city, he knew it would have to be a last-minute thing which would give Bird no chance to interfere with his plan which was slowly formulating as he drove.

Looking down into the footwell of the big utility he could see that Bird was exhausted and beaten. That was fine by him because he wanted him to stay that way until the last. He realised that he had to give himself at least five minutes between dumping him and getting to the Consulate. If Lebedev was playing it straight then he would be able to just dump the utility at the gate after he rang him, walk over quickly to the rear gate and go in. If he left Bird in the utility, there would be an immediate connection between him and his captive which would be a hot topic on the news. No, he would get rid of him over the road in Fawkner Park. It wouldn't look strange driving into the park because there were actual roads going through it and he would look just like some maintenance guy doing his rounds. He would find one of the park sheds where they kept the mowers and equipment, knock him out and dump him in a green waste hopper. It would be up to Bird to get himself out before they fed all the tree offcuts and other such stuff into the waste shredding machine. To Antonov's delusional brain it seemed like a perfect plan.

He then turned his mind to the *'you're not getting in'* scenario. That required a lot less thinking. Simple answer was that if he got onto Consulate grounds, the State or Federal police couldn't touch him. Lebedev was obliged to take him in. He would worry about the rest when he got in. He smiled to himself as he drove, thinking about the massive bull bar on the front of the utility. Who needed a gun when you had a ton of Australian steel attached to the front of your car? *'Well, I have both and I am coming in.'*

As he drove along St. Kilda Road he went past the Russian Consulate. Everything looked normal but he had no faith in Lebedev. In his mind he put himself in his shoes and it became clear to him that the best outcome for Lebedev was to cut his losses and keep him out. If he got into the grounds, it was game over for the Consul General. He would be obliged to treat his visitor as a Protected Person. With Antonov's history and what charges he would face it would make life very difficult indeed if he got past the front or back gate.

He swung the big Ford left off St. Kilda Road and left into Slater Street which did a big right-hand loop into Fawkner Park and stopped near the maintenance sheds. Turning off the motor, he waited a few seconds before speaking down to Bird, who was whimpering meekly on the truck floor, hands tied behind his back.

"We are parting ways here, my card playing friend. It will be down to you whether you have played your last hand. I don't care at all what happens to you because I think all politicians are parasites. You no longer matter," he said as he waited to see if there was any movement near the sheds. After waiting several minutes, he could see that there was no movement inside or outside. He started the vehicle and slowly drove around to the rear of the large shed. His guess was correct. There was a very big hopper in the open yard which had tree branches sticking out of it. With his hands tied, Bird was never going to be able to climb out of his green gaol.

Antonov stepped out of the driver's side of the vehicle, walked around to the passenger side, opened it and dragged a now crying Steve Bird from the footwell and shoved him towards the big bin. It stood at over two metres in height. Antonov jumped up onto a metal attachment on the side of it and peered over into the deep receptacle. *Perfect.* Stepping down, he went quickly back to the utility, grabbed a roll of black gaffer tape and then spun bird around so he was faced up against the hopper. He ripped off a piece of the tape about half a metre long and proceed to wrap it around Bird's head and over his mouth.

"I am a fair person, so I have not put the tape over your nose. You will be able to breathe. You will either get yourself out somehow or you better be prepared to be put through a tree shredder. The bin is only half full, so you may have a day or two to figure it out. Bird's moans through the tape became almost hysterical as the big Russian grabbed him by the neck, lent down, picked him up by one leg and held him over his head like an award-winning weightlifter. With very little effort he threw Bird over the edge and into the bin resulting in a very large sound of someone or something striking the metal base. The one thing you could hear was a guttural scream coming from within the metal walls.

Antonov walked quickly back to the utility. The sound of the scream faded into nothing.

Now it was up to himself. Driving slowly around the loop he went back out onto Slater Street across to the other side of St. Kilda Road and into the service lane to travel back to the Consulate.

'Here I come Dimitry, ready or not.'

Looking at his watch quickly, he could see the digital read out saying it was just past three o'clock. Antonov had never been one to back away from a situation and he didn't really know what he would strike when he arrived at the Consulate. Either way, there was no backing down now. He reached for his pistol and placed it on his lap as he slowly drove around to the back entrance of the Russian Consulate.

Chapter Fifty-Seven

Once Phil Stone was off the phone from Lebedev he briefed the complete crew on the situation and then took Tony Signorotto to one side.

"Mate, I stuffed up by accepting Bobrov at the station. Should never have happened. I think I was looking a bit too much at my upcoming promotion to Commander and took my eye off the ball. I know in my mind that if I knocked back the plan to put Bobrov at Carlton then there was a possibility it would upset my chance at promotion. That sticks in my craw. It has now escalated to this. Totally my fault and I should have listened to you when I first brought it up. After all, you were always going to be 'Johnny on the Spot' with this and I wished you had dragged me aside and given me a rocket," a war weary Stone said quietly.

Tony Signorotto knew this was a bad plan from the start and, in hindsight, he should have seen this decision by his old friend as not only wrong, but plain dangerous. Giving bent coppers a second chance was tantamount to stupidity, and if there was one thing that Phil Stone was not, it was stupid. That aside, he could see that all the years of fighting the system of the Victoria Police Department from within had left its mark on his friend. Now up at Commander rank there was no way that Stone would be let outside again. It would be email tag from now on, and that was not Phil Stone's way. Tony Signorotto would go down punching along side his good mate if he had to.

"My fault too, Phil. I had big doubts about letting Bobrov keeping on going after what he had done. We should have just charged him and given him the boot from the Force. All good in hindsight now but I was the one who made the decision not to tag him that day when he met up with Antonov. I should have known better. Guess we are both getting too old for this job, mate," Signorotto said smiling at his friend.

"If I can't get out and about and tag along on some real jobs then I'm past my use by date, Tony. Anyhow, let's finish this and tidy things up. What do you say?"

"What are your plans for getting Antonov at the Consulate?" Signorotto said looking carefully at Stone. He was not liking what he saw on his Commander's face. This was looking like a fight where, under no circumstances, Phil Stone was going to lose. Signorotto knew he was going to have to keep a close eye on his boss today.

"Let's just hope he does come to the back gate because if he gets in, the Russians are obliged to give him asylum. Lebedev won't want to, but he has no choice. We need to take him outside. I don't care what it takes but I want that bastard to answer to the courts here. Two murders, one attempted murder, kidnapping and God knows what else. I want this mad Russian. He's treating us with complete and absolute contempt."

With that, Phil Stone walked off in the direction of the watch-house. Signorotto followed and was concerned when Stone not only issued himself with an automatic pistol but also one of the two Mossberg pump action shotguns that were kept at Carlton. Signorotto knew he had to go into bat for Stone, so he issued the other one to himself. Ted Conlon was standing to one side of the Commander and grabbed Signorotto on the arm as he turned in his direction.

"Keep an eye on him, Tony. We can't stop him from going, but I know he hasn't given Command in town any updates, because they keep ringing me. If Antonov wants to go down in a blaze of glory, let him do it by himself. I have a bad feeling about this afternoon."

"Is it too late to call in the SOG with some sort of plan?" a now anxious Signorotto said.

"Department doesn't want them anywhere near a foreign consulate or embassy and Phil knows that. I think they are prepared to throw him to the wolves, so if there's going to be a gunfight, let it be on Consulate grounds. I personally don't care if Antonov goes back home vertically and talking or horizontally and inside a body bag. It will save us a lot of hours of paperwork. Let's you and I keep Phil safe," a serious sounding Tony Conlon said.

"I'm with you on that. I'll get the troops sorted and then head down to the Consulate. If you can keep Phil distracted until the last minute and then come down with him. I won't tell him I'm going right now. I'll get them all in position by the time you arrive."

Signorotto went out to the back yard and gave car keys to the various units. He split it into four crews besides Johnny Petran and Mick York whom he knew would stay in the background because they were in plain clothes. He wanted bodies in uniform so hopefully Antonov could see some sense in his futile attempt. He teamed Kate McLaren with Paul Romano, Max Tyler with Chloe Schaeffer and decided to take a car by himself. He gathered them all together in the rear courtyard.

"I'll sort the positions out when we get there but I don't want any heroics at the Consulate. This has got to be as clean a takedown as we can make it. Understand."

No words were spoken. None needed to be. All the members got into their vehicles, armed for war but hoping for peace and headed off to the Russian Consulate.

Chapter Fifty-Eight

Tony Signorotto was not going to let Pavel Antonov manoeuvre his way out of the trap that he had set. He had a feeling in his blood that this particular Russian would definitely not be giving up without a fight. The unknown factor was the whereabouts of the missing politician, Steve Bird and, because of this, they would be giving Antonov every chance to surrender. As Signorotto stood near his vehicle, pump action shotgun in both hands, he looked around at the location of his members. At the back gate were Kate McLaren and Paul Romano standing, fully armed, outside of their marked Police vehicle which was parked directly across the entrance. If Antonov was going to get in, he would have to drive through this barricade. Max Tyler and Chloe Schaeffer were also in a marked car on the other side of the small street opposite the rear entrance. Signorotto was looking at the concealed position of Johnny Petran and his crew and was pleased that they had backed up a laneway further up the road. Part of his overall plan no matter what happened was to box Antonov in. Truth be known, after that, the next move would be up to the Russian. He would be facing at least one shotgun and six or more members with handguns. Adjusting his Kevlar vest, he looked up to see Phil Stone's car pull up. Stone stepped out, as did Ted Conlon. Both wore Kevlar vests and Signorotto noticed that Conlon had the other Mossberg pump action shotgun in his possession. Signorotto hoped he would keep it away from Stone, because if this was going to be Phil Stone's 'last rodeo' then Tony wanted it to be one where his good mate didn't end up being charged with anything whatsoever.

It was just after two thirty in the afternoon when Stone, after having spoken to all the members, came back to Signorotto.

"Right, Tony, this is what I want... "

"Not your show, Phil. I took over ever since you started blurring the lines with retirement. Right Ted?" Signorotto said in their direction watching the bemused look on Stone's face.

Ted Conlon was not slow on the uptake regarding the comment.

"Spot on. Phil, you said you were retiring so as far as a Command-and-Control situation goes you are now an observer. I'm the next rank in line and because I've been out of uniform for a while, I'm giving Tony here the control of the whole show. No arguments will be entered into," he said with a serious look on his face.

"You think I'm going to hand out some blue justice, don't you?" Stone said flicking his eyes between Signorotto and Conlon.

"It's not that Phil," Signorotto said. "If you stuff up here and give the Department half a chance, they will demote you back to Superintendent or lower. Think of the superannuation you will forgo. It'll be thousands. I want you paying for all the dinners at Dom's restaurant when you go, not just a few beers you miserable sod."

"Okay, but you'd better have a plan for this idiot," Stone said retreating to his car.

Planning on the run, Phil, Tony Signorotto thought.

He turned to speak to Ted Conlon but as he did, a call came over the radio from one of the traffic units he had roped into the day.

"Traffic 400 to Carlton 250, that ute you are after has just passed us and will be heading towards the rear of the Consulate in about sixty seconds. It's got different plates that were reported stolen a few hours ago in Doncaster, but it's definitely Antonov in the driver's seat. Do you copy?"

"Copy that, Traffic 400. All units, Antonov's vehicle is just about here. Stand by and take your lead from me," Signorotto said authoritatively.

All eyes were glued on the big Ford utility with the massive bull bar as it entered the street behind the Russian Consulate and slowed to a crawl about fifty metres past Johnny Petran's car located in the alleyway. Nothing happened for what seemed an eternity. Antonov could be seen behind the wheel of the big truck with the loudly rumbling V8 motor, but he wasn't moving, just staring ahead.

"Johnny Petran, slowly move your vehicle out and block his exit. Keep your distance and get all members out and behind any cover you can find, but don't use your car for it," a calm sounding Signorotto said. Phil Stone and Ted Conlon had moved up closer to Signorotto. Conlon indicated to him that he wanted to speak over the radio. Signorotto nodded his approval.

"Listen up everyone. All our calls are being recorded back at headquarters, so I just want to say this. We will wait him out. We will not make the next move. He can only go forward towards the back gate and what's more important is we don't know if Bird is in the vehicle. If it means sitting on our hands, so be it. First priority is to the politician."

Everyone waited. Signorotto and his crew had time on their side, and they were going nowhere. Seconds turned into a few minutes before the peace was shattered by an urgent call on the police radio.

"Traffic 430 urgent."

"This better be important 430. We're a little bit tied up here," a frustrated Signorotto spat back into the handpiece of the portable radio.

"I have a very dirty and now untied Senator Bird with us."

Tony Signorotto looked at Phil Stone's now smiling face. "Game on," Stone said.

Chapter Fifty-Nine

Pavel Antonov sat behind the wheel of the rumbling utility as he sorted through his options. He believed he had an ace up his sleeve because he thought the police had no idea that he had dumped Steve Bird in Fawkner Park. He had to get into the Consulate without involving the politician. Lebedev would not be a party to the kidnapping of Bird, but if he could make it into the gardens at the rear without Bird, he had a fair chance of claiming Diplomatic immunity. Even if Lebedev found out about the kidnapping in detail it would be too late. Under Diplomatic status he would have to be sent home and not turned over to the local or Federal police.

What he didn't know was that while Bird was lying at the bottom of the green refuse bin in Fawkner Park and he had made his exit, there were two teenage boys who had lost control of their very expensive drone further over in the park and as he turned into St. Kilda Road the boys could see their expensive purchase nose diving behind the trees next to the rubbish area. The only clue they had to its landing site was a loud metallic banging sound. When they ran into the refuse area, they immediately saw the large bin. Presuming that their drone had done a crash landing in it, one lad hoisted the other up to look inside.

"There's a guy in here tied up," a gobsmacked youth said as his mate, who was holding him by the legs, was staring at their drone which was now a crumpled mess up against the brick wall of an outbuilding only a few metres away. The elevated youth jumped down as he heard a muffled yell coming from inside the bin.

The first lad immediately grabbed his phone and called triple zero. Within minutes, a black BMW traffic car came skidding into the rear yard. The lads indicated to the bin as they held the mangled remains of their drone. Minutes later, a now freed but filthy Steve Bird was out of the bin and yelling at the police.

"He's on his way to the Russian Consulate, tell your bosses."

Being detailed as a lookout for the Russian and his vehicle, the leading Senior Constable summed up the situation immediately. He knew what Bird looked like and he knew who he was referring to, so he didn't even speak to him as his offsider looked after the politician. He just jumped on the radio to Tony Signorotto.

If Antonov had realised the police were now looking at him as the single occupant of the utility, he may have reacted quicker. He believed that he held an ace up his sleeve, so he was caught off guard when one older police officer stepped out onto the roadway in front of him and yelled towards the utility.

"First round to you back at the house Antonov, but not this time. Turn the motor off then take both your hands off the steering wheel and keep them in my sight. I have eight solid slugs in this shotgun so don't put me in a position where I even have to use one of them. This Mossberg will put a hole right through that big engine block, so you can imagine what it will do to the parts of you I can see from here," Signorotto said as he adjusted his stance in front of the truck. Sweat was running down his face and his back under the heavy and now extremely warm Kevlar vest. His breathing was getting very rapid. Antonov decided to play his ace.

"You will take the chance of killing one of your Ministers, policeman?" he yelled out of the driver's window. His breath caught in his throat when the reply came back just as fast.

"We have Steve Bird with a police unit, Antonov. Give it up."

Antonov kept the game going. "You are bluffing. He is unconscious on the floor here with me."

Signorotto kept the Mossberg aimed directly at the windscreen of the Ford as he reached down with his left hand and turned the volume button of his radio to the loudest position.

"Traffic 430, over," he said into the handset. The reply came back immediately.

"Speak loudly and clearly and explain the way you located the Minister."

The experienced traffic member read between the lines and could picture the other end of the conversation.

"Traffic 430. Senator Bird was recovered, hands tied, from a large green bin in the waste removal area of Fawkner Park by us. He was, minutes before found in there by two teenagers searching for their lost drone, over."

The air hung heavy with silence as Signorotto turned the handpiece away from Antonov and clipped it back on his vest. His free hand returned to steady the shotgun he still had levelled at the windscreen.

Antonov knew he had no choice now. They had forced him into a position where he had to throw caution to the wind. If he didn't move now, it would be all over. His hand shot down to the large calibre pistol in his lap. Bringing it up he whipped it out the driver's window and let two shots go in the direction of the shotgun wielding police officer as he stomped on the accelerator. With a deafening noise, the vehicle shot forward collecting Signorotto with the corner of the bulbar, spinning him around but not dislodging the shotgun from his grip.

Signorotto let one round go and pumped the Mossberg slide action and let a second shot go. The first took out the driver's side front tyre and the second shredded the driver's side taillight assembly. Signorotto never saw Stone grab the other shotgun from Conlon and step onto the roadway as the roaring vehicle aimed itself towards the gate. It hit the marked police vehicle of Tyler and McLaren and pushed it into the gate. Antonov's arm was still holding the pistol outside the driver's window when his hand exploded into a red mist and the pistol was blown into pieces. Stone racked the gun again and approached the driver's door just as Antonov threw himself out of the passenger side door, blood pumping from his now handless arm. With a mighty effort he jumped up onto the bonnet, grabbed the top rail of the steel gate with his left hand and was just about over the top when six or so gunshots slammed into his body bringing him crashing to the ground on the inside of the gate onto Russian Consulate territory.

As Stone and others from the crew raced around to the passenger side of the vehicle, black sheets of steel were suddenly slid from the other side of the gates forming an impenetrable physical barrier into the grounds. You couldn't get inside or see inside.

All the Task Force gathered outside the black gates as they looked at each other in stunned silence. They were left with the big utility and a badly damaged police car.

Phil Stone threw the shotgun to Conlon and grabbed his mobile phone, quickly dialling the person he knew now controlled the scene. Dimitry Lebedev.

Chapter Sixty

Dimitry Lebedev never had any intention of granting any form of asylum to Pavel Antonov. He also had no intention of swapping his lifestyle in sunny Australia for the frozen tundras of Russia.

From the first visit of the very nervous State Minister for Licensing and Gaming, Steve Bird, Lebedev knew what had to be done to keep his position safe. The fact that he had the two staff that had been assisting Antonov locked downstairs awaiting direct transport back to the homeland meant he was serious. The two had been stupid and would pay for it when their flight landed in Moscow. It was very coincidental that at the last minute, the Russian government had offered to fly an Ilyushin military cargo plane to Melbourne for the International Air Show which was being held at the Avalon airport near Geelong. Getting three passengers, albeit one dead, on board for the return trip would be simple because they would be classified as diplomatic baggage.

Lebedev had been running the protection of the Consulate from a vantage point inside the spacious back yard where he could deploy his own trusted security guards if and when he needed. He had the full intention of letting Commander Stone and his troops handle the situation, but when the badly injured asylum seeker had almost scaled the back fence, he had no hesitation in ordering his execution. He would have preferred the Victoria Police to be left with the mess, but he had quickly thought that it would be better handled from his side of the fence, out of sight of the prying eyes of police. They could take back any story they liked to their hierarchy, but he was sure that they too would want nothing to do with the goings on inside the Russian Consulate. They would also not hand it up the line to any form of Government body because it would involve one of their own and that was Steve Bird. The last thing the Victorian State Government wanted so close to the state election was the story of Steve Bird. In truth though, a change of State Governments would mean nothing to the Russian. The majority of big trade deals were done Federally. The states might think they offered a lot, but it was very small compared to the deals that he helped set up through his contacts at the Russian Embassy in Canberra. State deals were small potatoes in comparison and with his reach he would keep the wheels of trade well-oiled in the ACT. He really didn't care who was running Victoria. Either side would still do deals with him. Politics was money.

Two ex-military security guards who had been in Lebedev's employ for some months had each put three rounds into Antonov with their DXL-Ravager sniper rifles loaded with 50 BMG calibre ammunition from their concealed positions. The fence scaler had not stood a chance of hitting the Consular ground alive.

Lebedev had then instructed his guards to close the sliding bullet proof inner gates so, short of the police quickly scaling the back fence, there was time to drag Antonov's body out of view to anyone.

The phone call that rang the Consul General's mobile phone was expected. Lebedev answered it and spoke immediately.

"Commander Stone, do nothing but listen to me. Understand?"

Stone's mind was spinning with what had just happened. Not only had Antonov been shot and most likely killed, he had nearly seen Tony Signorotto dispatched as well. As he began to listen to Lebedev he looked around at the scene near the gates. Antonov's right hand, or what was left of it, was lying by the back gate still dripping blood onto the pavement. Pieces of his pistol were fragmented around it. Looking up he could see Signorotto taking off his ballistic vest as he talked to Conlon and McLaren. Max Tyler had walked up the street to explain to the DRU crew what exactly was going on.

"Commander Stone, I can tell you that Pavel Antonov died whilst unlawfully trying to gain access to Russian property. As you know, under your own Federal and State laws any type of unlawful forced entry onto Consulate or Embassy grounds of any country can be met with deadly force because it is considered an act of terrorism by the perpetrator. There has been no crime committed here and we will repatriate his body back to Russia through diplomatic channels."

Stone took in what had just been said, but he knew Lebedev was correct in his understanding of the situation.

"Antonov was wanted for questioning regarding two murders, attempted murder and kidnapping. I can't just pretend it didn't happen," Stone said with an exasperated sounding voice.

"Who had he kidnapped?"

"A Victorian State politician," Stone said turning to see a Highway Patrol car pull up and a very dishevelled looking Steve Bird climb out.

"Would that politician's name be Bird?" Lebedev said looking down from the second story window he had now positioned himself in, which had a clear view of the outside of the rear gate.

"Yes. He is here with me now," Stone replied.

"I think you need to take some guidance from the Minister, Commander. I'm sure that your State Government does not want one of their leaders embroiled in a scandal that involves illegal gambling and kidnapping on the eve of the election and I'm also sure your Chief Commissioner does not want the apple cart upset." Lebedev said terminating the call.

Stone had by this time been joined by Conlon and Signorotto. He indicated to all others to move the police cars out of the way and park back up the street.

Phil Stone was beyond tired by this stage. The only remnant of what had just happened was Antonov's mangled and bloodied hand lying on the ground. As the three of them walked a few metres away towards where Bird was standing, the rear gate quickly opened and a what appeared to be a gardener quietly picked up the remnants of the hand and pistol and put them in a bucket after which he poured water from a large watering can onto the blood on the pavement. In seconds he was back inside with the gate closed. Kate McLaren had moved to stop him taking the parts, but Stone put out his arm to stop her.

"Let it go, Kate. You didn't see that." McLaren went to say something but didn't. She too was taken back by the whole situation.

"This situation is now yours, Minister. I am officially handing this mess over to you," a grim looking Stone said in front of his senior members. "What are your instructions?"

The things that were going through the mind of the Minister were many. First off there was keeping the Press out of this till after the next weekend's state election. This would ruin his career and most likely bring down the incumbent government. He looked gravely at the group of police officers.

"I will handle this with the Russian Consul. You are not to discuss this with anyone, and you will brief any and all Police here and tell them the same thing. None of this will be talked about till after the election. I am now in control," a now confident sounding Bird said as he went to step past Stone and his group until a right fist from Tony Signorotto slammed into his jaw, knocking him to the ground. Conlon and McLaren looked on along with a not surprised Phil Stone. Signorotto picked Bird up and dragged him around to the other side of a nearby tree, slamming him up against it.

"If you think that I will shut up until after the election you little prick, you've got another thing coming. You and your gambling mates started the ball rolling on this and we are going to close it. You can go in there and go along with however Lebedev wants to handle things from this side, but by God this will hit the Press tonight. I don't work for you; I work for the people of Victoria, and they are about to find out what happens when the Minister for Licensing and Gaming decides to play by his own rules. They have the right to know now. The Press are going to be told about your little illegal midnight soirees which have now been directly connected to the murder of Marco Toscano, your driver and the attempted murder of Ricky Bobrov and me just minutes ago. Your whole little kidnap episode will come out also. I am not going to sit back here and be dictated to by you. If that means that you must resign tomorrow, I don't care. I am proud of the people I work with. We at least have integrity which is something you don't. Antonov might be dead, but you are not hushing this up just to keep your job," Signorotto said as he let Steve Bird slide to the ground.

"Commander Stone. You have this man arrested right now for assault. Do you hear me?" a shaking Minister said as he readjusted his clothes and rubbed his jaw. I went to Lebedev because you told me to originally."

"You went to Lebedev not because you wanted to assist us, but also to keep your name clear. Well, it has all gone a fair way past that now and the whole story must be told whatever the consequences are. We won't even get a Coroner's hearing on Antonov because of the diplomatic situation which I reckon you are all in favour of. Antonov gone may be one thing but hushing up two murders even for a day or so is another thing. Marco Toscano needs some sort of justice and so does your driver. What were you going to do about him, huh? Tell someone he called in sick?" Stone screamed at Bird.

"This coming out now could change governments at the election next week. The Premier could be defeated. That would also mean big changes in the Police Force. There could be promotions for all of you if this was kept out of the Press. Just let the Russians handle it," an incredulous sounding Bird said to the group of police, whose jaws dropped at his statement.

"Let the Minister past, Inspector," Phil Stone said quietly as they all watched Bird walk quickly to the rear gate of the Consulate.

Tony Signorotto held up his mobile phone to show Phil Stone.

"I'm ringing the Crime Desk of the Herald Sun," he said to the group, but to Stone in particular.

Stone looked from member to member with a calm and relaxed look on his face.

"I'll give you the direct number," he said, scrolling through the index on his own phone before reading it out to Signorotto. "Hang the consequences for him and his political mates."

Chapter Sixty-One

The Press hounds were lighting up the switchboard of the Russian Consulate and were very soon going to descend like a pack of wolves, which would catch Steve Bird inside begging with Dimitry Lebedev to get him out of the premises by any means available, which, in political speak meant to put him in the boot of an official car and drive him out. Bird could have gone back to Phil Stone outside and ranted and raved at him for disobeying his instructions about calling the Press but now he had more pressing matters, the first being to make sure Dimitry Lebedev wasn't going to say or do anything regarding the situation.

Little did he know that Lebedev thought as much about him as something he scraped off the bottom of his shoe. He was very gracious in arranging the quick exit of Steve Bird. The quicker his life turned back to normal the better. His superiors back home had been notified about the impending arrival of packages via air over the next few days and were impressed about the way Lebedev had handled the situation. All they wanted from him was the truth and he told them the whole unfortunate saga. Job done; job finished.

When he gave his security permission for Bird to come through the back gate, Lebedev didn't just open the rear side gate, he opened the big rear gates. When Bird walked through, a black van drove out some ten minutes later, windows blackened. Tony Signorotto thought about stopping it, but it was now all out of their control. There would no doubt be a fallout from the police hierarchy regarding the way the Task Force had handled the original part of the Antonov affair, especially with the using of Ricky Bobrov. This was something that would come down the line after the state election.

Phil Stone had gotten rid of the crews at the scene but was still there with Signorotto, Conlon, McLaren and Tyler when the van drove past them driven by a black suited security guard with another in the passenger seat. Just visible in the rear seat were two more males dressed in what appeared to be scruffy clothes. Those two looked terrified.

Stone had read the memo from the Chief's office some days prior regarding the surprise visit of the Russian Air Force and their military cargo plane to the Avalon Air Show and it didn't take a Rhodes Scholar to guess who and what were in the van and where it was headed. He turned to the others before they went to their cars.

"Front two will be the shooters, back seat will be two more headed home and I bet in the rear will be a body bag with Antonov and whatever weapons that were used to execute him.

Lebedev is not mucking around. The van has diplomatic plates so the driver can't be booked and if they are stopped, they claim diplomatic immunity for whatever and whoever is in the van. That van will come back with a new driver who knows nothing. Very slick operation, Dimitry, very slick," Stone said as they watched the van disappear.

"Well people, I suggest we adjourn back to our office. I for one am going to try to empty that bottle of scotch I have in my desk. You are more than welcome to drown your sorrows with me."

As the members got into to their cars, Tony Signorotto put his hand on Stone's shoulder.

"Phil, I have been in this man's Police Force as long as you and both of us know that even though the top floor will hear about this tonight, they won't mention it till after the election. They are all playing musical chairs, and some will end up without one. We may have a problem with how we've handled the Bobrov bit, but if the government changes, this Chief will be out and the new one will not under any circumstances want to be thrown a live grenade. Once he knows the Russians have handled it, he will be more than happy to avoid any further conversations about it. The Press will concentrate on Bird if he gets back in or not. He will be thrown under the bus by the Premier. That's where the story is. It's a Polly in charge of gaming and he did the wrong thing by going rogue with the all-night card games. They will only look at Bobrov being an undercover cop who has been injured, not one we put out there. After all, for what it's worth, it's partly our fault what happened. We really didn't give him a choice, but he is still a cop and I think we must help him in this. He's paid his dues and we owe it to him to get him back on his feet. He only ever hurt himself with the gambling and by the way, they won't get any other names of celebs from Bird because someone will sue him. After all, he is the only person who shouldn't have been there as far as his job goes. There are too many high up connections with the others to throw them in the pot. They might have been at an illegal card game, but they weren't hypocrites like Bird."

"I know you're right, Tony but I feel like I've slipped up on this. As I said before, I was too busy looking at my promotion and I took my eye off the ball by putting Ricky out there. Admittedly the Department wanted to find out about Antonov, but I should have stood my ground I'm going to have to live with that. At some stage soon I'm going to see Ricky and see what we can do. The last report I got on him was that he will recover fully but it might take some time. I am going to reassure him that we are standing by him. I know it's a turnaround, but we must."

"I just wish he'd taken up my idea of following him and Antonov that day, but I reckon he was trying to prove to us that he was still a good cop and wanted his life back. I think the whole station would be behind him if he got back to Carlton."

"Let's just see if this government goes down. Bird's life will be put up there in lights. This Premier will abandon him, but it will look bad sacking a Minister on the eve of an election.

Shutting the barn door after the horse has bolted," Stone said getting into the car.

"Let's hope it's Bird's bad luck and Ricky's good luck," Signorotto said.

"Fingers crossed for a bit of good luck for us, too," Stone sighed.

Chapter Sixty-Two

The press had a field day with the goings on with Steve Bird and the Russian Consulate. After hours of trying though, the information coming out of the Russian Consulate was everything the news hounds didn't want: Absolutely nothing.

The blow torch was soon turned on the State Government and, in particular, The Honourable Steve Bird, MP. The heat only intensified as the flames licked under the door to the Premier's office. With only a few days to the state election, the Premier was constantly blindsided by questions he had no answers for. That was until he called his wayward Minister to task, and, after only thirty minutes of a one-way grilling and tongue lashing, Steve Bird emerged to a press conference in the Parliamentary Gardens where he immediately not only resigned his post as a Minister but announced he would be taking immediate stress leave from his duties, which basically meant that he was unavailable to properly represent himself or his party at the upcoming election. The bomb might have gone off under him, but it had shock waves that rolled right through the ballot box on election day. The government was whitewashed. This last piece of two-faced deceit was enough to turn the tide. The voters were sick and tired of waking up to the news of another polly saying one thing and doing another. Even the Premier only just kept his seat. The government changed hands.

The Press had tried everything to get some information about Pavel Antonov, but try as hard as they might, the Russian Consulate and even the Embassy in Canberra uttered only one word. Nyet! It would be no today, tomorrow and ad infinitum in regard to talking about the incident. They were all covered by diplomatic immunity, which was something that the new State Government was very glad about.

Days after the election, Deputy Commissioner Craig Stewart, who had not long before told the Task Fore to refrain from mentioning Steve Bird in the investigation, was duly promoted to the position of Chief Commissioner. With the State Government changing, the Night of The Long Knives had quickly taken place in Police Headquarters and Stewart had the sharpest one of all.

Stewart was seen very quickly, smiling with the incoming Premier and as far as he was concerned the chapter was closed on anything that happened with former Ministers of State. In that environment he had an even bigger ally, that being the new Premier of the State of Victoria. He would have liked to have brought Stone, Conlon and Signorotto to task for what happened but he couldn't be seen to be running a vigilante party when one body was gone, and it was a lay down misère that the future Coroner's verdicts on Marco Toscano and Bird's driver would pin the Russian for the two homicides. He also didn't give a toss that Tony Signorotto was nearly run over twice by Antonov and that an attempted murder had been committed by the same madman on Ricky Bobrov.

It was going to be business as usual as far as Stewart was concerned but at some stage soon, he was going to let Phil Stone know that his probationary period as a Commander was finished and he was going back to being a Superintendent, never to be promoted. The same was going to happen to Tony Signorotto. The rank of Senior Sergeant would be his last also. If only he knew that Signorotto was a man at peace with himself at Carlton looking after his beloved station. He never wanted to go higher than the rank he was at.

Phil Stone had heard the same whispers from above through one of the Public Service staff who had previously worked at Carlton and had been recommended for a higher level and subsequent pay rise. Stone had always looked after those around him, so the phone calls that came drifting down to him with the 'gallows' information made him smile inwardly. Stewart would never have the loyalty that Stone and Signorotto had with their troops.

While he was thinking about his future, Stone was walking through the foyer of the Royal Melbourne Hospital in Carlton on his way to visit Ricky Bobrov. He had rung him on several occasions, but Bobrov had been tied up with doctor's visits and other medical intrusions so more than two weeks after Antonov's body had been snatched out of their grasp by Dimitry Lebedev, he entered Bobrov's ward with the intention of laying bare his soul. He knew in his heart he shouldn't have forced the undercover operation on the young sergeant and that it was really nothing short of blackmail. Entering his room, he went to say hello but was taken back by the presence of Tony Signorotto, already seated in plain clothes and appearing to be having a very casual and friendly conversation with the injured member.

"You didn't tell me you were coming in here?" Stone said with surprise.

"Why should I tell some soon to be demoted Commander everything I do?" Signorotto said smiling at Bobrov who was sitting up in a chair beside his bed.

"Looks like Stewart's wasting his time telling me then if I've already been told by an expert like you," Stone said in reply. "Anyhow, I've come in here to have a serious talk with Ricky. You want to take a coffee break while I do?"

"If you think I'm leaving one of my sergeants at your mercy then forget it."

Stone could sense the vibes between the two.

"Okay you two, let's talk."

Chapter Sixty-Three

Phil Stone sat on a chair next to Bobrov, but before he could say a word, Ricky started.

"Please don't come in here talking about apologies and all that sort of shit. I've had quite a while getting over Antonov and what he did to me, and I just want to move on," the rather gaunt looking Bobrov said.

"Ricky, the Department gave you to me to basically see how corrupt you were and probably how far you'd go. I should have said no from the start but at that time a while back I was just looking at my upcoming promotion and wasn't thinking about the outcome of what could happen. I don't think any of us realised fully what we were dealing with. I should have looked further into Antonov and realised that the scheme he was running with the Asian migrants was really something I should have handed over to the Feds, but I just wanted to show the top floor that I was up for the Commander's job. What you did with the gambling house was done because you have an addiction more than anything really to do with corruption. You were just corrupting yourself. The payments were coming out of your pay for the problem in Bendigo and that's what we should have concentrated on: You getting better, not us, or in particular, me trying to let you hang yourself," a very sorrowful looking Stone said as he lowered his head.

"Me too, Ricky," Tony Signorotto said. "I should never have let you make the play on us following you and Bobrov. I knew in my bones that it was fraught with danger. The Task Force knew he was connected with the Russian mafia and that the street begging shit was most likely having its strings pulled by Canberra at their Embassy. Phil and I here have had long talks about the whole thing, and we reckon Dimitry Lebedev, although not connected with Antonov, knew more than he would say and just wanted peace in Melbourne. We'll never prove anything against him or Canberra, but the fact that they sent that Russian plane to Avalon was no surprise to him. He must have arranged that through Canberra and came out of it with an enhanced reputation as a very good operator for them. It saved us a lot of paperwork and ended up bringing down the State Government and in a roundabout fashion helped you because we now have a new Chief Commissioner. Not that any of us like him but he wants it all swept under the carpet."

"What's happened to all the illegals swept up after the scam was caught out?" Bobrov said.

"The Feds have got them all in detention centres but there are moves to get their families out here. They were all under extreme duress while they were begging for Antonov. Pictures of their family members were found in folders at the places they were housed. They were having them waved in their faces to keep them working. The Russians in Canberra are working with the authorities in their home countries to get their families here because they don't want to be connected to any form of illegal immigration. I think all of those bagmen will be okay in a year or so," Stone said, smiling. "What we have to do is see what we can do for you out of this mess that I pushed you deeper and deeper into."

"You weren't the Lone Ranger, Phil. We both handled this badly," Signorotto said

"I've been keeping a close eye on your medical progress, and I am so pleased that the bullet the mad Russian put into you went straight through without any real damage," Stone said.

"Yeah, it did. No long term damage. I think I've used up all my punter's luck on that shot. I just want out of here. I've finished with any sort of gambling. Not that I deserve it, but if I could get a reference from one of you, I'm going to start searching the job adds when I get out next week. I've got to find myself some new digs because I don't think Police Welfare would want an ex bent cop taking up room in one of their flats, do you?" Bobrov said with a sad grin.

Stone and Signorotto looked at each other sheepishly before Stone nodded.

Signorotto spoke.

"Actually Ricky, No they probably wouldn't."

Ricky Bobrov put his head back on the headrest of his chair and looked at the ceiling before Signorotto continued.

"A lot of talking has gone on about you back at the Task Force and at the station also. Inspector Conlon put his job on the line and demanded an appointment with the new Chief and told him there was no basis for getting rid of you and that if the whole story came out about how all of us pushed you to the dark side it wouldn't look good for him in his new position. After a lot of arguing, the Chief backed down. Well to a degree and with some compromises that Ted, myself and Phil have gone along with. The fact is, we are all quite happy with them, but for Christ's sake you didn't hear me say that."

"What are you getting at?" a completely puzzled Ricky Bobrov said.

Stone looked the dressing gown clad figure in the eye.

"Like this, son. I have had my Commanders rank pulled and I'm back to being a Superintendent. Tony here has been told that Senior Sergeant is his final rank and Ted Conlon has been sent packing to the lovely seaside port of Warrnambool as a uniform Inspector. Main thing is though you are staying, that is if you want to. You'll be busted back to Senior Constable for a minimum two years and on a strict probationary set up and a lot of psychological counselling for your gambling addiction. That stunt you pulled with the money from the Property Office, which unbeknown to you, was seen, will also come out of your pay quick smart. You are on sick leave and in a couple of weeks, you will be back at Carlton. There will be a Disciplinary Hearing about the Property Office money where you will be told about your demotion, but at least you know that you still have a job and in a few years after proving you have turned a new leaf, you'll be allowed to go for promotion again. Your resignation papers were only fake, and they seem to have disappeared. Tony will work around it all. The Chief will be keeping out of it because frankly, the whole thing could blow up in his face. In his defence, he wants to move forward with his career, not backwards. Any mention of the word Russia and he nearly has a breakdown. I'm told by my source at his office that he refused to eat caviar at a recent function," Stone said laughing out loud.

"That's unfair on all of you. I don't even deserve to keep my job, but you lot are copping it for stuff you didn't do," Bobrov splurted in a loud voice before collapsing back into his chair, crimson in the face.

Stone looked at Signorotto who had a slightly sad look to him.

"Mate, the boss here has decided that this is his last rodeo. He's pulling the pin and going on a long-earned holiday with his lovely wife. I'm as happy as a pig in shit because I've never wanted the illustrious rank of Inspector. I'm Carlton born and bred. As for Ted Conlon, he was told to go somewhere, so he picked Warrnambool. The Chief didn't know that he has a beautiful holiday house down there on the coast. He and his wife are selling up from the city and he can't wait to get down there in uniform away from all the bullshit here. Thing is now though; can you handle working under me at Carlton? You'll be behind a desk for a quite a few months until you find your feet, but I'll have you working the front counter so you can deal with all the social issues of the United Nations of Carlton, as we all refer to our lovely suburb. What do you say? Oh, forget that Welfare flat, too."

Bobrov's head was spinning. He didn't know how to respond for about ten seconds, after which he took his hand away from his mouth, looked at them both and spoke.

"What about the flat. Does Welfare want me out of that place?"

Phil Stone lent back and spoke.

"You can stay there if you like, but a good friend of mine by the name of Carlo Genessi, a Real Estate agent owns a couple of nice places in Carlton, one of them being a flat in Pigdon Street. You owe him a huge favour, because he's the man who owns the house you held that card game in, but you probably already know about that because you got the information from the Holiday Book. The main reason he hasn't had you charged with burglary is that he was a big gambler himself when he was younger. He managed to turn his life around and now he's one of the biggest Real Estate agents in the northern suburbs. He and his family are going overseas for twelve months, and his brother Sergio will be taking over the business. He's looking for a person to mind the flat for him, no strings attached and rent free which will allow you more money to pay back the five hundred dollars and finish off the payments in Bendigo. Much more upmarket than what Welfare can offer. He wants someone solid in there. I told him I had someone in mind. Interested?"

The emotion charged room dissolved into silence before Bobrov spoke.

"Second chances don't come around too often. I've stuffed up badly but if you want me back on your team, I hope you realise you'll never get me off it," he said holding his hands to his head as tears rolled down his face.

Tony Signorotto stood and put his hand on Bobrov's shoulder.

"One last thing, Ricky. There's a rather big party at a very well-known restaurant in Lygon Street in two weeks' time. You'd better be there. Everyone's invited except the new Chief."

"Yeah." Bobrov replied with a quiet hesitant tone as he shook his head slowly.

Chapter Sixty-Four

Lygon Street had seen many big functions and parties over the years from the well-known street being packed by crowds when Ferrari had won the Australian Grand Prix and the Scuderia Ferrari flags took over the restaurants and the precinct to the famous navy-blue flags of the Carlton Football Club dominating the scene when they had won the Australian Football League Grand Final. It was the heartbeat of Melbourne for a lot of reasons. This night was not nearly as big or etched in folklore, but it certainly meant a lot to those in the navy blue of a different uniform, that of the Victoria Police that had cut their teeth in the surrounding suburbs near Carlton, Collingwood, Richmond and Fitzroy. There were many a past and present member that wanted to show their respects to their retiring Superintendent, Phil Stone.

No matter what the occasion that was being held by the members at Carlton, there was only one place where the night was celebrated and that was at Dom's family restaurant. It had always been known as Dom's after its owner of thirty years, Dom Santino and his wife Maria took over the run-down eatery and gradually turned it into a Lygon Street institution. This night was going to be a big one.

Fellow Police of every rank right up to Assistant Commissioner were gradually pouring into the restaurant, and Dom had even enlisted the help of his old friend Bernardi from his own restaurant next door to help. The speeches and such would go on for hours, but that was what Lygon street was all about. Family and friends.

Kate McLaren was there with her husband Tom Cole and their lovely little daughter Summer along with retired members such as Jill Norton who had been the mainstay of the watch house for many years. She was being swamped by other members who had climbed the ranks of the Department, some because they never forgot how she trained them at Carlton. They always claimed that if she taught them anything, it was always worth remembering. Members of the recently disbanded Task Force that had been involved in the Pavel Antonov affair, Johnny Petran and Mick York had actually put on clean shirts for the occasion, albeit flannel ones.

As the wine and beer flowed and Phil Stone and his lovely wife Mandy were feted with more speeches than an incoming Prime Minister, Tony Signorotto and his wife Susie sat down in exhaustion from too much dancing. They were joined by Ted Conlon and his partner.

After a couple of drinks and watching the younger members from the stations cavort on the dance floor, Ted indicated to Tony that they needed a private conversation. They excused themselves and went down the hallway to the kitchen entrance.

"Everyone's here except Ricky," Conlon said.

"Don't worry. He rang me today and was unsure about attending. Thought some of the members might not like it. I told him that was bullshit, but I put a backup plan into place," Signorotto said as he pointed towards the front door. Conlon broke out into a smile when he saw Max Tyler and his new fiancé Chloe Schaeffer enter either side of Ricky Bobrov.

"You sent them? Good idea," Conlon said.

As the three members entered, Tyler and Schaeffer left Bobrov to the other members who were coming towards him with hands outstretched in greeting. Suddenly he had half a dozen or so fellow officers of various ranks around him. Bobrov was overcome but with a hug from Chloe Schaeffer and a bit of a shove towards an approaching Phil Stone and his wife Mandy he wiped his face and stood in front of them. Mandy put out her hand to shake and spoke.

"I know the whole story, Ricky and I've got one word to say," a serious looking Mandy Stone said. Ricky Bobrov said nothing but just waited to be rebuked by her for what was basically something that was his fault, that being the retirement of her husband.

"The word is thanks. I've being trying to get him out of that uniform for the past couple of years. I'm sorry it happened this way, but I know you will be okay with Tony, Max and Chloe looking after you. You are welcome at our house any time, that is if we are there," she said elbowing her husband. "I have booked the first of a few overseas trips which we are both looking forward to. Fate works in strange ways, Ricky, but it does work."

Mandy Stone took Ricky and gave him a long hug which ended in a handshake from Phil Stone.

"It's good to get my life back, Mrs. Stone. I think with this mob around me, I can do that," a smiling Bobrov said as he was dragged away by a few uniform members, beers in hand.

Phil Stone wandered towards Tony Signorotto and Dom Santino who were gradually heading towards the seat of power, which in fact was as always, three huge unopened tins of olive oil which were located just inside the kitchen door. Stone and Signorotto sat as Dom handed Tony a large Coke with ice and a glass of Chianti for Phil. He held up his own in a toast to his great friends.

"This place will always be here for you, Phil, retired or not. In fact, I would think you may be here more often than usual," Dom said seriously.

"What makes you say that?" Stone said.

"Well, that young couple Max and Chloe will be having their reception here. There will be no arguing about that. They're Carlton, so no choice. Then there will be birthdays for Kate and Tom's little Summer and well, this restaurant will always be here for my friends. I am glad I heard about your upcoming trip Phil. The going away party will be here too," he said raising his glass again.

"Can I handle another party here? My oath I can, mate," a smiling Phil Stone said.

Tony Signorotto had been quiet during Dom's little talk but now he wanted to speak. Standing, he held out his glass.

"To great friends, great memories and more great times to come."

The old friends clinked their glasses. They spoke as one.

"Salud!"

About the Author

Phil Copsey served with Victoria State Police Force, Australia, for forty years. His hard-earned experience fighting crime on the streets of multicultural Melbourne compelled him to write his true policing trilogy, **Blue Justice**, **The Calibre of Justice**, and **The Hand of Justice**. His depictions of characters and crimes are infused with authentic operational details, told through the eyes of his composite character, Sergeant Tony Signorotto. Phil is a natural storyteller who returned to study towards the end of his career to begin his Tony Signorotto crime series.

*

You are welcome to email the author at *philipcopsey@gmail.com*

By the same Author

Blue Justice is the first of a gritty new crime series published by in case of emergency press.

Don't look for puzzling cases, corpses in locked rooms, ingenious criminal masterminds, this is a novel about police on the beat: ugly, raw, and morally uncertain. It's not about solving crime. It's about solving problems.

Sergeant Tony Signorotto has good friends, plenty of enemies, and the sort of family connections that just might get him killed.

Buy **Blue Justice** from
https://icoe.com.au/bluejustice.html

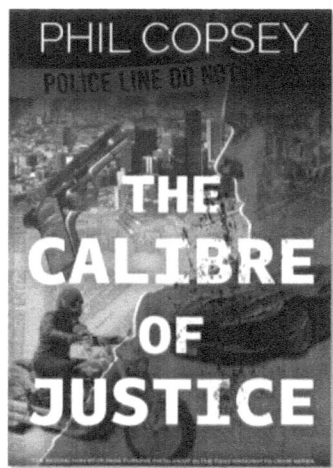

The Calibre of Justice continues the story of Tony Signorotto, now newly promoted to the rank of Senior Sergeant, at his beloved Carlton Police Station. Now married to his long-time girlfriend, Tony is looking to extend his career and look after his charter of the safety of the suburb of Carlton in Melbourne's north.

Life should be less complicated. He has made the sacrifice of life on the edge for nine-to-five and the paperwork routine surrounding his mahogany foxhole—until the rumours of a possible firearms raid on the Victoria Police Department. Enough handguns, if stolen, to flood the streets of Carlton and every major city in Australia.

Fast-paced, and brilliantly plotted, **The Calibre of Justice** is also frighteningly real!

Buy **The Calibre of Justice** from
https://icoe.com.au/thecalibreofjustice.html

www.ingramcontent.com/pod-product-compliance
Lightning Source LLC
Chambersburg PA
CBHW020354120726
47904CB00002B/552